ARAKIBA
ALIEN LEGACY BROTHERHOOD BOOK 3

KERI KRUSPE

STARCHANCE PRODUCTIONS

I hereby declare this is a work of fiction. However, locales and public names are sometimes used for atmospheric purposes. Everyone in this story is a product of the author's vivid imagination (this includes names, characters, businesses, places, events, incidents, and/or aliens). In no way does this story resemble actual persons, living or dead, or actual events. If it does, it's purely coincidental. For gosh sake's, this is a work of fiction! Even so, the facts and events in the story may not be accurate except in the universe where the book takes place.

Just so you know... I've used several editing programs, which include Prowritingaid and ChatGPT. These tools were used to support brainstorming, refine ideas, and enhance the writing process.

Cover art by Jacqueline Sweet

Edited by ELF

CONTENTS

ARAKIBA

Alien Legacy Brotherhood Book 3

*W*hat if your only chance of survival laid in the hands
of a man who can't even remember his own name?

Arakiba wakes up on a derelict ship run by ruthless Ozevroc
aliens—galactic gangsters with no mercy and a taste for smuggling
human captives. His body aches with the aftermath of battle, but his
mind is blank—no memory of who he is, why he's there, or even his
own name. His only certainty is a woman named Morgan, a fierce and
captivating female who has dragged him from the brink of death. With
no one else to trust, she becomes his anchor in a sea of uncertainty.

Morgan is no stranger to danger. Determined to prove her worth
and stop an alien threat, she never expected to find herself enslaved
by the brutal Ozevroc. Now, her only chance at survival lies with the
mysterious man who seems as lost as she is. Drawn to him by more
than just circumstance, she feels an undeniable connection, as if fate
has bound them together.

Too bad Morgan's convinced he is more than he appears. In a galaxy filled with betrayal, she refuses to listen to her heart. How can she trust a stranger who is a stranger to himself? Would he be a friend or foe against a looming galactic invasion?

As danger surges and enemies tighten their grip, Morgan has no choice but to place her life in Arakiba's hands. He may be lost in the fog of a forgotten past, but her fiery resolve ignites something primal within him, stirring a force he can't ignore. As their bond intensifies and passion flares between them, the looming shadow of Arakiba's buried memories threatens to tear them apart.

They suspect the key to their freedom lies buried in his lost memories. But if his truth is uncovered, will it be more treacherous than the enemies hunting them?

Is it possible for two strangers to rely on their fated bond to defeat the deadly forces closing in, or will the dark secrets buried in Arakiba's past shatter their chance of survival—and each other?

CHAPTER ONE

S wimming to consciousness was a never-ending battle. One minute he was on the brink of awareness, the next, a yawning abyss dragged him back into mind-numbing darkness. The relentless tug-of-war between consciousness and empty bliss soon became unbearable as a throbbing ache gnawed at him. His stomach twisted, nausea creeping in as his head pulled with the constant, vicious, never-ending struggle between light and shadow. After an eternity, he finally found the strength to open his eyes.

Sort of.

Stupid eyelids fluttered like a nervous butterfly wrestling against a high wind. And what did he get for all his efforts? A sharp, piercing pain that felt like his skull would blow off his shoulders.

Throwing his forearm over his face, he shielded his throbbing noggin from the weak, yet blinding, light. A groan rolled out from his scratchy, dry throat. Taking a chance, he flopped his arm to his side and peeked through slitted lids.

Well, shit. All that effort was totally worthless. High above him, a flickering glow of a malfunctioning light danced, creating erratic shadows that crisscrossed over rust-streaked metal walls. His nose twitched as the odor of burned wires and engine grease filled his nostrils, acrid and heavy. A sharp stench coated his mouth, leaving behind a vile aftertaste.

Sucking in a deep breath for courage, he opened his eyes wider. Where was he? Wait a *goddess-damned* minute. More importantly... who was he? The dull hum of engines reverberating through the floor didn't supply any answers. It only provided a relentless, rhythmic vibration that echoed into his very bones. Every muscle ached as he pushed himself upright, his hands slipping on the slick, oil-smeared surface of a hard floor. He glanced at his splayed hands as if they held the secrets of the universe.

Nope. Nothing. He blinked. His only claim to fame was a humongous dose of zilch. Zero. Nada.

An oncoming wave of blankness threatened to suffocate him with a cold dose of hard reality. Forgotten memories pressed, clawing for attention at the edges of his mind. His heart pounded as a mix of confusion and unease threatened to take over. In stark desperation, he surveyed the wide, cluttered space, littered with abandoned tools and tangled cables.

A movement to his right caught his eye. It was... a person? Yes, that sounded right. A person crouched next to an enormous... machine? He blinked. And what was that person doing? He watched their profile as they tapped their fingers against full lips, their eyes narrowed at the tablet settled on the floor between their crossed legs. This person wore tan, one-piece, baggy overalls layered and streaked with grease and grime. Wild golden spirals that hid the side of their face escaped from some type of ball cap covering their head. Across the floor were strewn several unfamiliar items, arranged by size in precise, evenly spaced rows. Each object sat at a measured distance from each other.

Obviously, an obsessive-compulsive type. How many times had he teased... An elusive memory slipped through his mind—a man with dark skin who had a penchant for trying to make him into a methodical ass like he was...

Agony scorched his mind as he tried to recall what he almost remembered.

"Where are you, you bastard? I know you're there..." That mumbling grouse from the mysterious person had a distinctly feminine tone. She shook the tablet.

Feminine? What... oh, that meant that person was female. Female. Woman, girl, lass, maiden, damsel... lover. Yes. That felt right.

Was he female? He glanced down at the strange clothing he wore. The black, stiff material covering his lower half was... jeans. Over his chest was a tight short-sleeved shirt in an airy material of the same dark color. T-shirt. He had on a T-shirt. He patted his chest, feeling the tight muscles under his hands. His covered feet caught his eye. On them was a clunky pair of... boots? Ah, the brand name filtered by. Doc Martens.

He glanced across the room. Nope. Not female. That meant he had to be a... male. Man, gentleman, masculine, lad, boy. Heh, he was no boy. That was easy to remember.

"You're finally awake."

He jumped. How did that woman end up in front of him so quickly? "Ah... yes?" He had no idea how to respond.

"Good, you speak English. Who are you?" Her fists were planted on her trim hips. She glared at him with narrowed eyes. Eyes that were a mesmerizing mixture of emerald green and brilliant gold. "What happened to you? Where are you from? Why were you on that ship?"

With a wry grin, he croaked. "English? Don't know. Can't remember. No clue. What ship?"

The woman snorted. "Humph. Okay, let's try this slow and easy." She crouched to meet him eye-to-eye. "What's your name?"

A shot of pain pounded his temples, making him wince. He rubbed the right side of the offending area. His name? What was his name? "Ar... Ar..." He glanced at her for help. "I don't know."

"Are you sure?" Her disapproval was clear, with her eyebrows pulled close and down, creasing her forehead. She stood. "I refuse to go around calling you, Arr. It makes you sound like a stupid pirate or something."

Pirate. A person who attacks and robs at sea.

Nope. At least he didn't think so.

He shrugged and grimaced as the pain in his head slithered down the back of his neck. "Sorry, but I really don't remember." He glanced around. "Anything. Where am I anyway?" He focused on her.

She crossed her arms, shelving her full breasts on them.

Now, his mouth dried for a different reason. He cleared his throat. "And who might you be, lovely lady?"

The caramel complexion of her face flushed.

It was a toss-up if she was angry or embarrassed.

"Look, buster." She pointed a finger at him. "Let's get one thing straight from the get-go. The only reason you're alive is because I pulled you out of that." She directed her thumb behind her, over her shoulder.

There, on the other side of the room, was an immobile... spaceship?

"I don't need or want you to flirt with me."

Flirt? The definition eluded him. Not wanting to look like a total ignoramus, he focused on where she pointed.

Despite the weak light, the ship's sleek design was unmistakable. The vessel had a seamless blend of elegant curves and smooth surfaces. Covering the hull was an iridescent sheen of organic materials that pulsated in gentle waves as if it were alive. Scorch marks and deep gouges marred its surface, clear evidence of a recent battle. Vines and tendrils snaked around obvious wounds, slowly knitting and repairing the damage. The ship's organic form had a preternatural vibe, even battered like it was. All in all, it gave off a sense of resilience and quiet power.

Out of nowhere, information about the ship spewed out of his mouth. "It is an organic 11-15 that was created by the WOL, the 'Warriors of Light', for the previous Chancellor of the Federation Consortium. Its designation is *Elemi*."

The woman's eyebrows rose. "You can remember all that, but you can't remember your own name?"

With a grunt, he stood on less-than-firm legs. He was tired of craning his neck to keep up with this weird conversation. He moved like an old man because his body screamed and ached in places he never knew existed. "What can I say?" He grimaced. "I'm a man of many talents, but knowing my name isn't one of them."

"Fine." She crossed her arms again.

Damn, he wished she'd stop doing that. The last thing he needed to do was ogle her tempting chest. He suspected that might be part of that flirting thing that irritated her before.

"Well, I guess I'll just call you Ari. Okay?"

He almost shrugged, but stopped himself since the last time he did it made his headache worse. "Whatever." He eyed her. Yeah, looking down at her was much easier for his aching head. Helped the pinch in his neck, too. "And what do I call you?"

Thankfully, she put her fists back on her hips. Too bad it didn't stop the urge he had to watch her chest rise and fall with each breath she took.

"You can call me Morgan." She waved an expressive hand around her. "I guess it's up to me to welcome you to the *Nebula Viper*, the supposed best smuggling ship this side of the galaxy."

The Hidden City of Aethralis in Antarctica, two months ago

"I swear to God, Morgan, you go out of your way to piss him off."

Morgan snorted. No, no, she didn't. He was just a stubborn old coot who never took her seriously. "Look, Seren. I'm tired of the High Guardian and his minions thinking we shouldn't get involved with anything outside the city. Especially when it concerns humans." She stopped walking and glared at her friend. "We could've ended the Akurn invasion before they got close enough to do the damage they did. I only want to prevent something like that from happening again."

She ground her back teeth at the memory of what those asshole aliens almost did to Earth. No matter how hard she and her small group of allies urged the ruling council to act against the invasion, their pleas were dismissed every time.

"We will not get involved," High Guardian Rummeh had stated in a flat, no-nonsense tone. "Not only for the good of Earth, but for the entire galaxy. We don't have the luxury of taking our attention off Tartarus, that holds the Titans, for even a minute."

Then the man had the nerve to chuckle.

"Don't worry, I'm sure Inanna and her people have things under control."

Take today. She'd gone to the council to tell them about the newest threat that had happened to her the previous night. As a reward for her efforts, the jerks gave her a hefty dose of humiliation, dismissing her without a second thought. As if they didn't deem her smart enough to recognize a disastrous threat when it fell into her lap.

Well, didn't that just sum up her whole life in one hard reality? Treated like an outsider in their psionic society. One who fell short because of her painfully limited psychic abilities. Her only claim to fame was having xenoglossy, the capacity to understand and speak a language after hearing a few words spoken. It took longer for her to read a foreign language, since her brain needed a little extra time to sort through and unravel the written word.

Seren chuckled. "Yeah, you're lucky your grandfather, the High Guardian, didn't put you into solitary for having the nerve to argue with him like that." She nudged Morgan's shoulder. "Good thing he's fond of you."

"He's too old to be my grandfather," Morgan automatically argued. While she couldn't deny she was one of his direct descendants, she was too uncomfortable with the immense age gap between them to use such a common title. Since he was a pureblood Akurn who lived one year for every 3,600 years that passed on Earth, she always had a hard time wrapping her head around the man's actual age. Not that he'd ever confessed how old he was to her or anyone else.

"You always say that." Seren chuckled, closing the high collar of her long, elegant coat to activate the heating unit within it. The luminescent designs on the coat displayed her status within their community.

Even deep within the ice shelves of the city, the temperature tended to fluctuate at the oddest times.

Morgan did the same and breathed a sigh of relief when her similarly styled clothing and boots wrapped her in welcoming warmth.

Tired of the same old argument, she changed the subject. "Well, I'm sick and tired of him not taking me seriously. Why can't he see this as an additional threat from aliens outside our solar system like I do?"

Although she expected Seren's deep sigh, it still hurt.

"Because, my dear friend, the only concern we have here in Aethralis is keeping the Titans under wraps. If they ever got out, we'd all be toast. And not just those of us on Earth." Seren stopped and gripped Morgan's upper arm, her clear, sky-blue eyes sure and steady. "Besides, I'm sure Queen Inanna and her crew have done their due diligence and made sure the alien Zerin running the exchange program made it more than safe."

"Safe? Ha! Not only did those aliens hack into my eReader here in Aethralis, but they somehow took me to their ship orbiting Earth while I was sleeping! Then they had the nerve to offer me a place in their so-called exchange program to find an alien mate. As if I needed their help to find a man." Morgan snorted and glared off into the distance. "What's bothering me is, how'd they do that? We've been told all our lives that the shield protecting Aethralis would prevent anyone from finding us, much less take someone from here without anyone knowing." She snorted again. "In desperation, I agreed to go with them, otherwise they'd have wiped my mind of the whole thing. Lucky for me, they let me come back to *get my affairs in order* before I left with them."

"Hmm, I'm glad they let you come back. I'd hate for you to disappear without me knowing where you went. I'd have been sick with worry." Seren let go of her arm, and they resumed walking back to their section of the private sector of the city. "But if the High Guardian doesn't think the exchange is a problem, why do you?"

How could she put into words the powerful feeling inside her, knowing her psychic abilities fell short compared to the gifted population of Aethralis? She'd had no precognition potential before. Why now?

Morgan hung her head and watched her feet move on the icy ground. The non-slip soles of her white boots gave her excellent traction on the slippery surface.

With a heartfelt sigh, she glanced at her friend and secretly envied Seren's delicate beauty. While they shared the same caramel skin tone, Seren's white-blond hair was thick and straight, while hers was a messy conglomerate of spiral curls that were hard to control. Damn stuff had a mind of its own, no matter how much product she put in it.

"It's hard to explain." Morgan admitted. "But I can't let it go. I've got to join that exchange and find out if I'm right or not. Not that anyone but you care if I'm here or not." With the ease of practice, she thrust the pain of losing her parents back to the deep pit where it belonged. Stopping, she took Seren's gloved hands in hers. "But I need you to promise me something."

Seren's clear blue eyes narrowed. "You're going to leave no matter what I say, aren't you? Even though the High Guardian warned you what would happen if you did."

Morgan squirmed under her friend's direct stare, but met her glare with one of her own.

After a moment of staring at each other, Seren closed her eyes with a dramatic sigh. "Alright, you win. You know I'll do whatever you ask. What is it?"

"Give it at least a day before you let them know I'm gone." Morgan grimaced. "By then, I'll be in deep space. Hopefully far away enough that my grandfather can't make good on any of his threats."

Seren chuckled. "I doubt that even if you made it to the other side of the galaxy, it'd stop him. You know how persistent he is."

Sighing, Morgan nodded. "Yeah, if nothing else, that's something I inherited from the stubborn ass."

Aboard the Zerin spaceship StarChance *en route to the Alien Exchange, two weeks later*

Morgan poked her head out of her cabin, looking left and right to make sure all was clear. Satisfied no one was around, she slid out and waited until the doors whispered closed behind her. Holding her breath, she concentrated on listening for sounds that might alert her someone was coming.

She grimaced at her whimsy. The golden walls and floors of the *StarChance* appeared solid, but had a soft, underlying feel to it. Firm enough to hold its shape, yet gentle enough to absorb the sound of her footsteps. Well, now was as good a time as any. Gripping her multicorder smuggled from Aethralis, she checked out the schematics she'd downloaded from the ship's computer. Widening the section she was interested in, she memorized the way there. All right, just a couple of decks below this one. Not that this was the first time she'd seen the layout. For the last couple of days, she'd diligently studied the workings of the ship in preparation for this chance to sneak around. The schematics written in Zerin were the only thing that took her extra time to learn. While most Earth languages had some common syntax, the Zerin language didn't.

At first, she relied on the translation injection the Zerin host gave her to understand what they said. But after a few days, she used the multicorder to eliminate the pesky potion from her system. It had gotten to where she was hearing double in her head whenever any of the aliens spoke to her. With her natural xenoglossy ability to hear and understand languages, she'd rather go natural than have the annoying foreign substance in her system.

Now that she could read and speak like a native, she studied everything she could about the ship during her off hours, since the Zerins put her and a hundred other women through vigorous training during the day.

While most of the areas in the vessel had known uses, there was a subsection deep in the bowels of the ship that didn't have any designation on the diagrams she'd downloaded.

Looked like that might be a great place to start tonight. Her urge to continue checking things out had only grown stronger since she came aboard. On the surface, it looked like the Zerin race was legit about their offer to take women to an exchange program to find alien mates. But still, something was off. Something she was bound and determined to uncover.

Yeah, take that, Grandfather. Won't it shock the crap out of you when I prove I'm right?

Heart racing, she bypassed the common elevator and headed straight for a service shaft only used by the Zerin for emergencies.

Changing the mode on her handheld, she pointed it at the entrance panel that needed a Zerin handprint to open it. Clicking the multicorder at the port, she gave the latch a satisfied smirk when it slid open. Yeah, that's right. Here goes.

Activating the flashlight on the multicorder, she aimed it into the black hole. Instead of rungs like those built on Earth, this one had a solid-looking floor disk large enough for one to use as an elevator. All she had to do was step on it, and it would light up and take her anywhere she wanted to go with just a verbal command.

"Sh'a'gaa." Morgan said the Zerin word for "down" in a confident tone. She then gave the command to take her to the unused section.

The disk beneath her feet seamlessly dropped. Leaning back on the railing provided, she jotted down what she'd experienced in her multicorder, and recorded a vid to document everything. That way, if she ever had to re-look at something, she'd have it handy.

The descent slowed before lurching to the right. A few more moments, and the device stopped. The panel doors opened to a sea of blackness. With a grunt, she pointed the light on her multicorder and swung it left and right. So far, empty corridor. Dusty, with a heavy smell of disuse, but empty.

She opened the visual mode on her handheld to study the schematics again. Down to the left, the narrow hallway ended. But if she went right, there should be several supposedly empty bays. Listed as available storage units.

Except, now that she switched the flashlight off, an ominous low light down the hallway caught her attention. *Aha!* And why was there a light over there? This had to be the reason for her unease since boarding. Yes, the suffocating urge to head that way almost overrode her common sense. Shaking her head to clear it, she returned the multicorder to the harness on her belt and headed toward the light. Keeping her back to the wall to remain as flat as possible, she concentrated on keeping her footsteps silent. The floor here was just plain, old-fashioned metal of some sort. Not the spongy, quiet stuff on the above decks.

As she neared the lighted open bay, she stopped to listen. At first, the only sound was a low, audible whine. Pulling out the multicorder again, she activated it to record. She watched the screen, and it wavered before it displayed a conversation taking place on a psychic level.

"Attention. Directive. You are to receive human females from the Zerin operative. Place each in stasis aboard your assigned ship."

A different decibel in the sound indicated another speaker. "Destination?"

"FiPan. Deliver to Dred Pirate Maynwaring. Return to *StarChance* for another cycle. Do not deviate," the first one answered.

A third voice. "Zerin operative. Trustworthy?"

"Zerin operative irrelevant. Task execution is primary objective," the first voice answered.

This one had to be the leader.

"Maintain communication. Report status upon delivery. No deviations tolerated."

"FiPan environment. Precautions?" The second voice spoke again.

"Standard protocol. Avoid local interaction. Deliver and return. No deviations."

The quiet shuffling of what had to be bare feet on the floor followed.

Morgan waited, making sure they didn't say anything else. When all was quiet, she took a few steps to the side. Not wanting her voice to carry, she frantically typed into her handheld. Good thing she'd downloaded all the data the Zerin ship carried.

Analyze conversation to determine species.

It didn't take long to get an answer. Her stomach dropped as she read through it.

Description: The Friebbigh are male/female hybrids originally from the planet Fibona in the North-Western section of the galaxy. They are gray in skin color with a large bulbous head and have enormous almond eyes with a black pupil. Two vertical slits for a nose and one small horizontal slit for a mouth. Small in stature, around 4'5" tall, with thin, stick-like arms and legs. They are adorned in a skintight outer-suit that is the same color as their waxy gray skin, giving the appearance of wearing no outer garments. They communicate telepathically with each other but refrain from doing so with all other species, which they deem inferior. To converse with other races, they have a "voice box" attached to their suit that transmits their thoughts into speech. Nothing is known about their reproductive process.

Warning: The Friebbigh rank as notorious criminals within the Federal Consortium. Wanted for arms dealing, kidnapping, slavery, and war crimes. Authorities suspect them in multiple unsolved assassination attempts against members of the known civilized factions. It is against Consortium law to interact with this species in any manner other than to kill or arrest. Any other form of interaction constitutes treason. All perpetrators will be prosecuted to the fullest extent of the law."

Wow, this was worse than she imagined. Known criminals here on the *StarChance*, ready and willing to kidnap human women. Without overthinking it, she sent everything she'd downloaded to her grandfather in Aethralis, even though it would take weeks for it to get to him.

She ended the missive by saying she wouldn't report her findings to the captain of the *StarChance* since the Friebbigh indicated they had a Zerin operative. No telling who that was. She'd have to dig deeper first.

Turning to head back to the service elevator, she almost ran into one of them. Squealing like a dolphin in pain, it held up its spindly fingers and waved them in the air. Before she could knock the creature out, a burning, sharp pain pierced her neck. Slapping her hand over the offended spot, she turned to see an unknown female Zerin behind her. The only thing she grasped was the female's deep red-wine colored hair and a long, clear cylinder device held in her three-fingered hand.

"Sleep well, *human*." The Zerin sneered.

Too bad the stupid alien didn't know Morgan wasn't all human.

Present Day aboard the spaceship Nebula Viper

Ari eyed the small streak of grease on Morgan's cheek. The temptation to feel her smooth skin against his was almost hard to resist. The only way to keep from touching her was to clench his hands into tight fists.

He tilted his head with a wide smile. "Morgan, eh?"

"Ari, eh?" Morgan returned his smile.

Ari chuckled with a shrug. "I guess so." He scratched the side of his head and glanced around the cluttered bay before focusing back on her. "So, what's a pretty girl like you doing in a dump like this?" He favored her with his best sultry smile and heavy-lidded gaze. At least he assumed it was his best. Hard to know.

Instead of his actions warming her up, her golden-green eyes narrowed. Her full lips turned downward into a harsh frown.

Ouch.

"I told you, we don't have time for that crap." She sliced her hand through the air. "The Ozevroc will show up before we know it, to see if you're alive. And I've got to finish something first."

Ari's eyebrows rose. "Ozevroc? What's that?"

She rolled her eyes. "Hang on. Let me finish this before we get into that."

Morgan thumbed behind herself to the place he'd first seen her sitting on the floor in front of an open panel on a large machine standing away from the metal wall. Without another word, she went back to it and sat cross-legged in front of it. Picking up a thick cylinder from the floor, she bowed her head over the open panel, pursed her full lips, and clicked on a thin blue light on the cylinder. It pulsated as if repairing something inside.

It didn't take a genius to figure out she'd zoned him out.

Glancing around, Ari looked for a chair to sit on. He rotated his shoulders, trying to loosen the ache. The last thing he wanted was to sit on a hard floor. Spying a square metal block against another wall, he went over and brought it near the woman, who was lost in concentration. Placing the block opposite her, he sat, leaning his back against the wall so he could keep her in sight. His tight thigh muscles screamed in protest, which he acknowledged with a grimace.

The silence stretched between them. Ari opened his mouth to break it, but she spoke first.

"The best way to describe the aliens that run this P.O.S. ship is they're typical gangsters."

He tilted his head. "P.O.S.? What's that?" An elusive memory came and went of a man smirking when Ari uttered that at one time.

Morgan kept her eyes on her work, but a slight smile poked free. "It's short for *piece of shit*. This ship—" Her head rose as her golden-green eyes glanced around. "—is the home base for their criminal activities. Their main claim to fame is smuggling." She scowled and put down her tool and picked up another. This one was larger and rectangle shaped. "The little creeps are all about greed. Their only known weakness is how much they admire strength and cunning. Especially within their own people. They're known to promote any of them who double-deals with another species and ends up not suffering any consequences for the betrayal."

Ari's stomach rolled. Well, that didn't sound like anyone he wanted to get friendly with. He hated to ask, but... "So, what do they smuggle?" He suspected he already knew.

"Goods, people, weapons, and a host of other things. Their favorite is taking any sentient species they can get their grubby little hands on to sell on the black market." Her answer was prompt and said in an absentminded tone. She squinted at the tool she held before glancing at him. "Especially humans whom they consider rare and valuable."

"Humans?" Another slippery memory floated by. This time, he stood in the middle of a crowd on a busy street, and the feeling of being overwhelmed rushed back. He remembered the solid feel of the sidewalk, the concrete beneath his feet, solid but vibrating with the constant thrum of passing cars and trucks. A thick sea of bodies moved around him, and a chaotic tide of hurried footsteps sounded as fragmented conversations filled the air. Neon signs flickered overhead and cast garish reflections on the shop windows accompanied by the piercing wails of sirens that pierced the cacophony. His chest tightened as he relived the stale stench of exhaust fumes combined with the overpowering scent of cooked street food.

In his memory, he'd held his breath when he looked up. He became dizzy as he gaped at the towering buildings that surrounded him. Their shadows pressed down as if the sky itself was closing in. A lingering remembrance of feeling small and trapped in the bustling and unyielding cityscape made his heart pound.

"Ari?"

He jumped. The sound of Morgan's voice made him blink, pulling him out of the recollection.

"You okay?" she asked with drawn eyebrows. Her connecting stare held him.

Ari swallowed hard. "Yeah." He cleared his dry throat. "Just peachy." Peachy? He rubbed his pounding temple. What the hell kind of word was that? He dropped his hand onto his lap and met her gaze head-on. The stupid metal crate he sat on dug into his ass and thighs.

"Are you one of their slaves?" He squirmed, searching for a more comfortable position.

Morgan's grin wasn't happy. "Yeah, and so are you." She fondled the thick, black collar around her neck.

He hadn't noticed that before. Startled, he reached up to his own neck. Yep, he had the same thing nestled against his skin. "What's this?"

"That, my clueless friend, is a *nutesh* snare. It's a painful reminder that we're under someone else's control." She resumed working, her lips pursed as she delved into the open panel again.

Ari frowned. "I don't understand. If we're slaves, why are we out in the open in this, ah, room?"

For the first time, he took a long, hard look at his surroundings. The place had an eclectic mix of machinery of every kind scattered around. He ignored the most amazing thing there, the silent, hulking spaceship at the far side of the room, sitting still and ominous. Instead, he studied the overhead dim lightning that cast long shadows, turning a maze of cables and conduits along the ceiling and walls into a tangled mess. Tools lay scattered across the floor, and not just around Morgan. He spied a wrench-looking thing teetering on the edge of a grated walkway above him.

The hum of the *Nebula Viper's* engine vibrated through the walls, a rhythmic pulse that matched the flickering overhead lights. Loose wires dangled through several open panels on every wall. Occasional sparks around the room sent out puffs of ozone into the stale air. Overall, the place had to be held together by sheer luck and duct tape.

"They need me to fix this mess." Morgan waved her tool around her. "Idiots don't have an engineer among them, so I'm worth more to them doing this than selling me to someone else." Her golden-emerald gaze trapped him. "And I convinced them I needed help when they found you. I don't suppose you have any mechanical talents, do you?"

A sour taste coated his mouth. "I have no idea." He studied the open panel she was working on. "But nothing in there looks familiar."

Her sigh made chills run down his spine. Was she going to hand him over to their captors?

"Well, it was a long shot at best." Morgan gave him a narrow glare. "Until you get your memory back, think you can do what I tell you so we can keep you out of a cage?" She pointed her tool at him.

"Hey, no worries." Ari put his hands up in surrender, his chest lighter. "I may not know much about myself, but I'm sure I'm good at taking orders."

Fingers crossed.

CHAPTER TWO

"That's what I'm worried about," Morgan mumbled to herself as she studied the man she named Ari. Did he just admit he was faking his amnesia? If so, why? It's not like it'd help him with the Ozevroc.

"So, what do you need me to do?" Ari rocked back and forth on the balls of his feet, his hands clasped behind his back.

What did she need him to do? Well, that was a loaded question. Her gaze lingered on him as the soft light accentuated the chiseled lines of his tall, muscular frame. His thick, wavy, blond hair cascaded around his shoulders, framing a face that was undeniably handsome. From his intense thickly lashed metal-gray eyes, to the tempting cleft in his scruffy, manly chin. The tight black jeans and T-shirt he wore clung to his form, highlighting every sculpted muscle.

He towered over her by at least a foot and exuded a raw, powerful presence that made her heart race.

The more Morgan studied him, the more unwelcome warmth spread through her and left her breathless. She wasn't delusional enough to deny the attraction she had for him. An attraction that simmered just beneath the surface. But she was the last person to let something as inconvenient as an attractive man get in the way of surviving this god-awful situation she found herself in. Her primary goal was to get back to Earth. Since being with the Ozevroc, she'd uncovered more dangers to Earth than anyone on Aethralis could imagine.

It didn't matter whether she felt drawn to the enigmatic, captivating man or not. He was a part of the solution or... he wasn't. If that was the case, she'd have no choice but to leave him behind. "I don't suppose you know how..."

A loud clicking noise echoing outside the open doorway interrupted her. It was the familiar sound of the Ozevroc clawed feet hitting the floor as a group of them headed to the engine/cargo bay room she and Ari were in.

"They're coming." She put up a hand as a warning to Ari. "Unless you can speak their language, I suggest you not say a word and let me do all the talking."

The confused look on his scrunched face as he scratched the side of his head was cute as hell.

Ahem, not cute, Morgan. Not cute.

Liar, her inner voice chastised.

"Okay." He turned to face the open doorway with his arms crossed. The action made the muscles in his arms writhe and tense.

Tearing her thoughtful gaze from him, she concentrated on the clanking sounds of the Ozevroc steps that matched their hissing and growling noises as they spoke to each other. Oh, great. She could tell their high chieftain, Welozz, was in a pissy mood.

He'd demanded the impossible from her this morning and was back to check on her progress.

"Human. Today you die!" Welozz boomed in the strange mixture of growls, hisses, and snarls that made up the Ozevroc language.

His hollow threat didn't worry her. It was his usual greeting.

When she first met the species that kidnapped her and the other women from their prison on FiPan, it'd taken her a few moments before she understood them. Fortunately for her, the high chieftain himself took her. As he dragged her to his ship out of the gangster headquarters, she quickly negotiated with him to spare her. She convinced him she'd be more of an asset as a member of his crew instead of selling her on the black market. That was how she ended up as an all-around fixer-upper for anything that went wrong on the *Nebula Viper*.

The Ozevroc might be crafty smugglers, but mechanics they weren't. You'd think a spacefaring species would have a full-time engineer on board. Not these guys. They were too busy stealing anything they could get their grubby paws on, rather than bother to keep their ship running. It's not like their lives in space depended on the vessel to keep working or anything. Short-sighted idiots.

Not for the first time was she grateful for the training she'd gotten back home as a general mechanical engineer. Her limited psychic talent for understanding and speaking other languages wasn't in much demand there. So, in Aethralis, they deemed her only fit for manual labor. Even though her first love was computer coding, she'd fallen into the role of physical work easy enough. Coding was more of a hobby, and it gave her a chance to keep track of the outside human world. Lately, she worried those humans were catching up with her people's advancements. She kept a close, obsessive watch for any sign they might use their growing technology to discover Aethralis. If they did, all that she held dear would be lost.

"Not today, High Chief," she gave her usual response in his garbled language. "Lots to fix."

Ari hissed a breath. He moved close and leaned down. "You can speak like they do?"

"Hush," she hissed and waved him away before turning to Welozz. "Tell me, oh, High Chief Welozz. What brings you to the lower levels?" She picked up an almost-clean rag and wiped her greasy hands on it. She kept her gaze away from the Ozevroc's four beady, black eyes. He'd consider it a challenge if she did. Dammit, she forgot to warn Ari about that. Hopefully he'd be too busy ogling the aliens rather than confronting them.

"You no fix consumable-maker! Seared *chichuld* not seared!" Gripped in the high chief's middle hand was an octagon cylinder that he threw at her feet.

The bronze-colored device rolled before stopping in front of her.

"Human die!" he announced, waving the wooden stick he took with him everywhere. The staff was thin and long as he was, about four and a half feet.

The egotistical creep claimed it was a gift from the ruler of his planet Gnilia as a show of favor. Which she doubted was true. If any of them spoke the truth, she bet their stupid tongues would fall off.

Morgan pursed her lips to stop a smile from flying free. In a fit of childish frustration, she'd programed the device he'd thrown at her to make everything it created either sweet or burned, which the carnivorous Ozevroc loathed. Served him right for refusing to give her a similar contraption for her own use. She'd rather go hungry than eat one more tasteless food-cube.

Good thing he did what she'd hoped he would. Now that she had her hands on the machine again, all she had to do was install it in the replicron she fixed this morning, to create one for herself.

"My sincerest apologies, oh great and wise High Chieftain." She lowered her eyes and put her hand over her heart. Gotta make it look good and all. "I will endeavor to repair this worthless consumable-maker for your personal use. Please, allow me to correct my mistake. I promise to deliver it to you before the end of the day cycle." She peeked through her lashes to see if he took the bait.

Above his snout, his four beady-black eyes glared at her.

His stubby tail, one that reminded her of a beaver's, thudded up and down on the metal floor.

Along his short torso were three pairs of arms. The middle pair held the staff in one hand while he kept his upper and lower arms crossed over the coarse fur of his chest. Unlike most of his crew, he wore a pair of shorts covering his lower half that exposed his legs with their dog-like paws and extended claws.

She kept her head down, waiting for his response.

The small group he brought with him was quiet as well.

She glanced at Ari, who appeared to be studying the small group of Ozevroc with a slight frown. As long as he kept his big mouth shut, everything should work out just fine.

"One chance," Welozz announced. "Still might kill human."

Fat chance. The Ozevroc might be a merciless criminal, but he'd never kill her as long as she remained invaluable to him. Which wasn't hard to do. It'd take a lifetime to fix everything on this bucket of bolts. Not that she planned on staying there much longer. Things were almost ready for her escape, now that she had a spaceship. She only had to wait for it to finish repairing itself.

And since Ari had come in said ship, fingers crossed, she now had a pilot. Plus, she'd found a bonus item aboard that ship she never showed the Ozevroc. It was something she couldn't wait to delve into. Once that was up and running, the galaxy was the limit!

"Fix now." Welozz stomped his staff on the ground. "Kill human?" He pointed his staff at Ari.

"No, valuable." Morgan kept her voice low and respectful. "I am ever grateful to your magnificence for providing slave to help with fixes. Much faster now."

Welozz tilted his head and studied Ari with wide black eyes. "Male? Human? Know how to fix broken ship?"

The only thing Morgan was sure of about Ari was that he was a male. She doubted he knew how to fix anything. Freaking man didn't even know his real name. She peeked in his direction. He might be human, but if he was, how did a human end up in the outer reaches of the galaxy in an organic spaceship by himself?

Morgan nodded. "Yes, wise one. Much help."

Welozz grumbled. The thin black lips on the side of his snout rippled. "Fix consumable-maker." He nodded to a shorter Ozevroc next to him. "Bugurr will be back to get. See done! Or both humans die!" Another stomp and he whirled around with a flourish and left, his beaver's tail thumping behind him.

Bugurr, the sub-chieftain who was shorter than the high chieftain, with light gold-ochre fur, snorted in her direction before he too left.

"By Tiamat's titties, do those boys smell!" Ari waved a hand over his face. As if that'd help get rid of the wet-dog smell the Ozevroc carried.

Morgan raised her eyebrows at that strange exclamation. Wasn't Tiamat the ancient goddess of Babylonian myth? She hadn't heard a human use that kind of language in... well, not in her lifetime, anyway.

Who the heck was this guy?

Ari doubted he'd seen anything like those Ozevroc creatures. He glanced at Morgan, captivated by how she interacted with them. He took this opportunity to study the aliens, who he surmised stood around five feet tall.

They circled her, their six muscular arms shifting, and their stubby, beaver-like tails swaying behind them. Their long snouts twitched while their four beady-black eyes stayed locked on her. Each Ozevroc wore minimal clothing, exposing coarse fur that varied from light gold to dark blue across their bare chests and hound-like legs.

Morgan's posture remained relaxed but focused, and she made subtle hand gestures as she spoke. To Ari, it appeared she was conducting an orchestra of sounds rather than conversing.

The Ozevroc responded with an array of growls, hisses, and deep grumbles, each sound carrying intricate meaning.

While Ari couldn't understand a damn word, the fluidity of their exchange suggested a level of clear understanding between them. He observed Morgan's expression and watched as her lush mouth turned down and she furrowed her brow in a slight frown.

Her lips moved, forming garbled sounds that blended with the guttural noises emanating from the Ozevroc. She'd emit a low hum or a sharp click of her tongue, which the Ozevroc mirrored. After a while, their conversation felt almost rhythmic.

Ari's mind raced, still trying to grasp and make sense of the scene.

The Ozevroc's growls varied in pitch and intensity, like the distant rumbling of thunder in a high wind. Other words were like the hiss of steam escaping a valve.

Interspersed were grumbles that came out low and resonant in vibrations that Ari could almost feel in his chest. Despite not understanding anything they said, he sensed the emotions around the room. The Ozevroc she talked to clearly had to be the one in charge. His arrogance and superior attitude reminded Ari of... crap. Nope. Couldn't remember who, but there had been someone in his life just as self-important as this one.

As the conversation continued, Ari's gaze shifted between Morgan and the Ozevroc like an outsider peering into a secret world. Feeling left out tore something inside of him, like an old unwelcome intruder. As if reacting to an old habit, he shoved that emotion down. Deep down.

The Ozevroc now pointed that ridiculous stick in his direction. They had to be talking about him. The other little fur balls clustered around the leader, their buttony little eyes locked on him. Tension rippled through them, like they were gearing up to strike. He clenched his fists under his crossed arms as he instinctively stiffened, as though preparing to defend himself. If he was lucky, he'd had some sort of protective training in his previous life and his body knew what to do. Because if he had to rely on thinking it through, he doubted he'd survive.

Ari's only hope was to trust Morgan's extraordinary communication skills. His eyes narrowed. Unless she wanted to get rid of him. But when she peeked at him beneath her lush lashes, the tension pinching his shoulders relaxed. Her expression wasn't one of malice, more of confusion. Hopefully, when they were alone, she'd fill him in on what concerned her. Since he couldn't remember much, he had to be extra careful to keep trust open between him and her. Until he got his memory back, or at least got a better understanding of his current situation, he was at her mercy.

The leader thumped his skinny staff on the floor and, with a hissing growl, exited with a flourish. A shorter, gold one remained behind. He glared at Morgan before snorting, then left.

The aliens might have left the room, but their lingering, pungent odor still hung around. It was an obscene mix of shit, thick musk, and a hint of some metallic stench layered with wet fur. The damn smell was strong enough to make his eyes water.

"By Tiamat's titties, do those boys smell!" He waved his hand in front of his face. Like that'd help. He swallowed the urge to vomit.

Morgan faced him with her fists on her trim hips, her gorgeous eyes squinted. Uh-oh. What did he say now that made her look at him like that?

"Tiamat's titties?" She crossed her arms, raising up those glorious breasts again. "Why would you use that name?"

"Well, you know…" His mind went blank. Again. "I have no idea." By Gilgamesh's balls, he was tired of repeating himself. Gilgamesh? Well, shit. Time to go on the offensive. "What did short, ugly, and smelly say? Especially about me?"

"Don't worry. You're okay for now. I told him you were needed around here." Her frown told him she might be dropping her earlier question, but no way would she let it go.

"Okay, needed. How so?" At this point, he'd take what he could get.

She dropped her arms and pulled out her handheld, checking the screen. She poked it a couple of times before showing him the screen.

It was a list of some sort.

"These are the major repairs that have to be done to the *Nebula Viper*." She grunted. "Like yesterday."

He took it from her and studied the list. Not that he could read it. Read. Could he read? He wasn't sure. At least he couldn't read whatever was on this stupid-ass thing. "I have no idea what this says." He gave it back to her. "You'll have to tell me what's on it."

Her smooth brow furrowed. "You can't read?" She glanced at the screen. "But I translated it into English, which is what you're speaking."

Ari shrugged. "You told me that before, but I don't have any idea what English is." Much less know what language he spoke. Did he know any others? Hard to say.

Morgan tapped a finger on her screen. "Well, we'll tackle that some other time." She looked him in the eye. "What I really want to know is, can you help me with the repairs needed around here?" She waved to the immobile ship on the other side of the room. "At least until your ship repairs itself and you can fly us out of here."

Ari glanced at the ship. No other sense of recognition came to him. He turned to Morgan and lied through his teeth. "Oh, you bet. Just tell me what'cha need and consider it done."

"Come on, then." Morgan pointed to a small crate behind him. "Sit over there while I check you out."

Ari's eyebrows rose. Check him out? He grinned. That sounded promising.

"Not like that, you idiot." She blew out a breath. "You've been unconscious for who knows how long. It's been at least twenty-four hours since I pulled you out of that ship, and I want to make sure you're not suffering any lasting effects."

"Other than missing my memories?" Ari grumbled and plopped onto the metal box.

Morgan ignored him and pointed her handheld at him, sweeping the thing up and down his torso. She did it twice, then pulled it to her and read the screen. She pursed her lips as she studied. Every so often, she'd tap or swipe across the screen.

The silence was getting on his nerves. He sprang from the crate and stood behind her to look at the screen over her shoulder. He scowled when the squiggly lines and swirls meant nothing to him. For *fruk's* sake, this was getting old.

"Well—" He crossed his arms. "—what does it say?"

"I don't understand this," Morgan whispered. Probably to herself. She seemed absorbed and said nothing else.

She stayed quiet, her eyes glued to the screen as she continued reading.

The growing silence gnawed at Ari. His nerves stretched tighter with each passing second, and his patience wore thin. Why wasn't she saying anything? What was so wrong about him that made her forget he was there? The tension built up inside him until his face heated and his body shook. Swallowing a growl, he clenched his fists tight enough to bruise his palms.

Behind him, a loose pile of metallic parts rattled and shook violently before flying apart and crashing to the hard floor in a series of sharp, echoing clanks.

The noise snapped him out of his growing irritation.

Beside him, Morgan jumped. With eyes wide, she glanced across the room at the scattered mess. "I wonder what made them do that?" she muttered.

"Morgan—" Ari pointed to the handheld. "—what does that damn thing say?"

"Oh, well. You're fine." She eyed him up-and-down. "Believe it or not, there's nothing wrong with you. At all. And I can't understand why." She glanced at her handheld before looking back at him. "When I found you aboard that ship—" She pointed to *Elemi* in the corner. "—I ran a scan over you. You had massive internal damage and several broken bones." Her head tilted as she checked the side of his head. "Plus, you were unconscious and had suffered a severe concussion."

Ari barked with laughter. "Didn't you say I'd only been here twenty-four hours?" He smirked and nodded at her handheld. "That can't be right. Stupid thing must be busted."

Her face flushed, and the caramel skin of her neck and cheeks became a nice rosy hue. "It's not broken," she insisted. "There's something odd about you." She peered at him. "If I didn't know any better, I'd swear you were an *Adamou*."

His nose scrunched. "A what?"

She shook her head, and waved her hand around. "Never mind. It's not important. I'd better take care of this before that ass comes back." She raced to the strange-looking bronze contraption the Ozevroc had thrown at her feet. Grabbing it, she made a quick adjustment before heading to another part of the massive room. "I might just have enough time to do this."

Ari watched in astonishment as she announced, "Display!"

Nestled against the farthest wall was some type of a rectangular machine that phased into sight. It appeared to have a brushed-metal finish and rounded edges with parallel compartments next to each other. The thing was taller than him, like a refrigerator on steroids. On one side was a control panel with holographic interfaces that made no sense to him. And on the other side were two separate oval-shaped chambers, one on top of the other.

Morgan approached the machine, gripping the cylinder in her hand. She pressed the screen and the top panel turned blue. She placed the canister inside, then tapped the holographic touchscreen again.

The crazy thing lit up with internal lights that shifted from blue to green. In the lower chamber, a green light surrounded tiny robotic arms that sprang to life. With blinding speed, they created another canister identical to the one nestled on the top shelf.

Ari's eyes widened when both chambers turned from bright green to a soft blue.

A sharp whistle sounded.

Morgan whooped with her fists in the air. She grabbed both cylinders out of the machine. "Refraction!"

The massive machine vanished from sight.

"Now let's see if they work!" She rushed to an obvious worktable and swept aside a pile of parts that clattered to the floor. With care, she placed the identical canisters next to each other. Her fingers flew across the surfaces with quick, deft precision. Soon the machines hummed to life, with bright-orange lights under the control panels.

"Are you hungry? Tell me what you're craving, and I'll make it happen for you."

Dang woman was practically jumping for joy.

"Huh?" Ari put the hair blocking the side of his face behind his ear. "Food? These things make food?" His stomach growled. Crud. When was the last time he ate? As usual, no clue.

The only thing that popped into his head was, "Steak. I want a rare T-bone steak with a baked potato smothered in real butter." Hopefully, that was something he liked.

Morgan looked him up-and-down. "Yeah, I can see that. I'll make sure it's a double portion. Any other veggies?"

Ari shuddered. "No, I don't think I eat those." Whatever "veggies" were. They didn't sound too good.

"What are you, a five-year-old?" Morgan turned to the chamber and pushed several buttons. "We'll start with that and try other things later."

After a few seconds, the upper part of the cylinder on her left opened. Resting inside on a plate was a thick, oddly shaped slab, its surface seared with mysterious grill marks and exuding a familiar, savory aroma. Beside it sat a brown, wrinkled oval, split open to reveal a fluffy white interior dotted with a melting yellow substance. Wrapped next to the plate was a white cloth with the tips of a fork and knife poking out.

The sight and smell from it might be foreign, but it was intriguing enough to make his mouth water.

Morgan jumped at the sound of clacking claws getting louder outside of the hangar. "Quick, take this and hide behind that machine over there." She slammed the cylinder closed with the food inside and shoved it into his arms. She pushed on his chest with the flat of her hands.

Gripping the cool metal of the canister, he stepped back. Glancing over his shoulder, he spied the area she was pushing him to.

"Hurry, before Bugurr gets here." She shooed him. "If he sees that, he'll steal it from us, and we'll get stuck eating tasteless protein cubes." She turned her back on him to face the doorway.

Was Bugurr the shorter gold Ozevroc? Not waiting to find out if he was right, Ari rushed to the hiding place she pointed to and crouched behind it.

Sure enough, the ocher-colored alien strode in with two of his buddies close behind, each carrying a weapon.

It didn't take Morgan long to snarl, hiss, and gurgle at the alien as she handed him the original cylinder.

He answered with a sputtering noise by pressing his lips together, then sticking his tongue out. With a huff, the Ozevroc turned on his clawed paws and left. His minions followed without a garble or hiss.

Ari waited to make sure they didn't come back before he came out of his hiding place. "Can we eat now?" The aroma from the cylinder in his hands was driving him crazy. The painful pinch gripping his stomach made his hands shake.

"Yeah. Take your food and sit over there." Morgan nodded to the same box crate he'd sat on before. Opening the cylinder, she took out his plate of food and shoved it back into his hands. Then she put the empty cylinder on the workbench and punched several buttons and knobs on its surface.

Ari picked up the utensils and cut a piece of the meat and took a bite, barely paying attention to the savory goodness as it melted on his tongue. Instead of taking his time to enjoy his food, he watched Morgan turn her back on him and create her own culinary choice. He couldn't help but feel a pang of isolation with each absent-minded bite. Even while he chewed, his jaw clenched at the impersonal way she acted toward him. Was she indifferent to him, or was there something deeper at play here?

He might not know much, but the quickened beat of his heart and the way his thoughts kept drifting back to her made it clear. Indifference on his part wasn't on the menu. The more time he spent with her, the more irresistible she became. She drew him in with every glance and gesture. But as far as he could tell, she didn't give him a second thought. More of a nuisance than anything else. He took another bite, and this time the food was tasteless as he chewed. The ache of this newfound solitude gnawed in his gut. Maybe he didn't want her to help him find out who he really was.

With his luck, it'd only make him more invisible.

Morgan sighed with a silly grin. Her taste buds and tummy sang satisfied tunes for the first time in a long time. After being kidnapped from the *StarChance*, the only thing she had to eat were dusty, dry, tasteless protein cubes. That is, when anyone remembered to feed her. Once she "joined" the *Nebula Viper*, getting something to eat was a dicey proposition. Since the Ozevroc were a hierarchical species with a harsh chain of command, as a female and a lowly alien slave, the only thing she got was leftovers... if she was lucky enough when someone remembered her. Or if they wanted her to fix something. She lived on the stale cubes she'd found in a crate in a forgotten chamber when she'd been scrounging for engine parts.

She licked her lips, savoring the lingering taste of the marinated coconut-and-ginger crab soup she missed from Aethralis. Paired with that were light-as-air buttery biscuits. Now, all was well in the universe. It'd been hard, but she avoided creating a succulent glass of white wine to go with her food. Instead, she did the practical thing and opted for a flask of ice-cold water. Which she made for Ari as well. The guy had to be parched by now.

Taking a chance, Morgan snuck a quick glance at him. No doubt about it, he was one good-looking man. From his messy, sexy, thick blond hair to the masculine boots on his large feet, he was a definite eye-turner. Too bad he couldn't remember anything. Well, if nothing else, he'd be useful for moving the heavy stuff. Those muscles looked fine. She coughed. Okay, more than fine.

Morgan, quit ogling the strange man and get down to business.

"So, Ari." Morgan swiped her hands over the thighs of her overalls. "Are you ready to go into that ship now? Maybe we'll get lucky and something there will trigger your memory." Fingers crossed, seeing a familiar place might cure him. And, if luck was with them, he'd know how to fix that ship so they could leave sooner than she'd hoped.

Even though the Ozevroc had stripped the ship of anything they could carry, she wondered if he knew about the little secret weapon she'd found tucked into a corner. She was pretty sure she could fix that on her own. But if going onto that ship gave him any insights, all the better.

Ari rubbed his scruffy chin. "I guess so." He lifted his clean plate. "What do I do with this?"

She thumbed over her shoulder. "Just toss it into that open barrel over there. We'll dump it into the incinerator later. Come on, this way."

Ari gave her a nervous smile with a slight shrug. "Okay, you da boss."

Morgan sniffed at him with a frown, then headed to the dark side of the hangar, expecting him to follow. Thankfully, he did. She stopped in front of *Elemi's* sleek form. As she touched the soft surface, the ship reminded her of a predatory creature resting. Its smooth hull had subtle colors that shifted, allowing the vessel to blend into the surrounding shadows. When she stood next to it, the air was noticeably heavier, with a bio-synthetic scent along with a faint floral fragrance.

Morgan went to the place where an open door had originally appeared after the Ozevroc used their tractor beams to bring it in, placing her palm on the surface. There it was, a gentle pulse beneath her hand, as if the ship was breathing and had a faint heartbeat. At her touch, a section next to her rippled and parted like the petals of an exotic flower. Inside was a soft, welcoming glow that came from the leftover bio-luminescent tendrils lining the walls. As the entrance opened wider, a gentle breeze brushed against her face.

Morgan glanced at Ari, hoping to see some spark of recognition.

He hesitated, keeping his eyes on the ship before entering first.

Taking a deep breath, she followed.

Inside, limp tendrils hung from the ceiling like veins devoid of blood. The walls, stripped of their once lush, organic coverings, now exposed the raw, skeletal framework beneath. Shredded membranes and frayed edges were a testament of the Ozevroc's violence as they stripped the ship of anything they could. The floor, once a soft, cushioned surface, was now hard and cold.

Morgan's heart ached at the sight. She turned her focus on Ari.

He moved with careful steps as his fingers brushed the bare walls, his eyes scanning the wreckage.

She watched him, hoping the remnants of the ship might stir some memory. Surely, the soft hum of the ship healing itself had to feel like a forgotten melody to him. A possible lullaby lost but not completely forgotten. "Anything?" she dared to ask.

His slack, blank expression said it all. "No, I don't think so." He crouched and fingered a loose wire and brought it up to study as he twirled it. "What happened here?"

"Once the Ozevroc stripped this ship of everything they could carry, it ended up like this." Morgan gestured to the surrounding mess. "I did my best to stop them as much as I could. But, as you can see, I wasn't much help." It'd been like watching a mob attack an already wounded, defenseless person.

"No one can blame you for what they did." Ari spoke in a soft tone, as if lost in his own thoughts. He frowned as he went from one section to another. He caressed an exposed counter. "I'm afraid none of this looks familiar, but it makes me want to punch that alien ass in his pie-hole."

Morgan nodded. "I was afraid of this. I'm sure it doesn't help that this doesn't look anything like it did before." She snapped her fingers. "Hey, wait. Look at this." She pulled out her multicorder and browsed through the pictures she'd taken before the Ozevroc destroyed the interior. "Look at these. Do they help?"

He took her handheld and swiped through the vids she'd displayed. After a few moments, he shook his head. "Nope, 'fraid not." He handed it back to her. His face reddened with a scowl. "Damn it! I wish I'd recognize something!"

The entire ship shook, making Morgan pinwheel to stay upright before it abruptly ended. She teetered and looked around. Did the High Chieftain make some kind of unscheduled move with the *Nebula Viper*? She rushed to the open doorway and skidded to a stop. Nothing moved or was out of place. Even the loose parts and tools she had scattered on several counters were where she'd left them. *What the hey...?*

Glancing behind her, she looked for Ari. He must have stayed inside. Once more she double-checked the outside, just to make sure she hadn't missed anything. Nope, nothing had moved from that violent shake, so she went back inside.

Ari was kneeling on the floor next to an open portal.

Morgan's heart raced. Did he find it?

"I wonder what this is." He'd raised his open palm eye-level to examine the strange-looking secret thingamabob Morgan had hidden, hoping the Ozevroc never found it.

"I'm not sure, but I was hoping at least that might jog your memory."

The spider-shaped gold-and-silver droid hadn't moved. Its bulbous body, with its four spindly legs spread on its side, didn't so much as twitch.

Ari flipped the lifeless bot over, bringing it closer to his face. "I can't say I recognize it," he murmured, his voice tight, "but I feel there's something about it." The steel gray of his eyes darkened, shadowed by a sudden intensity. "Something important I should know."

CHAPTER THREE

Ari studied the strange spider-looking contraption. The more he observed the bot, the more his throat tightened as a creeping sense came over him. The urge to do *something* hit him hard. No, not something. To find someone. He glanced at Morgan. Her bright eyes followed him. He returned her stare. For some reason, being in the same room with her calmed his nerves. How strange was it that this particular woman calmed him? And, he suspected, she did it like no one ever had before.

Well, okay. At least as far as he knew.

Keeping the little bot nestled in his palm, he stood. "What do you think is wrong with it?" An inkling of a memory floated by. It was him looking at this droid surrounded by other bots that looked very similar to it, but in different colors and sizes. He frowned when nothing else came to him.

"I'm not sure," Morgan stated, looking at the unmoving bot. "But I have some experience in computer mechanics, and I thought I'd try to repair it." She smiled. "I'm hoping it has a working knowledge of how to fix *Elemi*, or at least tell me what I can do to help her heal. That ship is our ticket out of here." She held out her hand, palm up.

With a grunt, Ari pinched the bot between his fingers and thumb and carefully dropped it onto her hand.

The small thing remained unmoving.

"Now that you're here, it'd be helpful if you do some cleanup while I thinker with Charlotte."

Ari's eyebrows rose. "Charlotte?"

Morgan nodded as she turned the spider-bot one way and then another as she examined it. "You know, after the popular book about a spider of the same name."

Ari shrugged. Like he knew what she was talking about. "Works for me," he hedged.

With careful, exaggerated deliberation, she placed the bot into the large pocket on the chest of her overalls. Patting it closed, she again focused on him. "I'll show you around, and we'll make a place for you to sleep." She grimaced. "I'm afraid I can't take you around the rest of the ship since we're confined here. We're not allowed to step out of this room without an Ozevroc escorting us. If we do, these stupid things will activate and blast us into dust." She tugged on the large, black, leather-looking collar around her neck. "Or just knock us out. Depends on their mood."

Reaching up, he fingered the thick material covering his neck. Yeah, staying here sounded good. At least the place was big enough.

It didn't take Morgan long to show him the main room, then the alcove where she slept. She handed him a few blankets from the rag-tag pile of bedding and linens she used, assuring him there'd be more if he needed them. Then, she pointed to another alcove not too far from hers where he could set up his own sleeping spot.

But the best thing she took him to was a cramped, separate room for private use. With a mumbled "thanks," he went inside, grunting when the doors swished closed behind him. It didn't take long to finish taking care of his personal needs. Once he finished, he used the obvious sink. He turned it on, and a single trickle of water came out of the spout. Cupping his hands under it, he splashed the captured water on his face. At least he hoped it was water. If memory served him right, water was usually clear and not dark green. Above the odd-shaped sink was a vid mirror. Ari leaned in and pushed back his wayward blond hair and studied his image. He fingered a small scar at the edge of his bottom lip before concentrating on his eyes. Their steel-gray color stared back, selfishly hiding many secrets.

Who *was* this man looking back at him? Would he ever know? He clenched his teeth and fisted his hands. The vid wavered before blacking out. *Gilgamesh's balls.* This was getting him nowhere. With a huff, he left the room to search for Morgan.

There she was, back at the workbench she'd been at when he first woke up. Ari took the chance to study her before she became aware of him. Even in her baggy clothing, she was one fine-looking woman with a killer body. Obviously smart, but she also carried a hint of hidden mischievousness. Yeah, and he was just the guy to bring that out of her.

He was?

Damn, this not knowing was getting on his last *fruking* nerve. Throwing his shoulders back, he tromped over to her. "So, what do you need me to do?"

Morgan turned to him, putting the spider-bot on the table. She nodded at a stack of loose metal parts combined with panels and goddess knew what else piled against the opposite wall. "See that mountain of junk over there?"

He nodded.

"Until we know what you're good at, you're in charge of cleanup." She gestured to the large barrel he'd dumped his plate into earlier. "Put everything in there. When it's full, you'll get rid of the contents in the incinerator over there." She pointed to a large, rust-colored contraption that dominated the far corner of the engine room. "I'm sure that's something you can handle." Her attention returned to the spider-bot.

Great. Just call him the King of Clutter.

It didn't take Ari long to fill the barrel. It hardly made a dent in the pile. The only interesting thing from the clutter was a whiff of an unusual odor coming out of it. The more stuff he removed, the stronger the stench got. It was a sweet and sour smell like... death? It'd been nice if she'd have warned him there'd be disgusting carcasses in there. He'd be damned if he touched any future fertilizer.

"Hey, Morgan." He made sure his voice carried across the room.

"Yeah?" She didn't look up.

It shouldn't annoy him that the tiny bot got more attention than he did.

"Anything dead in here?"

She gave a ladylike snort and continued to work on the bot. "Nope. The Ozevroc eat anything organic, even their own comrades. They believe the spirit of their dead belongs with the living. Believe me, they never get rid of anything they could consume."

Well, wasn't that just disgusting? Freaking buzzards. He examined the outside of the full dumpster barrel and located a panel on its side. He was about to push one of them to see what it'd do when Morgan spoke up.

"That's the controls to make it hover, so it's easy to move around. The bottom button makes it lift off the ground, the left button guides it to the right and the right button makes it go to the left. When you want it on the ground, punch the top button."

"So, everything is the opposite of what common sense says it should be? Got it," he muttered, activating the contraption to move it to the other side of the room. You'd think an advanced civilization would at least have a way to put their discarded parts inside the incinerator instead of throwing things around so someone else had to go and pick it up. But, no...

Ari halted in front of the incinerator and squinted at it. The thing was a rectangular beast made of thick steel walls that absorbed the dim light. He brushed his fingers against the rough, gritty texture of the surface that was coated with years old grime and oil. One side had an embedded narrow control panel with flashing red and orange lights glowing in an erratic pattern. His hand hovered over the symbols he couldn't read.

"Remember, the idiots make everything opposite," he mumbled to himself and pressed a prominent blinking red button. With a low mechanical groan, the front panel slid open with a hiss. A puff of hot air made him step back.

Inside was a small, rectangular chamber lined with scorched, blackened metal grates. Residue of countless burnings with charred bits of unrecognizable materials clung to the walls. A conveyor belt ran through the chamber, littered with twisted scraps of metal, burned fabric, and ash.

The smell hit him. A pungent mix of tainted ozone and something acidic, almost chemical. He grimaced. The scent triggered a vague, unsettling memory he couldn't quite grasp.

"Everything okay over there?"

Thank the goddess Morgan's voice pulled him out of his musings. He didn't want to stand here any longer than he had to. "Yep. Having the best time of my life, right here," he replied without looking at her. Grabbing the stuff on top of the pile, he threw everything into the hot opening of the incinerator as quick as he could. The sooner he finished this, the better.

When it was full, he pushed the steady orange light.

The doors slid close with a grinding noise.

Satisfied it was working like it was supposed to, he hovered the empty barrel back to the junk pile and started over.

Things were going along in a mundane fashion when his fingers brushed against something different. Fur. Fur? He poked it. Didn't Morgan just tell him the Ozevroc ate anything organic? This one might be squishy as all get out, but it still had some meat on it. He grabbed the surrounding metal parts and panels to expose whatever it hid.

Sure enough, it was an Ozevroc. A really dead one.

"Um, Morgan?" he raised his voice without taking his eyes from the carcass. "Can you come here, please?"

"What? Why?"

Ari flicked a glance in her direction. "I thought you told me the Ozevroc eat anything organic, even one of them."

Her sigh echoed in the large room. "Of course they do. They save more credits that way."

"Well, no one told this guy he belonged in his friends' gullet."

The sound of her footsteps stopped when she stood next to him. "What are you talking about?"

Damn woman crossed her arms again, causing her plump breasts to lift up. It almost made him forget what he had to show her.

Almost.

The decomposing body of the Ozevroc drew his attention again. The nauseating sweet-sour smell of rotting flesh mingled with the corroded odor of the surrounding iron and rusty steel.

Morgan gasped, with her hand covering her mouth. "Oh my god, that's Xalgrim!"

Ari covered his nose and mouth with the palm of his hand. Not that it helped to keep the stink out. "Who?"

"He's in charge of security," she responded. "Or at least he was."

"Looks like he sucked at his job, since someone killed him." Ari pointed to the side of the dead Ozevroc's head. It looked like it was bashed in with something heavy.

"What? That's impossible." Morgan turned to him, keeping her mouth covered. "The Ozevroc may be cannibals, but if one of them went against Welozz, he'd just blast him into dust. They'd never leave one of them like this."

Ari's stomach sank. He could see him and Morgan getting blamed for this. And it didn't take a genius with full memories intact to know their captors wouldn't believe them when they claimed their innocence. "So, what do you say we throw it into the incinerator and forget the whole thing?"

What a day. Morgan couldn't remember the last time her emotions scrambled all over the place. Which annoyed her even more. The only thing she craved was sleep and not thinking about the crazy chain of events she'd just lived through. Getting settled in her nest of discarded blankets and rags, she did her best to clear her mind to let slumber take over.

But the last few hours were hard to forget.

She and Ari had wrapped Xalgrim's dead body in a flammable, raggedy blanket and tossed it into the incinerator. Keeping her lunch down was a struggle by the time they were done. Ari must have felt the same way since claimed he was done with trash and demanded something more important to do.

Knowing a hard wall when she saw one, she relented and led him to *Elemi*. Coming to the side of the ship, still open, she patted the sleek machine. "Since the Ozevroc don't care what happens to this ship now, if you screw anything up, they won't be any wiser." Turning to him, she narrowed her eyes. "But don't make things worse. While I believe she's self-repairing, I'm sure she could use some help. Just tinker around and see what you can do."

His answering grunt was all she got before he disappeared into the dim interior. Morgan blew out a breath. Maybe now she could concentrate on the little spider-bot in peace.

"Hey, Morgan—"

No such luck.

Ari stuck his head out of the entryway. "—I don't know what I'm doing here. It's not exactly my area of expertise."

She swore only a few moments had passed. How could he be bugging her so soon? "How do you know? Ari, you need to give it some time before you give up." Aha! She finally got the small panel on the bot's belly to open. Now all she had to do was...

"How am I going to fix this ship if I don't know what I'm doing?" The frustration was obvious in his strangled tone.

Morgan closed her eyes and took a deep breath. "I get it, but like I said, you've got to give it some time. Maybe your memory will come back if you don't try to push yourself so hard. Go back inside and wander around. If something makes you pause, sit down and study it. Let your subconscious absorb what the ship is trying to tell you."

"What, you think I'm a psychic or something?" Ari groused.

Morgan grinned. If only. She opened her eyes and peered at him standing in the doorway of the still ship. Once again, his handsomeness took her aback. She'd never been attracted to blond men before, but there was something compelling about Ari's overt masculinity. And she was a sucker for tall men. "Wait, hang on, Ari. Let me get you something that might help."

When she first repaired the replicron, she made a copy of her multicorder. While the thing wouldn't work as well as the original from Aethralis, it had its uses. She'd almost lost her precious device more often than she cared to admit since being kidnapped. Thank the goddess, the thing flattened into a compact, paper-thin mode easy enough for her to shove under one of her breasts to hide it when she had to.

Morgan marched to him with the copied unit in hand. "Here, this might help. You can use it to scan specific areas to see what might be wrong. It should even give you advice on how to fix that area." She held it out to him. "Want to try it?"

"I guess." He shrugged his massive shoulders.

Morgan bit back a groan as his muscular chest rippled under his tight shirt.

"Show me what to do."

Handing him the device, she pointed out the various functions and capabilities, activating the verbal response for him. When her hand brushed against his, an unexpected jolt shot through her. She glanced at him.

He didn't look at her, his attention absorbed in the handheld.

Pursing her lips, she swallowed her disappointment. She'd never been insecure around men, but for some reason, this one had her second-guessing herself at the oddest times.

The tense lines on his face relaxed as he studied the device, turning it over and back again. "Okay, this I can handle." He went back inside.

The rest of the day proved uneventful. But various images of Ari doing normal stuff wouldn't leave her mind. Even watching the man eat made her warm.

She snarled and turned over, punching the pocket of rags she'd made into a pillow to make it conform better. She plopped onto her back and stared at the darkened shadows in the dim light overhead. What was going on with her? She should keep in mind the man suffered from amnesia. If nothing else, she should be looking for a way to cure him, not obsess over the way he looked. Who knew what kind of man he was under all that confusion? For all she knew, he lied about everything. She laced her hands behind her head. Ha, she doubted anyone would go through the painful process he'd endured just to come aboard the *Nebula Viper*. If the Ozevroc had anything he wanted, all he'd have to do was to negotiate with them.

And that ship. If the Ozevroc had any idea how rare and valuable that organic ship *Elemi* was, they'd have already sold it on the black market. Even as stripped as it was, the ship would still command a high price. The proceeds would set them up for a whole galactic year. Maybe it'd be better to concentrate on the ship and not Ari. Especially since the only thing he accomplished was making himself angry over his lack of progress. When he came out of the ship, he'd tossed the faux multicorder onto her workstation and announced he was done for the night. He grabbed a pile of blankets and stomped to the other alcove.

Dang man sure was hard on himself. She watched him tug off his boots and lie down, his back facing her. It didn't take long for his breathing to even out and let her know he fell asleep.

Dang, if only she was so lucky. Sleep was the last thing...

"Human! Today you die!"

Morgan jerked awake. It took a moment before her groggy mind worked. She groaned and sat up, rubbing her eyes.

"Not today, Chief. Lots to fix." She yawned and scratched her head. The only thing she wanted was a steaming cup of hot coffee. Not dealing with some egotistical alien.

Rough hands grabbed her forearm and yanked her to her feet.

"Hey! Let go. What do you think you're doing?" Morgan jerked her arm out of the tight grip of a small Ozevroc. Great, it was Grozzik, one of the nastiest Ozevroc around. She deliberately turned to High Chieftain Welozz and ignored the annoying little shit trying to grab her again. When he placed his grimy hand on her, she stepped on one of his bare foot-paws and ground her heel into it. She smiled when he squealed like a stuck pig and hopped out of her reach.

"Sacred gone!" The navy-blue fur on the Chieftain's neck bristled. "Return or die!" He thumped his ever-present staff on the metal floor. The two sets of his dark, beady eyes narrowed as a growl rumbled out of his thin, black lips. "Human die!"

Crap. By the looks of him, he might really mean it this time.

She held up her hands, hoping to calm him down. "I'm sorry, Chief. I don't know what you're talking about. What is sacred?" It was hard to believe anything was sacred to these guys.

The High Chieftain's growl increased in volume. "Talon of Ancients... sacred. Must return to Sanctum of Reverence now! You die!"

"Hang on, hang on." Morgan spied her multicorder on her workstation. "Give me a chance to see what I can find. Okay?" She edged away from the angry alien and shuffled to the workstation, keeping her eye on the furious Ozevroc leader and his handful of protective goons.

Welozz snarled, but that didn't stop her from moving away. Holding back a sigh of relief, she powered up her handheld and inserted the name Talon of Ancients. Good thing she'd been smart enough to interface her device with the Ozevroc computer system when she found herself their prisoner.

Her eyes widened when the information came back with a picture. She sucked in a breath and skimmed the information.

"Talon of Ancients" is a striking and intricately crafted object that is approximately a foot long, shaped like a curved claw, and made from a combination of precious metals and crystalline materials. The surface is adorned with elaborate carvings and symbols that glow faintly with an ethereal blue light, a representation of its holy stature. The metal is a deep, lustrous black, while the crystalline segments shimmer in shades of blue and green.

The Talon of Ancients is embedded with small, polished gemstones at key points, each representing an element of Ozevroc culture and history. The base of the claw features an ornate handle wrapped in a silken, dark-blue fabric that is both durable and soft. The artifact exudes a sense of ancient power and reverence. Its very presence invokes awe and respect in the Ozevroc.

Aboard the Nebula Viper, *The Talon of Ancients is housed in a special chamber known as the Sanctum of Reverence. The Sanctum is a small, dimly lit room in the most secure part of the ship, accessible only to the highest-ranking members of the Ozevroc delegation. The room's walls have intricate tapestries depicting the history and legends of the Ozevroc people. The air must be maintained with a faint, soothing fragrance of sacred herbs.*

At the center of the Sanctum stands a pedestal made of the same crystalline material as the Talon itself. A protective energy field surrounds this pedestal, bathing the artifact in a shimmering blue light. The Talon of Ancients rests on a velvet cushion atop the pedestal, prominently displayed for all who enter the Sanctum to see and venerate.

The Sanctum of Reverence is not just a place of safekeeping, but also a site of ritual and meditation. The artifact is more than just a way for the Ozevroc to pay homage to their ancestors. It's the absolute seat of their governmental power. Whoever possess the Talon of Ancients has absolute authority over the species. The loss or destruction of the artifact would not only be a cultural and spiritual catastrophe, but would throw the entire Ozevroc civilization into a quagmire of civil unrest. This item must remain secure at all costs.

Morgan gulped. Holy God, if this damn thing was missing...

She peered at the High Chieftain. "You say it's gone?" Her voice came out raspy. "When did this happen?"

The clank of metal being thrown around made her jump.

The little troop the High Chieftain brought with him was tearing the place apart.

Not that she blamed him. If this Talon meant as much to them as she read, she could understand their single-minded devotion to finding it.

Speaking of finding things, where was Ari? She glanced at the alcove he'd gone to sleep in. The only thing there was a discarded pile of blankets and rags. Where in the hell did the man go?

And how did he leave the room without the *nutesh* snare zapping him unconscious?

Ari stumbled. Pinwheeling, he righted himself before he planted face-first on the hard floor. Blinking, he glanced around. Where was he? The last thing he remembered was lying on a lumpy pile of mismatched blankets and rags trying to fall asleep. Damn alcove Morgan told him to use barely gave him enough room to stretch out.

It was obvious he wasn't in the alcove—he wasn't anywhere in the massive engine/hanger room. He blinked against the dim, artificial lighting, his eyes slowly adjusting to the unfamiliar surroundings. The air carried a metallic tang, mingling with the faint scent of something earthy and musk-like. His footsteps echoed softly on the metal floor. He had to be in the *Nebula Viper* somewhere. With no other choice, he ventured ahead into the unknown, keeping in mind Morgan's warning about being found outside without an Ozevroc guide. Lined on the scruffy, unwashed walls were exposed circuitry and conduits. Taking the rhythmic glow as a guide, he kept close to the walls.

With each step, his senses sharpened with cautious curiosity. Each corridor seemed to twist and turn, a labyrinth of metallic passageways. Every once in a while, he'd stop and listen for any sign of movement. All remained eerily silent. The farther he went, the more alien the surroundings became. Strange symbols adorned the walls, and he passed rooms filled with unfamiliar technology—machines that hummed with energy and devices that blinked with erratic lights.

So far, so good. No one was in sight. He just might find something familiar before anyone saw him.

As he rounded a corner, Ari's breath caught. Damn, he shouldn't have gotten so happy-clappy.

Ahead, two Ozevroc were in some king of argument, their long snouts bobbing animatedly as they gestured with their six arms.

Ari's heart raced, and he pressed himself flat against the wall. *Tiamat's titties!* The only thing to do was wait. Every muscle tensed, making his headache grow as he watched the Ozevroc continue with their gibberish discussion. When one of them glanced in his direction, Ari held his breath. With every fiber of his being, he willed himself to become part of the shadows.

With agonizing slowness, the Ozevroc turned back to the conversation with his partner, oblivious to Ari just down the hall. Seizing the opportunity, Ari edged backward, retracing his steps with painstaking care. He navigated the maze of corridors, using the gentle hum of the ship and the faint glow of the walls as his guide. He kept each step deliberate, every movement painstakingly slow to avoid detection.

After an eternity, Ari heard voices. Random hisses, growls, and grunts in male tones. When Morgan's female tenor matched the same sounds, he grinned as his heart raced. Look at him, finding his way back without getting caught.

Peeking around the corner to the open hatch of the engine/hanger room, he spied the dynamics going on. There was that chief guy... Well-oz, or something like that. Boy, this time, the alien really looked pissed. He was spitting more than usual in his language and waving that ridiculous staff around as if he was going to hit Morgan with it.

Ari's neck burned. He had to get in there and protect her. If only he could somehow create a diversion...

A remaining pile of discarded steel and metal not only crashed into a single heap on the floor, but it captured several Ozevroc under some of the heavier pieces. The chaos that followed came with high-pitched screams among the rush of Ozevroc claws clicking on the floor as the ones not caught in the avalanche raced to their comrades.

By the unending abyss, how did that happen?

No time to wonder, time for action. He quickly assessed the situation and saw his chance to slink across the back wall where no one was looking. He snuck up behind Morgan and placed his hand on her shoulder. She jumped, then turned around, her golden-green eyes wide.

"Dang, girl. How dare you have a little party and not invite me? Shame on you." He smirked.

Morgan swallowed hard to calm her racing heart. She slapped his hand away in reflex. "What the hell, Ari?" she hissed. She glanced around, making sure none of the Ozevroc was paying attention to them. "Where have you been?" The sight of his naked neck made her suck in a breath. "And where's your *nutesh* snare?" How in the hell did he get the damn thing off?

Ari's gray eyes widened as he fingered his thick, muscular neck. "By the horned crown of Enlil, I have no idea."

Moran narrowed a glance at him. Enlil? What was with this guy and ancient Babylonian gods?

The commotion was winding down as the Ozevroc dug their comrades out from the mess as Welozz hissed and sputtered commands at them.

Spying a black neck scarf she sometimes wore when the heat was on the fritz, she grabbed it and waved it in front of Ari. "Quick, wrap this around your neck so Welozz doesn't notice your collar is gone."

Breathing a sigh of relief when he didn't argue with her, she watched him wrap the cloth around his neck. As the High Chieftain stomped back, she smoothed her face and looked at his feet after he stopped in front of her.

"Listen, High Chief," Morgan raised a hand to forestall the alien berating her again. "Have your troops finish searching this area so you know for certain we didn't take your sacred object. In the meantime"—she gestured between her and Ari—"let us help you find it. You know, a different perspective might be all you need to locate where it went. And the sooner the better. Am I right?"

Welozz snorted, making loose bits of snot flare out. Tense moments passed before he decided. "Human find or human die." His four black eyes studied Ari, then her. He turned his staff on the shorter, ocher-colored Ozevroc at his side. "Bugurr, watch troops. If sacred talon found, say immediate." He headed for the doorway. Over his shoulder he snarled, "We go. Follow." A small group of Ozevroc went with him.

"Does that mean they're sparing us?" Ari asked.

"Yeah." Morgan clipped her multicorder to her belt. "Lucky us, we're going to play Sherlock and Watson." She could tell he wanted to ask her what that meant, but she didn't give him a chance. "Come on, we've got to find a priceless relic for the Ozevroc so they don't kill us."

Ari whistled and shoved his hands into the back pockets of his jeans. "Sounds like fun. Can't wait to see how this turns out."

CHAPTER FOUR

Morgan's head spun as she followed the group of Ozevroc to their Sanctum of Reverence. There were so many questions rattling around in her head it was hard to concentrate on one thing.

Like, who took the sacred relic of the Ozevroc? She doubted it was any of them. It couldn't be any of the slaves they usually had on board. They sold all those beings at their last stop, which left no one else around to steal it. She knew she didn't. That left only one other person. The man walking next to her. Not only had he somehow taken his *nutesh* snare off, but it left him free to leave the engine room and disappear.

So, did he take the relic? If so, why? And what did he do with it? If he didn't take it, then where did he go and what did he do?

She took a step back and studied his backside, at first looking for where he could carry the Ozevroc relic. Nope, nothing between this man and his tight jeans. Pursing her lips, she stole a precious moment to appreciate the flow and ebb of his thick thighs and glorious ass working as he walked.

When he turned to look at her over his shoulder, she tilted her chin up and resumed her place next to him.

No way was he carrying that thing on his person. Did that mean he took it somewhere and hid it? Hopefully not in the engine room. No way she'd convince Welozz of her innocence then. Her pulse sped up, bringing heat to her neck and cheeks. What kind of game was Ari playing? Did the man really have amnesia?

Her shoulders slumped. Yeah, she had every reason to think he did. When she'd first scanned her multicorder over him, it confirmed he suffered from memory loss. But that didn't answer where he went after she fell asleep. Or what happened to his slave collar.

Well, the only way to get her answers was to talk to him. A private sit-down was on the agenda. She needed answers. But she'd have to do it away from the Ozevroc.

High Chieftain Welozz stopped before an obvious doorway, causing Morgan to jerk out of her musings. She glanced around, and her eyes widened when she noticed they were on a whole other level of the *Nebula Viper* than she'd been in before. Great. Instead of paying attention to where they were going, she'd moved around in a fog, worrying about Ari. She resolved to not let that happen again.

With a snarl and growl, Welozz prayed for the door to open with a flourish of his staff and open arms, all six of them.

The covering dissolved open with a reverent hiss.

"Humans. Come." Welozz demanded, entering the darkened room. His troops stayed outside, their ever-ready weapons held in tight grips.

Morgan followed the Ozevroc and stepped into the dimly lit Sanctum of Reverence.

The air was thick with the scent of sacred herbs and carried an aura of solemnity. The room was small but ornately decorated, with tapestries on every wall that looked like a depiction of the rich history of the Ozevroc people. At the center, an empty pedestal stood, the Talon of Ancients conspicuously absent.

Her heart sank. Damn thing was really gone. Sucking in a fortifying breath, she refocused on the task at hand. "Okay, let's see if we can find out what happened here." She kept her voice steady despite the tension pinching between her shoulders. Pulling out the multicorder, she scanned up and down the pedestal.

Ari nodded and glanced around the room with narrow eyes. "I'll take a quick look around. Just to make sure no one came in except through the main door."

"Find now. Only I Chieftain! Must have." Welozz claimed, smacking the staff on the pristine metallic floor. His six muscular arms twitched with barely contained energy, making his navy-blue fur glisten in the low light.

Morgan studied the readings as they coalesced on the screen. "Don't worry, High Chief. We'll do our best. I'll find clues that will point us to the thief."

She circled the empty pedestal again with her handheld, its soft hum filling the air. She swept it over and around the intricately embossed column. Her multicorder screen lit up with data. The readings showed traces of an unusual crystalline residue, faint but unmistakable.

"Well, this is weird," Morgan murmured, flipping the screen around to show Ari and Welozz. "The only organic residue is from the Ozevroc. But there's some kind of crystalline remnant all around the pedestal and the floor." She aimed her handheld above her to the ceiling. "It's faint, but there's even some here." She brought the screen down. "It has a strange conglomeration of amethyst, quartz, and some kind of alien compound I've never seen before."

"Hey, Morgan. Point that thing over here." Ari gestured to a section of the wall that seemed to glitter.

Turning around, she brought the multicorder to where he motioned. "You're right, it looks like this wall is thick with the same combination the pedestal has." She brushed her hand over the smooth surface. "It doesn't feel any different from this section to the next." She focused her scanner around the room, and the multicorder picked up more traces of the crystalline substance leading back and forth from the pedestal to the wall. "It looks like our thief somehow came through this wall. Where does it lead?" She addressed Welozz.

Welozz's snout tightened. "Outside ship."

Morgan translated what the Ozevroc said for Ari.

"Bummer," Ari muttered under his breath.

Morgan glanced at Ari with a frown. She turned to Welozz. "Has this been here before?" She gestured to the shimmering glow left behind on the wall.

Welozz snarled, which didn't need a translation.

"If you'll allow, great High Chieftain, Ari and I will go through the ship and..."

Bugurr raced into the room. "High Chieftain! Quick, come!"

Morgan never imagined she'd ever see that look of panic cross the Sub-Chieftain's snout. His four eyes were wide enough that a hint of white surrounded their onyx color.

"No obstruct!" the High Chieftain demanded, pounding his staff on the floor.

"Lurvath killed!" Bugurr rumbled as he fell to his knees with his head on the ground. Just informing the High Chieftain that one of them was dead without him being involved was a cause for severe disciplinary action to the messenger.

"What's going on?" Ari leaned down and whispered to her.

"Looks like someone murdered another one of them." Morgan glanced up at him. "And this time, they found him."

Ari's lips twisted into a grimace. "Well, at least we won't have to fire up the incinerator this time."

Ari sucked in a deep breath when they stepped out of the small sanctum room. The confined space made his skin crawl, and the cloying scent of the incense the Ozevroc used made his nose burn. Saying his mood was darkening would be putting it mildly. And the narrow-eyed looks Morgan gave him didn't help. Not that he blamed her. No telling how he ended up on another part of the ship. The black *nutesh* snare should've zapped him awake before he left the room.

Ari fingered the thick scarf around his neck. What happened to that snare? He glanced around to make sure the Ozevroc didn't notice he wasn't wearing their slave collar. An image shot across his mind. One of him with three other men as each ripped the offending thing off their necks with loud whoops of celebration. Had he been a slave on another ship? That might explain why he'd never noticed the collar until Morgan pointed it out to him.

A sharp shove to the middle of his back made him stumble. He glared over his shoulder at the short Ozevroc poking him with the cylinder pole he carried.

The alien hissed and growled.

Ari didn't need a translator to let him know the guy wanted him to pick up the pace. "Hey, take it easy, fur-ball four-eyes." He shrugged his arm away from the pushy guy. "No need to damage the goods."

"Keep up," Morgan hissed a whisper as she stepped closer to him. "We're walking on thin ice as it is."

She pursed her luscious, lickable lips and glanced at the Ozevroc around them. Her statement confused him at first. The floor was metal, not ice. Oh, wait. She was making a metaphor. He fingered his earlobe. Now why would he know what a metaphor was? *Gah.* This amnesia shit was getting on his last damn nerve. Especially since he didn't know why he woke up walking the hallways of a hostile alien ship.

He had to be mental.

One of the Ozevroc, something that looked like the offspring between a howler monkey that did the nasty with a beaver, growled at Morgan.

She held out her hand to stop Ari from following the self-important chieftain into a room. "We'll wait here until they say we can go in."

Ari peered into the room.

A scattering of tables and benches were built close to the ground, small enough to fit the short Ozevroc. Lumpy, worn padded material covered the benches that had to give their stumpy tails stability. The tables had round, built-in trays. Probably to keep the food in place when the ship jerked around for whatever reason.

But it was the strange smell that came out of the room that told him this had to be their communal eating place. The air had a thick scent of cooking meat mixed with a faint, sweet order of something pickled and fermented. Not to mention that underlying musk of wet dog the aliens carried. At least he hoped this was their version of a cafeteria. If they used this disgusting room for anything else, he might bolt for the hills. Well, if there were hills to bolt to.

The four-eyed member of the snout squad poked him again with more growls and grunts. This time on his side. He scowled at the beastie. He reached to grab the idiot's pole when Morgan gripped his wrist.

"No, it's okay. They want us to go in." Morgan led him inside. "I'm going to activate my multicorder around the body. Please just stay behind me and don't say or do anything." She turned her imploring gold-green eyes his way. "Please?"

Ari huffed with a frown. "Okay, I'll do my best." He glanced down at the stubby little shit with his weapon still aimed at Ari's midsection. "But warn mini-ugly here no touchy, or I won't be responsible for what shape his weapon will look like after I shove it up his ass."

Morgan rolled those expressive eyes at him, but leaned down to the Ozevroc and grumbled and hissed at him.

The creature's burned-orange fur bristled, but he stepped back and brought the tip up, narrowing his two sets of black eyes in Ari's direction.

That settled, Ari followed Morgan into the room. The place was a mess. Plates, along with eating utensils covered in congealing food, littered the floor. Every messy table overflowed with the same discarded, smelly crap untouched for goddess only knew for how long. He sniffed. If he wasn't mistaken, some of the Ozevroc had to have relieved themselves around the place. *By the everlasting gods, these are some disgusting beaver-tailed barf-dogs.*

Taking shallow breaths, he stood behind a crouched Morgan, who ran her multicorder over the still form of an unmoving Ozevroc.

The alien's mouth was slightly ajar, the thin lips tinged in blue. A thin trickle of dried blood crested at the corner, and his black tongue hung out the side. The creature's four eyes were wide-eyed, the orbs protruding. All six sets of his clawed hands were unnaturally bent and stiff. His beaver-like tail was curled in a way that spoke of agony and resistance. A clear bite mark from blocky, wide teeth stood out on one of his upper arms. As Ari looked it over, he found no similar wounds on it.

"Did someone strangle him or try to eat him?" Ari crouched next to Morgan, studying the body closer, trying to grasp every detail the corpse offered. The creature's coarse hairs might have been a dark brown, but the color was covered in a dried, caking goo and lay matted against his stubby chest. "Is it okay if I touch him?" he asked Morgan.

She took a quick glance at her multicorder and at the High Chieftain behind her. She hissed, and he growled back.

"Okay, just be respectful."

Ari grinned. "Hey, you bet. Respect is my middle name."

Not waiting for a response, he took extra care when he lifted the Ozevroc's head. There, around his neck, were deep, crescent-shaped bruises like powerful fingers had dug into the flesh. The skin beneath the fur bore the unmistakable imprints of a struggle, the force of the attacker's grip clear in the dark, mottled marks.

Ari laid the head down and studied the Ozevroc's long, coarse fingers, most bent unnaturally. Looked like the guy tried to pry away the hands that had stolen his life. "Morgan, aim your multicorder at his hands, especially his claws, and see if you can get any DNA from them." He sighed, rising to his feet. He stood with his hands on his hips, taking in the cluttered surroundings. While the place was an overall mess, it was easy to tell the Ozevroc died trying to save his life. Overturned crates and scattered cooking tools bore silent witness to his final, frantic moments.

"What do you see?" he asked her.

"Well—" Morgan rose, still reading her device. "—this here is, er, was Lurvath, the head cook."

"Wow, hard to believe anyone would object to something this guy cooked." Ari pointed to the rest of the room. "If this room is an example of his master chef capabilities, no wonder the High Chieftain wanted you to fix their food-thingy."

"Yeah, well. Now you know why I was desperate to make one for myself," Morgan responded in a quiet voice. She looked up at him. "I'm going to tell his highness over there that I've found the same crystalline traces here that were in the sanctum room." She pursed her lips. "Not sure how he's going to take that."

"I dunno—" Ari crossed his arms with a grin. "—we've lived a whole hour without getting a death threat. I was beginning to feel left out."

Morgan grimaced. "Yeah, well, let's hope that's the least he'll do."

Luckily, the High Chieftain let Morgan scan the rest of the room.

Sure enough, the crystalline trail was in there, but nowhere outside it. The corridor was clear.

"Maybe it popped in and out like a magician." Ari offered an unhelpful analysis. "Did you ask them if anything was missing from here?" He gestured around the chaos of the Ozevroc cafeteria. "Now that'd definitely be some kind of magic trick."

Morgan frowned, tucking a strand of her golden curls behind her ear. Most of them sprang back. The man might've hit on something. It was general practice for the psychics at Aethralis to teleport around the city all the time. Could this be something similar?

Shaking herself out of her musings, she faced Ari. "Nothing is missing as far as they know. But look here."

She led him to a mound of glass that sparkled in the dim light. Crouching, she aimed the multicorder over a deep impression on the side of the pile. Running her handheld over it, she studied the readings. "If I didn't know better, I'd swear it was a footprint."

Ari settled next to her and focused on where she indicated.

His warm, masculine scent drew her in, making her take a deep, appreciative breath. She sure loved the masculine scent he carried. Musky goodness mixed with an unfamiliar spice that made her pulse thrum. Images of them in an intimate, naked embrace made her bite her tongue. What was it about this guy that made her react like that? She'd never behaved like this with anyone so quickly before.

Ari whistled low. "Damn, if that's someone's foot, this here is one heavy sucker. Look how deep it is." He fingered around the side. "And what's sticking out the sides? It looks like spikes."

Morgan peered closer to the real thing before adjusting the multicorder. "Those spikes are part of the footprint itself. They're appendages just like the toes are. How odd." She tried to get her handheld to create an image of what could have made that print, but the 'corder stated it needed further information.

With a reluctant sigh, she stood and looked around. "I don't think there's anything else we can do here." She clipped her multicorder to her belt. "We'd better get back to the engine room before they begin their funeral ritual." She shuddered. "I vowed I'd never watch them do that again if I could help it."

Not waiting for his answer, she approached the High Chieftain, keeping her eyes focused low and to the side. "Oh, great and mighty Chieftain. May we lowly humans return to the engine room? Lots to fix."

Welozz thumped his staff with a snarl. "Find Talon of Ancients!"

She nodded, keeping her head bowed. "Yes, yes. With your permission, I wish to study the layout of the *Nebula Viper* to discover where the sacred artifact might be. I need to plan where to search further."

Morgan kept her head down as the silence stretched. She tensed when Ari took a step beside her, but at least he kept his smart-aleck self quiet.

"Done." Welozz announced. "Or humans die."

She pursed her lips to keep from groaning in relief. Welozz wasn't stupid. He had to realize she was his best chance at finding the artifact.

"Grozzik take back. You find," the High Chieftain announced, turning away to announce the festivities of cooking Lurvath for the funeral feast.

Morgan shuddered. "That's our cue." She announced to Ari. "Let's get out of here." She nodded to the khaki-brownish-yellow Ozevroc glaring at them. "Just follow Grozzik as he leads us back to the engine room."

"Okey dokey pokey." Ari watched the short Ozevroc with a mischievous gleam in his steel-gray eyes.

She nudged Ari with her shoulder. "Whatever you're planning, don't. Let's not give Grozzik any reason to stay with us once we get there. We've got too much to do." Between fixing the small spider-bot to help with *Elemi's* repairs, to cleaning up whatever mess the Ozevroc left after they searched the place. Not to mention she had to come up with a plan to find the missing artifact. To top it off, she was starving and couldn't wait to activate the replicron to whip up some breakfast. Along with a much-needed cup of coffee.

"Fine." Ari huffed. "He's safe." He grinned. "For now."

Morgan stifled the threatening grin. Damn clown. She wouldn't put it past him to trip the Ozevroc into the nearest airlock.

"Good." She nodded. "Let's get some breakfast and figure out what to do next."

"Yeah." Ari nodded. "Gotta admit finding a murdering thief is way easier on a full stomach."

When Ari, with Morgan beside him, followed Grozzik into the engine room, he hooked his thumbs into the loops of his jeans and glanced around. If he thought the place was a mess before, boy howdy, was he ever wrong. The mountain of discarded metal and tools he'd worked on yesterday might have been in a neat pile, but any sense of order was completely gone. All of it was every which way, making it impossible to move without stepping on something.

"Wow, good thing having nothing to do today isn't on the agenda," he quipped.

Morgan snorted, plucking up some of the clutter covering her workstation and tossing most of it into the trash bin he'd used before. "This is ridiculous," she muttered, wiping her hands together. "I'm hungry. Let's eat. Replicron display!"

It didn't take her long to pull her food replicator out of the larger machine where she'd stored it. Since he couldn't remember anything that resembled what she called breakfast, he told her to surprise him with something.

Soon, he joined her sitting on an upturned crate, devouring what she called an omelet. Best thing ever. The cheesy goodness smothered the veggies, as well as sausage, ham, bacon, and potatoes. She'd also brought him a container with a bright orange liquid. After his first tentative sip, he gulped it all in one swallow. When he finished everything, he asked her to show him how to make more.

"Later," she replied. "For now, I'll do it. We don't have a lot of time to get this place cleaned up. Patience isn't Welozz's strong point, so we've got to concentrate on finding that artifact as soon as we can." She shook her head. "I can't believe anyone took something that important to the Ozevroc without them noticing."

Morgan brought him another glass of the orange drink. His fingers brushed over hers, surprising him when a bolt of lust tightened his cock. The need to lay her back and lick every inch of her as part of his breakfast feast made his mouth water. *Dammit.* Had he always behaved like that with a female? With a tentative grasp, he put his other hand over his lap to cover his hardened member. No need to advertise how attracted to her he was. No telling how she'd react to that.

Too late. Her lips twitched.

Those sweet, pouty lips. Mesmerized by the sight, he imagined those plump mounds sliding against his naked chest... and lower. Much lower. His dick twitched in agreement.

Sliding his eyes to look anywhere but her, Ari drank the now-tasteless juice as fast as he could. Putting the glass on the counter, he sat back and turned his attention back to Morgan when it was safe to do so. He watched her every move. Even though she wore baggy overalls, the fabric cupped and held her breasts like a lover as it draped over her succulent form and accentuated her round, firm ass. She'd rolled the pant legs up to expose her trim, shapely ankles and calves, along with her dainty feet encased in some kind of slip-on shoes made of a canvas material. Every movement she made was as smooth as a burning flame, smoldering and hot.

"So..." Ari cleared his throat. Back to business. "What's first on the agenda for today, *irnini*?"

Morgan's eyebrows rose. "*Irnini*? Sweet-smelling lady? That's a weird name to call me." Her eyes narrowed. "Why would you use an ancient Babylonian name like that?"

All he could do was shrug. "Who knows?" He let his lips curl suggestively. "But you've got to admit I'm not lying."

Her only response was to roll her eyes. She went back to her workstation after discarding her plate and cup.

Ari's jaw tightened. He meant every word he said. "Why does it bother you when I say something nice to you?" He went over to her, bending so he could catch her eye. "I may not know a lot about myself, but I know I'm not a liar." Leaning close, he caught a whiff of her sensual scent, an exquisite blend of sandalwood with a hint of earthy balsamic. Honesty, he was sure, had to be the best policy. Why not admit it?

"I want you to know how attracted to you I am." He grasped her hand and exposed her palm. With deliberate slowness, he traced his finger from her inner elbow across to the middle of her hand. Just this simple touch made his heart thunder. "Is it normal for me to feel like this when we touch?" His voice came out low as he searched her expression for an answer.

Morgan jerked her hand away. "I don't know what you mean." She scowled.

Ari flattened his lips, ready to make a retort when he looked closer at her. Her face and neck were rosy, her cheeks darkened. And the pulse at the base of her throat throbbed. When she licked her lips, his tense shoulders eased. She was either fooling him... or herself. An unexpected sensation of burgeoning desire slammed into him.

And that feeling didn't come from him. Where did this... this passionate sensation come from? Well, it didn't take an emotional genius to figure it out. Without a doubt it came from her. Interesting. She was as attracted to him as much as he was to her. But why did she deny how she felt? He ignored the question as to why he was sure he knew that.

"Do you have someone back home waiting for you?" Ari held his breath. That would explain her reluctance.

"What?" Morgan exclaimed before clearing her throat. "No. Why would you ask that?" She turned away from him and went back to the replicron. "Just drop it. We've got a lot of other things to worry about besides... that." Waving a dismissive hand, she took out the small spider-bot from its hiding place in the wide machine. "Refraction replicron," she said over her shoulder. Her attention was wholly on the small droid as the machine fizzled into invisibility.

Ari took a moment to study the now-busy Morgan. Crossing his arms, he brought his hand up and tapped a finger on his chin. It appears patience wasn't one of his virtues. The urge to pull her into his arms to make her face what was happening between them was hard to resist. Especially when he envisioned doing so with his mouth, hands, and body instead of words.

He frowned. That wasn't right. He was the last person who'd force someone to do anything against their will. It had to be voluntary. A challenge then. Get Morgan to admit how she felt about him... with a little nudge. Time to craft a carefully planned seduction.

Yeah, that's right. He eyed Morgan nibbling on the corner of her mouth as she worked on the bot, seemingly oblivious to him.

The enticing woman didn't stand a chance.

CHAPTER FIVE

F ace heated, Morgan kept her head down and did her best to concentrate on the small spider-bot spread out before her. *Damn
man*. Who did he think he was, touching her like that? All seduc-
tive-like. She shivered and pursed her lips. When his finger slid across
the sensitive skin of her inner arm, she swore she could feel the heat of
his flesh pour into hers until liquid goo pooled between her legs. As if
the separate parts of herself ended up intermixed somehow. To top it
off, through the tip of his finger, she experienced his throbbing heart
pounding faster than it should have. Like touching her affected him
as much as it did her.

Morgan sucked in an impatient breath. They didn't have time for
this. *She* didn't have time for this. With the relic missing and now, with
another unexplained dead Ozevroc, time was running out. The High
Chieftain wasn't a patient creature. He'd have no trouble making
them an example for his merry little band of gangsters to keep control
over them. Didn't matter if she and Ari were innocent or not.

She snuck a peek at the seductive man as he went around the room,
tossing the loose metal and discarded parts into the trash bin. Once
again, his overt masculinity struck her as something unique. While

there were plenty of good-looking men in Aethralis, none came close to Ari.

In addition to his obvious man-beauty, he had a lot of traits she admired. Here was someone who suffered from amnesia but remained resourceful in an unfamiliar world. His curiosity was second only to hers, even when he was in the middle of trying to protect her from the Ozevroc if he thought they threatened her. A small smile crept free. *Silly man*. Unlike other Aethralians who were powerful psychics, she'd taken self-defense classes from an early age. She could take care of herself.

That didn't explain the strange things that had happened on the ship since he woke up. First Xalgrim, then Lurvath dead. Murdered by an unknown assailant. Now the surprisingly precious artifact of the Ozevroc was missing. Who would take that and why? She watched Ari fire up the incinerator and then throw in the items from the full trash bin. Sweat had broken out on him, giving his muscular torso a glorious sheen. She swallowed hard.

Damn. She had to find out who was behind all of this. Hopefully, before anything else happened.

"Hey, I've been thinking."

Morgan jumped when Ari spoke behind her.

"Why don't we see if the replicron can make a replacement for that sacred thing for the Ozevroc? That way, we'll have enough time for you to fix that bot to get *Elemi* going."

Morgan sat back and contemplated his suggestion. It didn't take long to decide. She shook her head. "I don't think we can do that without having the genuine artifact. While the machine can create something similar, without the original to copy, it'll miss something, making it obvious it's a fake. Nice idea, though." She turned back to the spider-bot.

"Are the Ozevroc going to let us do some investigating? It'd be helpful if you could aim your doohickey around to see if we can find any more of the crystalline stuff."

She turned back to watch him.

He'd found a broom somewhere and crossed his hands over the handle and leaned his chin on it. The gray of his eyes was lighter, as if he were deep in thought. "I don't suppose you have access to a printout of the ship so we can figure out where to start?"

Morgan smiled. "Yes, as a matter of fact I do. But I'm already having the multicorder running a program within the Ozevroc system to see if it can uncover those elements anywhere else." She checked the device. "It's still running, so I'm guessing we've got some time before it's done."

Ari shrugged. "Okay." He pulled the handle of the broom down and started sweeping. "Let me know when it's done."

She agreed and took a few precious moments to watch him work. *Hmm,* maybe she should check something out. Opening a different program on her multicorder, she had it run an analysis on the room they were in to check for that alien substance. It didn't take long to complete. The results surprised her. While there wasn't anything close to it in the room, it pointed a faint reading toward the ship *Elemi*.

She glanced at Ari, wanting to make sure he was busy. His back was to her as he continued to toss stuff into the incinerator. Doing her best not to draw attention to what she was doing, she approached the still-open door of the ship, keeping her handheld aimed ahead. The readings were faint, but stronger. How could there be remnants of this stuff in here but not out in the room?

"What'cha doing?"

Morgan jumped at Ari's baritone behind her. Her face heated as if she'd been caught red-handed doing something she shouldn't. She jutted her chin. "There are crystalline readings on this ship, but not on the outside." With a frown, she turned the handheld in his direction and walked around him, sweeping the device over him. "You actually have some on you as well, but it's really faint." Clicking the multicorder off, she hooked it on her belt and crossed her arms, facing him. "I don't suppose you have any idea why you're covered in this stuff?"

Ari matched her stance, crossing his arms with a smirk. "Oh sure, I do. But I've got to keep it secret for my health and all." He dropped his arms, his expression serious. "If I had a clue what this stuff was, believe me, I'd tell you." He circled a forefinger around the shambles inside the ship. "The sooner we solve these annoying hullabaloos, the sooner we can get off this bucket of bolts. I may not understand what that Ozevroc was saying, but I can tell when someone feels like they're getting pushed into a corner. And keep in mind your little high chieftain is no friend to you or me. He wouldn't hesitate to make examples of us of in a heartbeat. And I don't mean by giving us a parade and keys to the city."

Morgan nodded. "Yeah, I agree. When you're done with cleanup, I'll contact Bugurr and ask he assign some guards to us so we can follow the clues I've got in this baby here." She patted her multicorder.

"You got a place to start?" He quirked a blond eyebrow with a smile.

For a moment she got lost in how the simple curl of his lips lifting upward made his handsome face striking. Swallowing with a dry throat, she grasped the first thing that came to mind. "Yeah, but we'd better replace that missing collar of yours first." Morgan pointed to the now-absent black scarf around his neck. He must've pulled it off when he was working with the incinerator. "Or we'll have a bigger problem to deal with."

"Sounds good," he agreed with a grimace. "But I gotta tell you I hate that damn thing."

Morgan cocked her head. Maybe he was getting some kind of memory on how painful the *nutesh* snare was when activated.

"Let's do this before I change my mind," he stated with a stubborn tilt to his chin.

Later that afternoon, Morgan stomped into the engine room with clenched fists and resisted throwing a tantrum like a toddler. *What a total waste of time that was.* She and Ari spent hours looking for any clues on where the Talon of Ancients could be on the ship. She'd rather stayed in the engine room to finish working on that little spider-droid. At least they got the fake *nutesh* snare around Ari's neck before Grozzik and some of his goons came for them. As long as no one inspected it or tried to use it, it'd be good enough.

That pout he wore when he clicked the leather collar on his neck was cute as hell. She half expected him to argue, but thankfully, he didn't.

The two of them spent hours scouring the ship where her multi-corder showed the strongest readings. Every time they found some of the crystalline residue, there was no way to determine how a small portion congealed in one place, but was absent around it. As if whatever carried the crystalline, popped in and out without using the normal entry points. Someone or something had to be using a teleporting device.

Morgan glanced at Ari. Or had the ability to do so.

When she'd last ran a scan on him to see if he had some of the crystal substance on him, she also ran a deeper probe. While inconclusive, it made her determined to get a blood sample from him and run that in her handheld. If he was what she suspected he was, he'd have no trouble going in and out of rooms without using the normal entryways.

The main thing that bothered her was he wasn't the one creating the strange crystal readings. What was on him wasn't strong enough to leave the different trails they'd found. But it meant at one time he was close enough to whatever created them. Inside that pretty little head of his was the answer. She just had to figure out how to get it out of him.

But not tonight. She was beat. A little shut-eye would help clear her fuzzy mind.

"I'm turning in for the night. See you in the morning," Ari announced, heading to the part of the room he'd claimed for himself.

"Goodnight," she said, watching him settle. She pursed her lips. How interesting he slept next to the wall by *Elemi*. She hadn't noticed that before.

After a quick visit to the refresher unit, she changed out of the mechanic's overalls and into a long shift she'd created in the replicron earlier. The material was soft but strong enough to help keep her warm while she slept.

The last thing she heard was Ari's light snore from across the room.

The first thing Ari sensed was impatience. Why couldn't they look around first? He glared at the man next to him. Which didn't faze the ass one bit.

Well, since there was no making his brother change his mind, he gave the guy a wide smile. "Come on, bro. Let's see what we can find."

"No funny stuff, *bro*." The guy bit the last word out with a frown. Yeah, the man hated it whenever Ari used that nickname.

But that didn't mean his brother had to be such a dick! Here they were, on an abandoned gangster planet filled with all sorts of goodies just waiting to be discovered. But the only thing his companion wanted to do was go around in this lame circular hallway to find some kind of hint where the missing human women might have been. And then, presto! A clue to where they all went would suddenly pop out.

As if.

"Hey, A-Man," the baritone voice on his shoulder had a subtle mechanical, whirring undertone to it. "Let's ditch this guy. I bet we can find those babes all on our own! As the great Latin proverb states, 'Fortune favors the bold'. Let's be bold and see what kind of fortune we can find here on our own."

Ari couldn't help the pain-filled sigh that rolled out. How he wished he was free to do what his companion suggested. Why, taking apart one of those sexbots alone would... never mind.

"Slow down, Sparky. I wish we could, but we agreed to find these human women. So, that's what we're gonna do." He glanced at the small spider-shaped sentient droid resting on his folded, spindly legs parked on Ari's left shoulder.

The bot's gold-and-silver body was aerodynamic in design, perfect to slice through the air using iridescent wings hidden under his back panels.

"You sense anyone here?"

Ari looked up at the sound of the deep rich voice coming from the male walking next to him. Turning away from the droid, he took a second to open his senses before shaking his head. "Nah, just us and the two oldsters goin' the other way." All was good. No one around. Whistling, he shoved his fingers into the back pockets of his jeans.

"I bet we'd find them faster on our own!" His bot companion jumped up. "Look, if we just ditch these guys..."

The scene changed.

The world around him dissolved, replaced by a surreal landscape that felt both familiar and alien. He found himself inside *Elemi*. But a totally different environment from the disaster he'd seen in the engine room of the *Nebula Viper*.

The surrounding walls were a deep, shimmering green, like the surface of a still pond catching the morning light.

He reached out to touch them. The exterior was soft, warm, and supple, as if preening beneath his fingers.

"Well, well, what do we have here?" The feminine voice coming from the ship was like smooth, rich velvet as it wrapped around Ari's senses. Her tone was low and husky, each word laced with a seductive cadence full of mystery and intrigue. She spoke with a refined elegance, a hint of sophistication that danced on the edge of her phrases, leaving a hint of allure in the air.

He couldn't help the shiver racing down his spine.

"Oh, you and I are going to have such fun!" There was an undeniable confidence in her voice, a dominant presence that demanded attention and respect.

Ari cleared his throat and glanced around. He was in the main cockpit, a place comfortable enough to fit a small crew of five or more. Its oval layout emphasized *Elemi's* organic base with flowing lines. There was an apparent pilot's seat in the center, elevated enough to provide an open view of the room.

He took in a deep breath of the sweet, earthy scent in the air. Like a forest after a rainstorm. The whole place was calming and soothing, melting the stiffness in his shoulders. Soft, ambient sounds surrounded him along with a rhythmic hum, like a distant heartbeat.

He headed to the center of the room, where a spiraling column of light rose from the floor, pulsating in time with the ship's organic rhythm. Beneath his feet, the surface was firm yet slightly yielding, shifting gently whenever he took a step—as if the ship adjusted to how he walked. As he got closer to the center, a sense of belonging enveloped him, warm and comforting, like an embrace. Wispy glimpses of distant memories vied for his attention, tantalizing him to explore.

Reaching out, he brushed his fingers against the column of light, and the image disappeared.

Once again, everything around him shifted. This time to a place as unfamiliar to him as anything he'd come across since he woke up and got caught in Morgan's mesmerizing gold-green eyes.

Ari stood on the edge of a floating island suspended high above the shimmering cosmos. The island was a breathtaking paradise, unlike anything he'd ever imagined. The scent of exotic blooms filled the air, mingling with a crisp, invigorating breeze that carried whispers of an unseen ocean far below.

He turned around and his breath caught at the sight of an endless landscape of lush greenery dotted with trees bearing vibrant, iridescent leaves that glowed gently in the soft light of the celestial sky. The sky itself was an ever-changing tapestry of colors, with galaxies swirling in slow motion and stars twinkling like distant jewels.

The sand beneath his feet was smooth like cool silk, a mixture of stardust and soft earth that shifted delicately as he moved. His barefoot steps were soundless, adding to the dreamlike quality of the world around him.

Taking in the serene beauty, he was drawn to a gentle waterfall cascading down from a crystalline cliff.

The water sang as it fell, creating a melody that harmonized with the rustling leaves and the distant calls of ethereal creatures hidden within the foliage.

A soft rustle nearby captured his attention. And there she was, the eternal beauty that was Morgan. She emerged from the dappled shadows of a towering tree. The sight of her was as astonishing as a sudden burst of sunlight, brightening the already luminous world around them.

Morgan's golden curls flowed freely around her shoulders, catching the ambient light and reflecting it like a halo around her head. Her attire was as radiant as the setting, a flowing gown made of golden fabric that shimmered with every step she took. Adorned with delicate patterns reminiscent of constellations, it subtly emphasized her elegance and strength. The dress glided across her body like liquid moonlight, accentuating her graceful movements as she approached.

Ari's mouth dried. Here, in this strange place, he saw Morgan in a truly different light.

Her golden curls were a heady mixture of blonds and browns, as well as fiery reds. So many shades he didn't even know existed. Bright eyes of leaf green blended with hues of gilded yellow under brows and lush lashes that matched the unique color of her hair. Her mouth was wide, curved at the corners, giving a peek of her small, even white teeth. Tiny laugh lines graced the sides of her succulent lips and wide eyes, evidence of a sense of dry humor he had to have overlooked. Her glorious light skin had an undertone of café au lait, rich and creamy.

As she neared, her gentle smile widened.

The action brought a hint of curiosity and an underlying sense of wonder. Warmth spread through Ari, as if she brought with her a feeling of contentment and rightness sorely needed within him.

"Where are we?" Morgan's voice was a gentle melody. "And what are you wearing?"

Ari hadn't paid any attention to his clothing. Not when she was around. He took a quick look at the tunic and trousers, golden fibers that seemed woven from the very fabric of the universe itself. The material was light and breathable, giving him a sense of freedom and ease. Their intricate designs mirrored those on Morgan's gown, as if to signify they shared this moment together.

"Don't know." He grasped her hands in his. "As for where we are, I'm not sure." He couldn't resist and brought her hand up to kiss her knuckles. "I think we're in a place that exists between worlds—a sanctuary created from our desires and dreams."

Morgan's snort of laughter made him grin.

"Oh, brother. Laying it on thick, aren't you?" She admonished with a mischievous grin.

Ari tucked her hand around the crook of his elbow. "Shall we?" He gestured ahead of them.

With a quick, carefree laugh, she agreed.

Walking side by side along the beach, they left their footprints as ephemeral impressions among the stardust-like sand. The musical symphony of the waves from a luminous ocean created a harmonious blend that resonated with the very essence of the island.

Morgan nodded as her gaze swept across the horizon where the sky met the sea. "This place feels like a haven." Her beautiful lips pursed. "A forgotten place untouched by the chaos of reality."

They reached the water's edge where the waves kissed the shore in a rhythmic dance. This was a place where words were unnecessary. Here he could indulge what he suspected were his feelings about the mysterious woman next to him. He turned to Morgan, drowning in her eyes, free to explore the depth of their connection without constraint.

Ari was aware of everything around them — the warmth of the air, the shimmering blend of colors of the ocean, as well as the cosmic cool breeze caressing their skin. But what captivated him the most was her wicked, sinful, tempting mouth.

"I'm going to kiss you," was the only warning he gave. He couldn't resist tilting her chin up with his forefinger before lowering his lips to hers.

Morgan's feminine mounds were soft, yielding, welcoming. Nothing prepared him for the unrelenting pressure that began to build deep inside of him. A blazing inferno coiling tighter and tighter, a detonation threatening to explode.

She yanked them apart. "What is it about you that makes me feel like this?" Her strangled confession came out hoarse, the words trembling out. "No one's gotten under my skin like you have."

"Well, I'm not just anyone, am I?" Ari asserted. "You and I are already bonded." He took another kiss, planting his claim over and over. Long drugging kisses that made him tremble. Even without his memories, he knew no one had ever affected him like this before. And so quickly.

The world around them faded, but he and Morgan remained together. Their combined sensuous warmth wrapped around them while creating a haven for the bond they'd forged together.

It surprised Morgan when she realized she was an outsider in her own skin. Some dolt masquerading as a delusional lovesick chump she'd never dreamed she'd ever turn into. Where had the strong, emotionally divorced Morgan Elara Jackson from Aethralis gone? And who was this mushy impostor taking her place? One that allowed some good-looking, charming stranger to take over her soul from just one kiss? Not that she could call what they shared merely a simple kiss. Oh, no. It was so much more than that. The minute her lips meshed with his, everything changed. When his mind-boggling tongue swept into her mouth and danced with hers, her entire outlook shifted. Harsh, lush passion built within her to a level she'd never imagined existed before. Oh, she might not be a stranger to the act of love, but not like this. Never like this.

When he declared them bound, she didn't resist. Instead, she surrendered completely to her desires. The surrounding scenery faded away, and she didn't notice it had changed until he pulled back. She looked over his shoulder, and her eyes widened. Instead of being in a celestial paradise, they were someplace quite different. Around them were walls made of polished stone, their surfaces adorned with intricate carvings that flickered in the soft candlelight. Ancient hieroglyphics and symbols told stories of forgotten tournaments and struggles of power in a language as old as time.

Her bare feet gripped the floor made of mosaic tiles, each piece a different shade of blue, gold, and terra-cotta. The patterns created an image of a sprawling, long dead cityscape of ancient Babylon.

The ceiling above her arched gracefully, painted to resemble a night sky filled with constellations and swirling galaxies. Tiny lights embedded in the surface twinkled like stars, casting a soft, celestial glow. The effect was mesmerizing, as though she once again floated among the stars.

Against one wall stood an opulent bed, draped in luxurious fabrics that shimmered with their own light. Silken sheets in rich hues of emerald and sapphire beckoned to her, promising a playground of comfort and wild passion. Embroidered pillows were plump and inviting, with golden threads that caught the light and created a tapestry of elegance and warmth.

Here was a decadent haven she secretly dreamed about.

Beside the bed, a low table made of dark, polished wood held an array of edible treasures. Delicate glass vials filled with the deep burgundy of lush wine sat alongside ornate boxes filled with every variety of tantalizing finger foods.

The surrounding air carried an allure of jasmine and sandalwood in a fine mist, adding to the atmosphere of passion and desire. Lush green plants, their leaves vibrant and full, adorned the corners of the room and brought a touch of primitive nature indoors.

Morgan turned her gaze toward the corner of the room, where the principal attraction beckoned.

There, an exquisite bath awaited. Nestled beneath a gently arching alcove, the tub was a stunning blend of ancient luxury and futuristic elegance. The smooth marble basin glistened in an ethereal turquoise glow under the candlelight.

"Oh my God," she whispered behind her fingers. Soaking in a scented filled bath was one of her weaknesses. Being raised in a perpetual climate of ice and snow, the luxury of being caressed in soothing warm waters was one of her secret cravings.

Ari's warm chest covered her back. He pushed her curls aside and placed his dangerous mouth on her sensitive nape. "Would you like to indulge in a bath, *irnini*?"

Wispy steam from the tub called to her. Not trusting herself to say anything, she nodded and went straight to it.

Soft, sheer curtains draped elegantly around the alcove, their fabric catching a gentle breeze from a nearby open window, causing the fabric to billow in the gentle rhythm of the night air. The curtains gave a sense of privacy and intimacy, enclosing the bath into a world of its own. A place where she could indulge in sensual exploration with the man close behind her.

Standing at the edge of the marble basin containing waters shaded a deep aquamarine gave her the sense of a tranquil, hidden oasis. The round contours of the tub were smooth and flowing. On the outside, the edges of delicate, gold filigree depicted scenes of mythical creatures dancing amidst waves and clouds. These intricate designs shimmered subtly as they caught the wavering light of nearby candles.

Beckoning waters gently swayed inside the tub, its glass-like surface reflecting the twinkling ceiling above. Tiny, luminescent petals floated gracefully atop the water, releasing a soft fragrance that mingled with the scent of jasmine already in the air. The aroma was a sinful promise of escape.

Around the bath, carved stone steps led down to the water's edge, their surfaces etched with geometric patterns that mirrored the mosaic on the floor. Lush greenery flanked the steps, potted plants with broad leaves and vibrant flowers adding a touch of nature's beauty to the elegant setting.

Beside the bath, a small wooden table held an assortment of luxurious bath essentials. Crystal bottles filled with oils and fragrant salts glistened, their contents promising indulgence and rejuvenation. An ivory comb lay nearby, its delicate teeth carved with floral designs, ready to untangle her unruly curls.

"Allow me."

Ari's soft words meant nothing to Morgan, but his masculine tone struck a hidden feminine cord deep within her. She squealed with a laugh when he swept her into his arms and carried her down the marble steps into the tub.

"Ari!" Morgan laughed. No one had swept off her feet before. "I can walk, you know." She clasped her arms around his thick neck with a huge smile.

"Yeah, but then I couldn't do this." The mischievous gleam in his gray eyes was her only warning. He lowered his head, his eyes at half-mast as his lips parted bare inches from hers.

She licked her lips as her own eyelids lowered

He dropped her.

She didn't even have time to scream before the water covered her. Opening her eyes in the water, she spied his thickly muscled calves covered in light blond hair. Holding her breath, she reached over and pulled.

He went down like a rock, his back hitting the surface with a loud splash.

Giggling, she surfaced and watched him flounder before he righted himself. Dang, he was so big he almost emptied the tub.

The ornate brass faucet, styled like a majestic serpent, stood poised above the tub, pouring a gentle stream of water, like a miniature waterfall.

"*Kashshaptu!*" Ari wiped his hand down his face, giving her a narrow-eyed glare. "You'll pay for that!"

Morgan giggled again. She threw her shoulders back to show she wasn't afraid. "Witch? Who you callin' a witch, you *idimmu*?" Yeah, evil demon. Take that.

The man might be big as a horse, but he was quick. Morgan found herself wrapped in his arms, his lips covering the side of her neck. She moaned, moving her head back to give him better access. Wrapping her arms around his beefy neck, she jumped up and wrapped her legs around his trim waist. Ah, yes. Skin. Slick, hard as nails, man-skin.

Morgan nipped the thick tendon at the side of his nape. "Are we just going to play, or are you smart enough to get down to business?" She had no trouble asking for what she wanted in the bedroom. And she wanted this man here and now. She was so primed she'd come apart the minute his thick erection entered her.

Ari pulled back to look her in the eyes. "Morgan, I... ah," his neck and cheeks darkened.

She captured his scruffy jaws between her palms. "What is it, Ari? You can tell me."

He dipped his chin and looked over her shoulder. "Um, I..." His head tilted up and his steely-gray eyes bore into hers. "I don't know what to do."

Morgan sucked in a breath. He was a virgin? No way. She pursed her lips. "Are you telling me you've never made love before?" She unhooked her legs from around his waist and let them slide to the ground, until the warm water lapped over her waist. "How's that possible?" Stepping back, she gestured over his magnificent chest. "I mean, just look at you. You're practically a walking advertisement for overt masculinity."

Ari grinned. "I am?" He shook his head and closed his eyes. The flush under his skin now darkened his upper chest. "I don't know if I've had sex before or not." He opened his eyes and pointed to the side of his temple, mussing his darkened blond hair wet from the bath. "Amnesia, remember?"

Her smile was slow. She stepped close to him. Standing on her toes, she wrapped her arms around his neck and yanked him close. "How 'bout you let me show you what to do?" She spoke in a soft whisper against his lips.

He groaned and pulled her flush against him. "Would it be okay with you if we do this horizontally... like on a dry surface?"

Morgan hummed. "I can't think of anything I'd like better."

CHAPTER SIX

The next thing she knew, Morgan was flat on her back on the luxurious bed she'd spied earlier, blanketed by Ari's slick body. Since she couldn't remember walking from the bath to the bed, she came to a startling conclusion.

"We're in a Dreamwalk, aren't we?" She stared at the throbbing pulse at the base of his muscular neck. She fingered his skin as she studied his handsome face. "This isn't real, is it?"

He pulled back, leaning his upper weight on his brawny arms as he stared down at her. "I don't know what a Dreamwalk is, but does it matter? It all feels pretty real to me." He closed the distance between them until the only thing she saw was the burning intent in his gray eyes. "And if it is a dream, I'd rather not wake up." His lips hovered close.

Energy crawled from the tips of her toes and swirled up her body as she studied his mouth. Her nipples and clit swelled. Damn man hadn't even touched her yet. The anticipation of his kiss made her mind blank. She couldn't think, couldn't move. Just stare into his eyes, her body tight with suspense. Her heart thudded in a hard rhythm as she caught her breath, waiting... waiting for that first touch.

After an eternity, his full lips once again caressed hers. His soft brushstrokes threatened to steal the last of her sanity. Deep inside, her muscles clenched as arousal teased her. To hang on, she wrapped her arms around his neck, entwining one of her legs between his. The action put her throbbing sex in line with his hard member.

Grabbing a bunch of her hair in one fist, he pulled her head to the side as the soft kiss turned into a blazing inferno. He widened his legs, splaying hers. Swallowing her gasp, he danced his tongue with hers, stroking in an all-consuming act. They moved as one. His free hand shaped her body, smoothing down her side, and cupped her butt cheek, bringing their groins even closer. She wiggled to rub his heavy erection against her, desperately trying to get the friction where she craved it.

Ari broke the kiss, closing his eyes with a moan before she once again became the focus of his intense hunger.

A shiver slipped down her spine.

"*Irnini,*" he groaned. "Have pity on this simple man. I'm having a hard time keeping control when you move against me like that. I beg you, take this slow so we may savor our time together." He nuzzled the side of her neck. "Let me discover what you like. Allow me to explore you more thoroughly."

He didn't wait for her answer as he bent and kissed the side of her neck. That dangerous free hand of his roamed under one of her breasts before covering it. He feathered kisses from her jawline to the underside of her chin.

Lifting himself, he dropped his heated gaze to her exposed breasts. He sucked in a sharp breath. "If there is anything more gorgeous, I'd insist that wasn't possible." His reverent whisper was a heartfelt prayer.

Morgan warmed under his regard, feeling sexy and wanton. For this fiercely beautiful man to say something like that was more than she dared to hope from any lover. Reaching up, she traced the minute lines on his face, the shape of his scruffy jaw, before outlining the contour of his luscious lips.

She allowed a sultry smile to peek out, peering at him through her lashes. "It's hard to believe you don't know what you're doing," she admonished him.

His only answer was to cup one of her breasts, his thumbs brushing her peaked nipples before dipping his head to run a trail of fire from her chin, down her throat, to the tips of her breasts. The erotic action of his mouth tugging and pulling her sensitive nipple caused the puckered skin to harden.

A small keening moan escaped her throat.

He let her breast go with a pop, then feathered kisses down her ribs to her flat stomach, with light licks here and quick nips there. Her muscles quivered and rippled under his masterful ministrations.

"Your skin is so delicious," Ari growled against her stomach. With almost languid movements, he traveled south to the curls at the juncture of her sex. "What's this?" he teased. "Must be a lush territory, just waiting to be conquered."

Oh God. She should tell him his corny words were stupid. Later. Much, much later.

"And what mysteries do we have here?" He breathed on her mound as he used a finger to part the curtain of her sex. "Ah, this little bud. What shall I do with you, my little friend?" He tickled her overly sensitive flesh with his forefinger, nestling his broad shoulders between her thighs, widening the juncture for his pleasure.

If the damn man was any better at this, she wouldn't survive his so-called fledgling inexperience. Morgan gripped his shoulders and moaned softly, unable to voice those directions she'd promised him. As if he needed guidance from her.

Ari turned his head, a lazy, languid motion. Those steel-gray eyes turned a dark shade, now tinged in molten silver. "Your scent has enthralled me, *irnini,*" he whispered. "If there is anything more riveting in the universe, I would argue it wasn't possible." He inhaled deeply, a self-indulgent grin creasing his full lips as he studied her womanhood. Stark, raw hunger stamped on the lines of his face. So seductive.

Her entire body clenched in anticipation as she held her breath. Every word, every touch from him, was killing her. Slowly. Inch by sizzling inch. His kisses. The feel of his hard body against hers.

She burned for him. Right the hell now.

"Please, Ari," she mumbled, squirming beneath him. Every part of her was trying to force him back up to align their bodies just where she wanted them.

"Now, none of that." He gave a smart slap to the edge of her butt. "I'm going to make sure you're ready for me, my beauty. I couldn't bear it if I somehow fell short of bringing you the ultimate pleasure."

Morgan gasped at the slight sting and grabbed the top of his head. She tugged his silken strands, trying once again to bring him over the top of her. "No... I'm... ready... now!" She wailed when his tongue swept over her straining bud, causing her to buck mindlessly.

He clamped an arm around her waist to hold her captive for his hedonistic attention.

Another short smack, causing heat to flare. Part pain, but mostly pleasure.

"Don't be so impatient, *irnini*. Stay still."

"I can't... no... impossible," she gasped her denial.

His head lifted, his glistening mouth now creased with a stern, reprimanding look.

Morgan's fingers fisted closer around his captive hair, but stopped trying to move him. She held on for all she was worth as the building pressure strained from her sex outward. It was almost more than she could bear.

Keeping his steely gaze on her, he lowered his head once again, his wicked tongue stroking her nub before stabbing deep inside her.

Morgan convulsed, bucking her hips despite the restraint of his arm. Her womb flexed hard.

He started out slow at first, leisurely assaulting her with his teeth and tongue, driving her insane with need. Masculine sounds of dominance escaped his throat, as if he couldn't get enough of her taste. His arms tightened, keeping her in place as he licked and suckled to his heart's content.

She writhed under him, her head tossing as she spilled more of her cream into his mouth. Sharp pleasure gripped her stomach as he inserted one of his thick fingers into her.

Morgan tensed as rapture rolled up. She wouldn't live through this. This decadent play coiled her body tighter and tighter, threatening to blow her apart.

Just when she was sure nothing would stop the cataclysm, Ari lifted his head, possession glittering in his molten-gray eyes.

He leaned away to sit on his heels. He lifted her hips, positioning himself at her entrance, her legs draped over his elbows, widening her womanhood. Skillfully, he burrowed his wide cock inside her.

Unbidden, her slick channel tightened around him, daring him to leave.

Instead of retreating, his hot, thick, velvet steel pushed in, inch by glorious slow inch, as if to claim his rightful place.

Her breath hitched as she grabbed his forearms to hang on.

His fingers held her hips tight as he relentlessly bore into her. He threw his head back with a low-pitched growl. *"Ninmulmulla!"* His face was a mask of raw intent as his hips plunged his manhood deep inside, reaching the end of her womb, fully embedded.

Morgan's body bowed. Throwing her legs off the shelf of his arms, she planted the soles of her feet on the firm mattress, finding leverage. She rose to meet the thrusts of his powerful hips, the musky scent of their joining ramping her pleasure to another level. Heat seared her, a scorching blaze she couldn't run from. The tension was just out of reach, stretching on and on, with no end in sight. She dug her fingernails into his arms and tossed wildly under him.

Surging forward, Ari fastened his mouth on hers.

The steel piston of his living flesh drove into her quivering folds. Over and over. Hard and unrelenting until Morgan's orgasm ripped through her, causing her to jerk her lips from his as her body clamped down hard on his. She shattered, and her bones and muscles melted under the explosion of shocking pleasure. She absently experienced Ari exploding inside her like a fiery comet, erupting with pulse after scorching pulse.

When breathing became possible once again, Morgan somehow found the energy to lift her hand to his face.

He turned his head to catch her fingers with his mouth, sucking gently. He opened his lips to release them. The slumbering joy in his eyes was an open invitation as he leaned toward her, his expressive steel-colored orbs lowered in half-lidded purpose.

Everything around her dissolved.

Morgan groaned, putting an arm over her eyes to block out the dim light of the Ozevroc engine room. She'd never experienced a Dreamwalk before, but she knew all about them from the way her psychic friends bragged how enjoyable they were. Especially Seren. The woman claimed the best way to judge a potential lover was to see how imaginative they were when they joined on that psychic plane.

Well, if that was the case, Ari passed with flying colors. She dropped her arm and groaned. And then some. Freaking man was a master. Not only creating several realistic scenes, but, Gods above... if that's what he did with a limited memory, how devastating would he be once he got them back? She sighed. No sense putting it off. She had to confront this head-on. No need to pretend it didn't happen.

Morgan frowned. But what if he didn't realize she was there with him? That the experience was more than just a dream? Should she push the point? To what end? Like she was ready to drop everything to explore a relationship with the guy? As if she didn't have her hands full with life-and-death issues right now. Getting out of this place alive was the only thing she should focus on. After she saved their lives, maybe she'd consider something different with Ari. That was a big maybe. The man was a walking mystery, and it might be foolish to even consider exploring anything personal with him.

A fleeting memory made her frown. She swore toward the end of their psychic lovemaking, he spoke in an ancient language that she hadn't heard in a long time. He called her *Ninmulmulla,* which was an ancient word that meant "lady of many stars." How was it he spoke in the native tongue of her grandfather, Rummeh, the High Guardian of Aethralis—who was an alien from the planet Akurn? Ari even had the same old-world accent the old man had. What did that mean? The only thing that came to mind was the *Adamou* created by the Akurn scientists over seven thousand years ago. But they were all accounted for. Weren't they? Morgan sucked in a nervous breath. Could he be a Titan that escaped their confinement in Aethralis? Her stomach dropped. Did that last invasion attempt by the Akurns somehow set them free?

A strong sense of urgency struck her. She had to get back to Earth, now, more than ever. But first, she'd better confront Ari for more reasons than just their little tryst in the dream world.

Scrambling out of her sleeping alcove, she strode with determined steps to the other side of the room where Ari slept. Only, he wasn't sleeping. He wasn't even there. Putting her fists on her hips, she looked around the spacious room. Maybe he was in the refresher unit. No, she didn't even have to get close.

The door to the room was open, and no sounds came from it.

Okay, maybe he was inside *Elemi*. With a firm purpose in mind, she marched to the ship. Since the arched doorway was open, she stomped inside and looked around. Nope. Not there either.

Now her sense of urgency took on another twist. He was gone... again? She closed her eyes and pinched the bridge of her nose. Now what? Even if she accessed the ship's computer to find him, what good would that do? It's not like she could leave here to find him. She blew out a breath and dropped her arm with a hard swing.

Okay, first things first. She'd be damned if she wasted another second not doing anything. Time to do what she could and not worry about something she couldn't. Going over to the replicron, she announced, "Display replicron!" The machine waved into sight.

Opening the storage unit, she pulled out the food replicator and the small spider-bot she'd put in there for safekeeping.

First off, a cup of coffee. Strong coffee. Yeah, if nothing else, that would set the world right. Then she'd get to work on this droid to see if it could help repair *Elemi*. Then she'd leave this goddess-forsaken piece-of-shit ship and go home.

With or without Ari.

A brutal squeeze of shattering pain squeezed Ari's temples. He moaned and sat up, rubbing his eyes before opening them. Instead of enjoying the gorgeous Morgan in a sultry bedroom, he was somewhere dark, cold, and smelly. He sneezed. *By Tiamat's titties!* He gagged at a stench so vile, like something died, decomposed, and filed a formal complaint about the accommodations. Even when he'd helped his family rescue humans in a destroyed section of one of their large cities buried under layers of refuse, it wasn't this bad. The image of dead animals packed along with rotting food swirling in streams of liquid from a broken sewer line popped into his mind. Even that smell didn't come close to this mind-numbing stink-o-saurus.

Startled at the memory, he tried to grasp it before it floated away. No such luck. He fisted his hand and hammered it on the unforgiving floor in frustration.

Anything loose around him floated up, then crashed hard on the metallic floor.

"Going up. Going down. Make pretty sound."

Ari twisted to look behind him at the singsong litany of a masculine voice. The room barely had enough light to see anything clearly. He squinted at a large shape across from him several feet away. At first, all he could make out was a huge blob of some kind of humanoid creature. Two legs, two arms, a torso, and one head.

No fur or short stature. Not an Ozevroc then. Ari scratched his head. Didn't Morgan tell him the only species on the ship were them and those fuzzy, creepy aliens? If that wasn't an Ozevroc, then what was it?

The dim lights in the room flickered before going out.

"Food. Food. Food. I need. I find." The deep baritone continued to sing. "Fuzzy no good. Taste bad. Find better food. Follow the light. Follow the light. As'ni follow the light."

Ari waited. No other sounds. Like the creature vanished. Great, alone in this disgusting place, wherever he was. Goddess, what he wouldn't give to have some light.

And just like that, his palm raised up, and a shining, rolling a ball of light perched just above his skin. He jumped back with a girly squeal and shook his hand.

Darkness took over again.

What the hell? He raised his hand to look at. *Duh, no can do in pitch darkness, moron.* Rubbing his opposite thumb against his palm, he was surprised there was no pain. Nothing singed or burned. Okay, he might not have an explanation for what just happened, but he couldn't stand here with his thumb up his ass all day. Raising his hand palm up again, he concentrated on getting some light.

The illuminating ball of fire returned.

Ari brought it closer so he could study it. His brows raised. Dang thing didn't generate any heat. Just light. How odd. Well, no telling how long this would last. Shining the light in front of him, it was clear he was still on the Ozevroc ship. In their disgusting garbage holding area. With a grimace, he searched his back pocket for the multicorder Morgan had given him.

Of course, it wasn't there. He wasn't wearing his jeans. Just some shorts he'd put on before searching for dreamland in his little niche of paradise in the engine room. Now that he noticed he wasn't in the climate-controlled engine room, chill bumps broke out, and he shivered. His breath came out in a foggy whisper with each exhale.

Ari turned around, casting the light on the walls to see if he could find a door of some kind. Nothing. The walls were solid. A shrill squeal was the only warning he got when a trap door slid open above his head. Seeing a load of unsavory items ready to tumble down, he leapt out of the way before a mass of garbage rained down, missing him by inches. The air filled with a choking stench—a fresh but nauseating blend of rotting food, burned electronics, and the acrid tang of spilled chemicals. His eyes watered as he surveyed the mess, seeing twisted scraps of metal, broken containers leaking dark, viscous fluids, and a tangle of wires sparking intermittently. The gleam from his ball of light cast eerie shadows on the piles, making them seem alive, like some grotesque, breathing monster.

Sucking in a shallow breath, he closed his eyes and hung his head. His heart raced, making it hard to concentrate. He had to get out of here. He had to...

"Take a deep breath, Ba, and relax." A distant, familiar memory of a man's calm voice filtered through. An exercise he'd been through before. Many times.

"All you have to do is relax and envision where you want to be." The steady tone made Ari's stiff muscles relax.

"That's it." The encouraging voice in his memory continued. "Can you see where you want to be?"

"Yes," Ari whispered out loud. He wanted to be with Morgan. He yearned to be with Morgan. Back at the chaotic mess of the engine room. He craved to hear the musicality of her feminine voice. To savor the way her body moved in perfect harmony, a person comfortable in their own skin. The intelligent, practical way she tackled everything without a hint of panic.

"Now imagine you are already there..." The name Azazel floated away as his tranquil voice faded.

"Where the hell have you been?"

Morgan's sharp demand shattered Ari's serenity.

His eyes popped open.

And... there she was. Standing with her lips pressed into a frown, her fists resting on her trim hips in all her annoyed glory.

Ari did the only thing a man like him could do. He swept her into his arms and kissed the living shit out of her.

Just the feel of holding the pliant, warm woman in his arms made everything fade into the background for Ari. The sensation of her open mouth against his became an invitation to dive deep inside. One he was eager to take, so he didn't hesitate. Tangling his tongue with hers, he grasped her firm yet supple butt and pulled her against him. He swallowed their dual groans as his hard erection rubbed against her soft belly.

He walked her backward, aiming for the beckoning allure of her makeshift bed just a few steps away.

Then the lights and gravity went out.

Free floating, their bodies separated.

Morgan cursed under her breath, giving him her location. Reaching out, Ari grasped her arm and pulled her close. "What the hell is going on?" he groused close to her ear.

"I don't know." Morgan wrapped her arms around his neck. "This is the second time it's happened in the last hour." She gripped the back of his head and pulled his hair to force his head back. "Where have you been?"

The lower part of their bodies drifted apart. Ari put his hand back on her ass and pulled her close. "Wrap your legs around my waist. I don't want you to get hurt when the gravity comes back on." Okay, that wasn't the only reason. But still.

Morgan huffed, but wrapped her muscular legs around him.

He swallowed a happy groan and nuzzled the side of her neck. Being in the dark brought all sorts of good things, as far as he was concerned. Holding her like this... breathing in her musky, womanly scent made his head spin. The tantalizing recollection of what they shared in that bedroom wouldn't leave.

"Hey." She tugged a little harder. "Answer the question."

"Hmm? What question?" Ari whispered, pulling her lower body tighter. Her covered breasts smashed against his naked chest. He ignored the slight tinge of pain from her tugging at his hair.

"Where have you... ah!" Morgan didn't get to finish her sentence before the dim lights blinked back on and gravity took hold.

Ari had just enough presence of mind to roll as they hit, making sure he took the brunt of pain the landing caused. Thank the goddess he'd cleaned the floor the other day. Landing on those hard metal rejects would've made things worse.

They ended up with her on top.

Morgan put her palms against his chest and pushed up, flinging her curly golden mop over her head and out of her face. She glanced down at him, then at where her hands were on his pecs. With a hiss, she jerked her hands off him.

He smiled, grasping her trim hips to keep her in place. Yeah, her sex was now snug in line with his. He bent his legs to give her a comfortable backrest.

Not that he expected her to take advantage of it. Which she didn't. She dismounted like he was some stallion. Now, there was a thought...

Her gaze flickered to his straining erection, tenting his snug briefs.

No way to hide that bad boy. He laced his hands behind his head and gave her a huge grin.

She snorted and stood over him with her hands on her hips.

He half expected her to wag a finger at him.

"Ari, get up," she admonished. Her no-nonsense tone made up for her lack of gestures.

"Spoilsport," he muttered with a provocative smile. Well, guess playtime was over. He rolled to stand before her.

"Now, look." Morgan crossed her arms. "Just because we ah, met in a Dreamwalk, it doesn't mean..."

"A what?" He cocked his head. "What's a Dreamwalk?"

"It's a psychic plane where people can meet to do, um, personal things if they want." The caramel skin across her cheeks darkened. She waved her hands. "But that's not what's important. What's important is..."

Ari's whole body tensed, spiking awake. "You created some kind of dream world where we could be together?" He reached for her. "Not that I mind, but I'd rather do what we did in real life."

"I did no such thing!" She scowled, twisting away, exasperation stamped firmly on her face. "Even if I wanted to, which I don't!" She waved a hand to warn him off. "I couldn't. I don't have that kind of psychic power."

Ari rubbed his scruffy jaw. One of these days, he'd find the time to shave. "Well, if you didn't, then who did?"

Morgan threw her hands up in the air. "Oh, for God's sake. Isn't it obvious?" She pointed her forefinger at him. "You did, you big lummox. You obviously have some psychic abilities." Her green-gold eyes narrowed. "So, the question is... what or who are you? Where did you come from? Why are you going around killing Ozevroc, and what did you do with their relic?" She moved in and poked his chest with her finger. "Are you here to enslave the galaxy like you guys tried to do before?"

Enslave the galaxy? Ari's stomach hardened. What kind of thing was that to accuse him of? First she claimed he was some kind of murderer and thief, now she was saying he's a tyrant poised to take over the galaxy. *What the everlasting* fruk?

Ari crossed his arms. Any warm, fuzzy feelings he'd had dissipated with each ridiculous accusation. Shaking his head, he lowered his eyes and studied the woman. He couldn't believe she had all these pent-up accusations without a shred of proof. The thought crossed his mind to tell her where he'd awakened, hoping it might convince her to help him figure out why these things kept happening.

Ari studied her mulish bearing. Like she'd be open to that now. Not with the mistrust written all over her face.

"Look, if I was the psychic you claim I am," he growled. "I sure as hell wouldn't stand here and listen to this bullshit." He'd had enough. If there was one thing he knew about himself, it was he hated it when people made assumptions about him—just like she had. The woman hadn't even bothered talking to him first before spewing stupid crap that had nothing to do with him.

"You may not have known me for very long..." Ari started. "Hell, I haven't known myself for very long." Face and neck heating, he leaned into her stiff finger. "But it should be obvious I'm nothing like what you accuse me of." With an impatient glare, he swung around and headed to the refresher unit, locking himself in. It wasn't until he stepped into the sonic cleanser that he realized he hadn't brought in any clothes.

Well, too bad. She could just suffer all his naked glory when he strode to his alcove to put clothes on when he was done.

CHAPTER SEVEN

M organ crossed her arms and frowned. What just happened? She went from melting into the man's kiss, then... *whammo*! A stormfront of accusations fly out of her mouth as she charged him with all sorts of heinous things. Her shoulders slumped. Maybe it was for the best. She was getting too caught up in him, letting important things slip through the cracks.

The lights flickered before going steady again. Dammit! She dropped her hands and marched to her workstation. Calling up the floating computer monitor, she accessed the ship's diagnostics to see what might be going on. Squinting, she found the problem right away. Some idiot had rerouted power from the critical systems to non-essential areas. Diving deeper, she found that life-support, navigation, and communications were failing intermittently.

Thank the goddess, it didn't take her long to correct everything.

The sound of the refresher unit door opening didn't catch her attention. But out of the corner of her eye, she zeroed in on the man wearing nothing but a thick, black leather band around his muscular neck. Her eyes widened, watching Ari traipse across the room to his alcove as if he didn't have a care in the world. She swallowed with a parched throat. Just that one simple act of him traipsing around naked transformed every other man she'd been with into ridiculous triviality. She couldn't look away as his profile cut a striking figure against the soft light. The line of his jaw was sharp and defined, leading to a strong, regal chin, while his high cheekbones gave him an almost feminine beauty. Her fingers itched to plunge into his thick, dark-blond hair that swayed across his tanned broad shoulders. Even in profile, the intensity of his unwavering gaze was palpable, and it wasn't on her. He stared straight ahead, not once glancing in her direction.

She pursed her lips as she continued to study him. His powerful, muscular frame exuded a quiet strength, each step deliberate and controlled, as if he held the weight of the world with effortless grace on his broad shoulders. Those shoulders tapered to a trim waist as each step flexed his drool-worthy, firm butt. Morgan clenched her fingers at the memory of caressing and squeezing that ass. Dream state notwithstanding. A man's firm, rounded derriere was a total weakness of hers. She snorted. Oh yeah, watching him walk around naked all day would never be a hardship. She'd never get anything done.

Morgan sighed, admiring the symmetry and perfection of his form. Putting a fist over her heart, she bit back a moan when he reached his alcove, then bent to pick up a pair of snug briefs from a pile of new clothing she'd made in the replicron for him. She hissed at the sight. Dang, stupid, weak female hormones. It was a complete shame he covered his perfect body with anything.

After putting on a new pair of black jeans, he pulled a black T-shirt over his head.

She blinked and turned her back to him, focusing on a bunch of nothing on the workstation. Last thing she needed was to get caught ogling him like a lovesick idiot.

"How does it look?"

Ari's masculine voice behind her made her jump. She squealed and put a hand over her throat, glaring at him over her shoulder. "You look fine."

His blond eyebrows rose. "Well, gee, thanks a bunch. But I wasn't talking about me." He nodded to the spider-bot laid out on her workstation. "I was asking about the droid. Figure out what's wrong with it yet?"

Her face and neck didn't just flush, the blood under her skin burned like an inferno. She closed her eyes, praying for strength before opening them to focus on the droid's open abdomen. "Yes…" she coughed to clear her throat. "Yeah, I think I know what's wrong." Taking a stylus, she pointed to a missing circuit in its "motherboard". While its configuration was familiar, using that word was the closest thing she could come up with on how to describe what she saw. "It's missing vital ah, let's call it wiring, that allows it to access its memory functions. I'm going to recreate something compatible in the replicron and see if that works."

Clenching her hands into fists, she threw her shoulders back for courage before turning around to face him. She jerked her head back when her nose practically smushed into his muscular chest. She took a step back.

"Look…"

"Listen…"

When they spoke at the same time, she shut up and stared into his charcoal gray eyes.

Ari put his hand up. "If you don't mind, I'd like to go first."

Taking a step back, she clasped her hands behind her and gave him a nod. It was only fair since she attacked first without giving the guy a chance to defend himself.

He pushed his hand through the soft waves of his light hair, taking the strands out of his eyes. "Listen, I admit there is some weird stuff going on with me, and it looks bad. But I swear it isn't what it looks like."

She cocked her head and hid a smile. Didn't most guilty people say that?

"I have no idea how or why I leave this room in the middle of the night." Ari continued, crossing his beefy arms over his wide chest. "And I don't know how I got back here last night. But I think it's important for you to know what happened."

"Okay, take a seat and tell me about it." She gestured to the other stool next to the workstation platform. Sitting on her own comfy counter chair, she put one of her arms on the bench and leaned in.

He went into a deep explanation of waking up the first night and finding himself in an unknown corridor of the ship. He regaled her with how he barely avoided stumbling into a couple of Ozevroc before finding himself back in the engine room. Then, last night, he ended up in one of the garbage rooms. The most interesting part of that story wasn't the strange creature he didn't have time to look at, but how he got out of the doorless room.

Now it was her turn to be honest. "I might know how you got out of there." She gazed into his troubled gray eyes. "I haven't had a chance to tell you a little about myself. Once I do, I think you'll understand when I tell you that you are, as far as I can tell, one of the most powerful psychics who's ever existed." She gave a winsome smile. "And believe me, being raised in a city full of them, I know one when I meet one."

Ari held himself still. Did he hear her right? She might know why these weird things kept happening to him? The rush of relief made him lightheaded. He smiled when she made him a cup of coffee from the food replicator she'd put on her workstation. He couldn't wait to hear where she was from. Maybe that would give him some unanswered details about her. Taking a grateful sip of the hot beverage, he focused on her. Had to be a big step for her to share some of her history with him. Damn, he was all for it.

Morgan sighed and ran a finger around the rim of her own coffee cup and stared off into the distance. "I'll try to be as brief as I can, but I think it's important for you to get a full understanding, so I'd better start from the very beginning."

She looked up at him, her full lips drawn into a thin line. "Do you know what a rogue planet is? Have you ever heard of a planet called Akurn?"

Ari's eyebrows rose. Out of anything she could have started with, this is what she came up with? He shrugged. "I don't think so." He took a second to think about it. Nope, didn't ring any bells. "Is that where you think I'm from?"

"Hmm, not directly." Morgan took another sip from her cup. "So, I'd better start there." She sat back. "The planet Akurn..."

"No, no, no. Wait just a minute." Ari held up his hand. "If you're going to tell me a story, you've got to begin it the right way."

Morgan blinked with her mouth in a perfect moue.

Damn, that was sexy. All too soon, her pouty lips turned into a slight frown.

"I don't know what you mean."

Yeah, now, that was better. When she got all serious and stern-like, her caramel skin took on an attractive darker hue and her golden-green eyes sparkled.

"You know. All the good stories start with, 'Once upon a time...'"

"Oh, for the love of..."

He gave her an innocent, wide-eyed stare with exaggerated blinks.

"Okay, fine." Her luscious lips curled in a miniature smirk. "Once upon a time—" She gave him a mock glare. When he didn't interrupt, she continued. "—there was this rogue planet called Akurn."

He nodded and sat back, lacing his hands across his flat belly.

"Just so you know, a rogue planet is an interstellar object of planetary mass that isn't gravitationally bound to any star or brown dwarf system. Akurn was such a planet. When their own sun died, they devised a way to generate enough power in their core to create its own self-sustaining eco-system. But that took an enormous amount of energy the planet couldn't create on its own. Especially since the planetary shield took an enormous amount of precious minerals like gold to keep it running. So they roamed the galaxy, plundering any system they deemed inferior to theirs to get what they wanted. Unfortunately, most systems didn't survive."

"Bummer," Ari said. "I'm surprised no one tried to stop them." The coffee was cool enough to enjoy a hearty gulp.

"You'd think so. But I'm not sure why..." She shook her head and glared at him. "Don't interrupt. If I have to keep answering your questions, I'll never get through this."

He opened his mouth to protest, but she put up a palm to stop him. "Ari, I mean it. Just sit there and be quiet."

His cock twitched. See, sexy as all get-out when she got demanding and bossy like that. He grinned, lifting his cup to salute her to continue.

"Anyway—" She eyed him, but sat back as if to get comfortable with her narrative. "—Akurn ended up at the edge of the galaxy in a solar system with eight planets, three of them with all the natural resources they needed." She sighed and took a sip from her cup. "To make a long story short, they got greedy in a civil war and ended up destroying one of those planets and decimating another one. Because of the horrific onslaught they generated in the solar system, Akurn became caught in the sun's strong gravitational pull and became a prisoner of that system in an elliptical orbit around it that takes about 3,600 years to complete."

"Now, that generated a huge problem for the war-loving race. They were desperate to find a way to replenish their dwindling supplies to keep their shields working. So, they sent a contingency of their top scientists to the remaining viable planet to mine the gold they had to have. To help with the dangerous hard work, those scientists did some illegal experimenting on the native population with various alien DNA they'd collected to create slaves." Her head tilted and looked him in the eye. "The name of the planet is now called Earth. Any of this sound familiar?"

Ari took a moment and finished his coffee as he considered her question. Putting the empty cup on the table, he shook his head. "Afraid not. That it?" He didn't see how any of that applied to him.

Her laugh held no humor. "Hardly." She held her cup in both hands, tapping her forefinger on the rim as she looked off into the distance. "The scientists were successful in creating human/alien hybrids they called the Titans. They were a nasty race of creatures that were immense in size and strength, coupled with almost unlimited psychic powers." She chuckled. "It's funny how their story has endured in human mythology over the years, depicting them as primordial gods who embodied different aspects of the natural world, regarded as one of the first divine rulers. Which was far from the truth. They were a violent race bent on total domination of the physical and the metaphysical realms. It was pure luck the scientists subdued then froze them into stasis in a place we call Tartarus, since they were impossible to kill."

"Nothing is impossible to kill," Ari stated, startling himself. Where did that notion come from?

"You'd think so, but no one has found out how to kill them yet." Morgan tapped her finger against her lips with a faraway look before continuing. She glanced at him. "Once the Titans were out of the way, those dense scientists tried again. This time they created a smaller race known as the *Adamou*. Instead of being out-of-control maniacs, these hybrids were intelligent beyond belief. And, unknown to those clueless Akurns, the *Adamou* learned at a very early age how to hide their psychic abilities.

The one thing the scientists didn't count on was their monarchy discovering their illegal creations. Sub-Prince Murduk vowed to destroy what he called the abominations by any means necessary." Morgan shrugged. "What happened next is still not clear to me why he did it, but he melted most of the ice plates of the planet and created a massive worldwide flood."

"Well, that sounded like a cesspool of stupid. Why destroy his planet's only hope of getting the minerals and resources they needed to survive?" Ari lifted his foot to the edge of the table and pushed with his foot to rock back and forth. It helped him think.

Morgan shrugged. "I'm sure there's more to this story, but I'm afraid I don't know what it is." She sipped her coffee and grimaced, putting the cup on the table. "What I do know is that the sub-Prince didn't kill all the *Adamou* and rogue scientists like he thought. One of my distant ancestors, an Akurn by the name of Rummeh, took a huge contingent of fellow Akurns and several of the humans and *Adamou* to a safe place, the southernmost continent called Antarctica. Deep in the ice, they created a city called Aethralis. And that's where I'm from."

She looked away, lost in her narrative. "Now Aethralis has one purpose, and only one. Rummeh took on the responsibility for the violent Titans and created a civilization whose primary goal is to keep watch over them so they'd never get out. Those monsters threaten not only Earth, but life as this universe knows it. Fortunately, the *Adamou* he surrounded himself with were all powerful psychics. Most of the humans who came with them left Aethralis to start their own civilizations, but some remained. As of today, pretty much all of the Aethralis citizens are powerful psychics, which are needed to contain the Titans." She frowned. "Unfortunately, lately their stronghold has been showing signs of weakening."

Morgan sat back and mimicked his stance by leaning back with her laced hands across her taut stomach. "Now here's where I come in. While I am a hybrid of human and alien DNA, my psychic abilities aren't that strong compared to others. My only claim to fame is having xenoglossy. I can hear a language and speak it immediately." She twirled her finger. "That's why I can talk to the Ozevroc like a native."

Ari frowned. "That doesn't explain how you ended up here."

"Yeah, well." Her cheeks flushed, but she looked him in the eye. "Here's what happened. An alien race called Zerin contacted me by taking me to their ship while I was sleeping. There they offered to enroll me in what they called an exchange so I could leave Earth and find a mate from the thousands of humanoid races in the galaxy suffering shortages of females."

Ari stopped rocking. His mouth fell open. "Are you kidding me? You... *you* had to leave Earth to find a man?" Damn. No wonder she left. She'd been surrounded by complete imbeciles.

Crossing her arms, she slid down in her seat. Her blush deepened. "Yes... I mean, no. I didn't leave Earth to find a man." She sat up with a huff. "I left because an alien race somehow penetrated our city shields to not only find me but to take me off planet. I felt it not only put us in danger, but that they'd somehow let the Titans loose."

Ari's brows furrowed. "So, your government sent you as some kind of agent to spy on these aliens?"

Morgan pursed her lips and squirmed. "Well... not exactly. When I approached Grandfather with my concerns..."

"Grandfather?"

Her eyes narrowed. "Yeah, the Akurn I told you who saved most of the people from that scientific outpost, Rummeh, is my distant grandfather." She raised a hand to stop him. "We can go into that later. Much later," she mumbled. "Anyway, they brushed off my concerns, so I went ahead and joined the Zerin exchange." She shrugged. "I figured I could investigate how they penetrated our defenses and then go back with proof of the danger they brought."

Ari sat back, stroking his scruffy jaw as he studied Morgan. What he got out of that narrative was more than she was saying. Here was a strong-willed woman who had grown up in a society where she felt less than those around her. Someone not taken seriously, even when she brought to light a danger they might be facing. His admiration for her grew. She was a woman who didn't let others define who she was and made things happen, with or without anyone's permission.

For some reason, he related to her circumstances on a personal level. Was he, too, viewed as someone less than those around him? What a sobering thought. "Go on," he encouraged with a nod.

"Not much more to tell." She shrugged and looked away. "A Zerin caught me snooping where I wasn't supposed to on their ship, someone who'd been secretly kidnapping woman to sell on the galactic black market." He once again became her focus. "And through several flukes, I ended up here with the Ozevroc."

Ari waited a beat. Just to see if she had anything to add. When she didn't, he gave her a wide grin. He couldn't resist ending the fairytale the right way.

"And then she met the man of her dreams and they lived Happily Ever After."

Morgan chuckled. "You're such a dork."

"Yeah, well, someone's got to lighten things up," he quipped. "Otherwise, it'd be all dull work and no funzies." His gray eyes narrowed. "But I still don't understand what that has to do with me. None of that sounds familiar."

Morgan watched his face twitch, as if he was trying to remember something. It was gone as soon as it came.

"Like I said, I'm pretty sure you're a powerful psychic." She took in a deep breath. Should she take a chance? Like, what choice did she have? With the ship's systems behaving more erratically than ever and dead bodies piling up, their window of escape was rapidly closing.

"I think you're a Titan that somehow escaped Aethralis."

Ari's whoop of laughter caught her by surprise. She frowned. Why was that so funny?

His deep belly laugh ended with a chuckle as he knuckled a rolling tear away. "Me, a Titan." He snickered. "That's rich."

"Why do you say that?" Morgan sat straight and fisted her hand on the table facing him. "It makes perfect sense! Let's look at the facts, shall we?" She raised her hand to highlight each point by ticking off her fingers. "You got rid of the *nutesh* snare. You teleported out of this room. Not once, but twice! You have supernatural healing. Anyone else would've died, as broken up as you were when you got here." She leaned forward to make sure he saw the intent in her eyes. "And last, let's go ahead and mention that Dreamwalk we shared."

His bright gray eyes darkened. "Yeah, I'm all for mentioning that Dreamwalk."

"Oh, for goddess's sake, Ari!" Morgan slapped the table with her palm. "Get serious, would you?" Trying to keep him focused was like catching a puff of smoke with her bare hands.

"I am serious, Morgan," Ari stated with a straight face. "I may not know much, but that's something I know for sure." He frowned and got a faraway look in his eyes before they swiveled back to her. "Listen, I bet you've got pictures of the Titans on your doohickey there." He pointed to her multicorder. "Now see if you can find me in there." He sat back with crossed arms. "I guarantee I'm not one of those big, dumb dickheads known as a Titan."

Morgan pursed her lips. Why didn't she think of that? She glared at him. It was his fault he had her so discombobulated she couldn't think straight. Grabbing her handheld, she deftly typed in the command to bring up the images. Scouring through each one, her frown deepened. He was right. He might be a tall man, around six foot five, with a muscular build, but he wasn't near the height of the shortest Titan at an even seven feet. And none of them had gray eyes and light-blond hair like he did.

She let out a hiss of relief. Him not being a Titan was reassuring, but she remained convinced he possessed powerful psychic abilities. Glancing at him, she narrowed her eyes. "Why did you think it was so funny when I called you a Titan?"

"Because I spent my whole life avoiding being confused with one of them." He blinked slowly, as if he surprised himself.

"Really? You were around when the Titans were created?" How could that be? He'd have to have been alive on Earth when they were. Okay, enough of this second-guessing. "No, never mind. Just give me your finger."

Ari's brows furrowed. "You want me to give you the finger?" He glanced at his middle finger as if stopping it from standing at attention.

Freakin' man. "No, not *the* finger. A finger." She waved her multicorder at him. "I'm going to take a sample of your blood. Which I should have done when I first saw you." See, discombobulated.

"Okay." He held out his hand.

It only took a quick prick from the tip of his forefinger for her to get what she needed.

Studying the readout, she glanced back at him. "You don't have enough original human DNA to make you a Titan, but you have enough of it to make you more than what the modern humans think is normal."

"Huh?" Ari's expression slackened. "I don't get it."

"It's a misconception among modern humans that only aliens have psychic powers, but it's actually the other way around." She explained, replacing Ari's readouts back on the home screen. "The original humans on Earth were the ones with the psychic abilities. When the Akurn scientists added alien DNA to them, it diluted that ability until only a recessive amount remained in the general population. So, the more ancient human DNA someone has, the more psionic powers they inherit. I haven't heard of anyone having this high of a reading since, well, since before the great flood."

If she didn't know any better, she'd swear he was an original *Adamou* like she'd thought before. But they all died thousands of years ago. Didn't they? She squinted at the handsome man before shrugging. "Oh well, let's get back to what we know. I'm really glad you aren't a Titan, but we've got to figure out how to access the psychic powers you do have. Have you done anything you could control?"

His grin was infectious. "Yeah, watch this." He held up his palm. After he scowled at it, a small ball of fire rolled over his skin. His wide smile made the corners of his eyes crinkle. "Cool, eh?"

"Is it hot?" Morgan asked, extending a finger just before touching it. No heat, just light. "Very nice." She glanced at him. "Anything else?"

His eyelids lowered, his sultry intent clear. "We could always try that Dreamwalk thing again." He waggled his eyebrows.

Morgan laughed. "You nut. You..." A sharp crackle split the air, instantly shifting the vibration beneath her feet. "What the..."

She never finished because the world around her erupted.

A deafening boom reverberated from the outside corridor. The walls pulsed with the force of an explosion.

Everything inside Morgan screamed for her to move, to run, but there wasn't time. A blinding flash of light seared through her vision, and an acidic stench filled the air with burning metal.

In the split second that followed, something—or rather, someone—slammed into her with the force of a freight train. Ari. His body, all muscle, collided with hers, knocking the breath from her lungs. She stumbled back, but before she could fall, his arms wrapped around her, strong and unyielding. The impact drove them both to the floor. Ari's weight pressed her down, shielding her from the worst of the blast.

Morgan coughed as her ears rang with the aftershock. Her skin tingled from the heat washing over them. Her heart thundered, each beat drowned out by the relentless ringing in her ears. Rolling vibrations of the ship's structure trembled under her, as if the explosion had caused the very bones of the vessel to rattle.

Ari's body was a protective barrier, his broad back taking the brunt of the heat and debris that rained down around them. The air was thick with dust and smoke, making it hard to breathe. Ari's chest rose and fell in a steady rhythm against her, keeping her grounded amidst the chaos.

For a moment, everything else faded away—the noise, the danger, the acrid smell of burnt metal. The only thing she was aware of was the solid, reassuring presence of Ari covering her. His face was close, his breath warm against her neck. His arms, still wrapped tightly around her, were like iron bands, unyielding in their resolve to protect.

Morgan's mind raced as she remained pinned beneath him. She wanted to move, to push him off and assess the damage, but she knew, instinctively, that he wouldn't budge until he was sure the threat had passed.

His voice, when it came, was a low, urgent murmur in her ear. "Are you okay?"

All she managed was a brief nod, her throat too tight to form words.

The heat from the blast dissipated, and the tension in Ari's muscles slowly eased.

As the smoke and dust settled, it looked like the immediate danger had passed. Tears filled her eyes. How close were they to getting caught in that deadly blast? But more than that, how close was she to losing whatever started between her and Ari?

As his grip on her loosened, just a fraction, her eyes met his. For a heartbeat, the chaos of the ship faded into the background as she connected with him in that one electric moment. A type of connection that went far beyond words.

It took everything Ari had to unwrapped his firm hold around Morgan. Placing his palms on the hard metallic floor, he raised up to check her out, just to make sure she wasn't hurt. Satisfied she'd suffered nothing worse than several bruises, he rolled and extended his hand to help her up. "What the *fruk* just happened?"

Morgan took his hand and stood, swiping a lock of golden curls out of her eyes. "I don't know, but it sounded like something exploded." She glanced around. "Thank the goddess it doesn't look like any vital systems were affected." She ran to her workstation and called up her floating, transparent monitor. After a few swipes and taps, she straightened with her hand over her heart. "Yes, all right. Everything is good."

The sound of hissing and growling from the outside corridor came close.

"Uh-oh. Here comes the scavenger patrol." Ari pushed her behind him. He might not know how he'd do it, but he'd make sure no one laid a hand on her.

The first alien rushing through the door was the smaller, dirty yellow Ozevroc waving his weapon in their direction, followed by a group of guards that swarmed around him and Morgan. Ari didn't need a translator to know they were warning them not to move. As they growled and mumbled, they poked their blasters or solid spears in time with the sounds they made.

"Buzz off, snout squad." Ari growled back, shoving the weapons away when it got too close to Morgan.

None of them moved. He'd become the target of the steady glare from four sets of beady-black eyes each of them had. At least they left Morgan alone and focused on him. Win-win.

One of them whistled, and the Grand Poobah himself waltzed in. High Chief Walls or Wells... something or other.

Morgan deftly whipped around Ari and faced the Ozevroc leader, who growled.

Well, he should have seen that coming. No way would this lady hide behind anyone. To show his support, he placed his hands on her shoulders and pulled her so her back was flush to his chest.

She said nothing but replied in a like manner to the Ozevroc with a small bow and her hand over her heart.

As the two of them growled, hissed, and snarled at each other, Ari took the time to study the other aliens.

Most of them looked pissed off, rumbling in gravelly noises that made their thin black lips ripple along their snouts.

Snorting in disdain, he looked over their shortness and surveyed the room. Where the replicron stood in its camouflaged mode, various sheets of dust covered its outline. Otherwise, it seemed in good shape. Hopefully, the crazy aliens wouldn't notice it. Glancing around, he noted that nothing was broken or cracked except the wall where the explosion happened. He was itchin' to see what that corridor looked like on the other side.

He checked Morgan and swallowed a grin. From his high advantage point, he saw her tight expression, pursed lips and all. Whatever Mr. *I'm the grand, my shit don't stink, pooh-bah* said irritated the holy hell out of her. Not that he blamed her. The guy's total superior dickness was loud and clear.

A few more rumbles and growls before Stubby and his merry band of Fuzzy Knuckleheads departed with lofty snorts.

Ari let Morgan go and stepped back. He waved a hand over his face as if that would get rid of the stench the Ozevroc left behind. "I don't suppose you could insist they take a bath before visiting again, hmm?" He exaggerated a gagging noise.

Morgan humphed and tapped her forefinger against her lips. "It seems like High Chieftain Welozz is having trust issues with some of his crew."

"Yeah? No kidding." Ari nodded at the warped and bubbly wall. "Nothing says 'surprise!' like redecorating with a bomb."

She nodded. "We're told to keep an eye out for an Ozevroc named Grozzik, who'd taken the place of one of the head guards. You know, the one we found dead here."

"Like I'd recognize him if he showed up with a blinking neon sign plastered on his forehead." Ari gestured to the wall. "Did Mr. Wizard know why the bomb went off in the first place? Seems like a dumb place for it to happen."

Morgan shook her head and crossed her arms. "He has no clue. But, that's the weird part. The blast did nothing but make a loud noise, generate some heat, and shake the ship up a bit." She dropped her arms and went to her floating monitor. Biting her bottom lip, she studied several readouts. "Look at this." She pointed to a page.

Ari leaned down and squinted at the image. "What am I looking at?" It appeared to be some kind of video. "Is that the corridor?"

"Just watch," she replied.

At first, it was only an empty hallway, then a blob of purple blurred into the scene. The image sputtered out and remained that way.

"What the hell was that?" Ari straightened. "Hey, did short, ugly, and hairy leave? I'd like to look in that corridor."

She narrowed her eyes at his throat. "That's right, you don't have a *nutesh* snare on." Laughing, she grabbed his forearm and led him to the warped entrance. "Peek around the corner to make sure none of them are there before you go out." She nudged him between his shoulders, as if he needed any encouragement to step out.

"Okay, super-snoopy." He grinned at her over his shoulder. "No need to get pushy. I got this."

With her hands up, she cocked her head. "Okay, just be careful. I'd hate to see you blasted into space dust."

He rolled his eyes. "Sheesh. You'd think this was my first rodeo or something." Not that he had any idea what a rodeo was or if he even had anything to do with one before. Not waiting for her response, he took a quick peek. The only thing to see was smoke listlessly floating around, several sparks popping in and out from the exposed wiring protruding from the roof and walls. He stepped out.

"Ari!" Morgan hissed a sharp whisper. "Wait..."

Not waiting to answer her, he slid out the doorway and kept close to the wall.

"Ari!"

At Morgan's raised voice, he glanced back at her.

She was waving her handheld at him. "Use this to take some readings!"

Okay, rodeos aside. It never occurred to him to use something to scan the area. He snuck back and took the offered device with a sheepish grin.

"Just point it around. I've got it all ready for you." She shooed him with both hands.

The corridor wasn't wide or long, so it didn't take him long to make a complete sweep of the blasted area. He made it back inside the engine room with no Ozevroc the wiser.

Morgan eagerly grasped the device he handed back to her. Her eyes moved back-and-forth as she pursed her lips.

"Oh, this is interesting," she said, showing the screen to him. "There's a huge amount of the same crystalline material all over here." She focused back on her handheld. "Just a couple of adjustments... there. Let me upload this on the computer and let's see where the highest concentration of this stuff is."

Ari followed her back to her workstation where she sync'd her device to the mainframe.

"Aren't you afraid the Ozevroc will see what you're doing and accuse you of something?"

She shook her head. "Nope. I've got this baby protected, so no one knows what I'm looking at." With a huff, she grinned. "Besides, they're either too lazy or too arrogant to think anyone could hack their system."

He snorted. "If you ask me, they're both."

Her eyes widened. "Oh, look!" She gestured at the transparent screen. "Oh, lucky you. It seems like the highest concentration of that crystalline stuff is in one of your favorite places."

Ari stiffened at the mischievous glint in her golden-green eyes.

"Time for you to go back to your favorite place. The stupendously wonderful... garbage chamber."

Well... *fruk*.

CHAPTER EIGHT

A ri glanced around the dim corridor inside the *Nebula Viper* that led him to garbage heaven. Oh joy. Looking forward to once again bask in the delightful aroma of rotting shit... or whatever that stench was that blended nicely with the acrid smell of sharp, musty metal.

He couldn't wait.

At least he wasn't alone this time. Well... kinda sorta, since Morgan had synchronized his handheld with hers. She also created earbuds from the replicron so they didn't have to rely on texting each other. Though she huffed at being left behind, she was smart enough to know if she stepped one foot out of the engine room without an Ozevroc, the *nutesh* snare would blow her head clean off.

They decided it'd be best if he went out late into the sleep cycle to avoid any of those aliens. Too bad her replicron couldn't create a weapon for him. He felt downright naked, with just his bare hands to defend himself.

"You're almost there," Morgan's sweet voice whispered in his ear. "I'll tell you when to stop. You're looking for a faint seam in the wall."

Ari's eyes narrowed as he scanned the walls as he passed, searching for the faint seam she mentioned. The metal panels appeared flawless, blending into one another with no obvious entrance in sight.

"There!" Morgan's voice rose. "It's right there."

If she hadn't warned him, his hand would have moved right past it. It was a small, grimy panel that was practically invisible under layers of soot and grime. Stepping closer, he reached out, his gloved fingers tracing the edges of the panel. It felt solid, unremarkable.

"Okay, press on it in this sequence with only two fingers." Her tone was excited. "And don't you dare get creative, understand?"

He grinned. Yeah, the woman was in her bossy mode again. Shoving the tempting scenario of her being naked while she was in that mood out of his mind, he pressed down on the tile in the deliberate sequence she described. He kept his touch light and sure. For a moment, nothing happened and...there—a subtle shift in the wall.

A nearly imperceptible seam appeared, the metal barely parting to reveal a narrow gap.

Ari pressed a little harder, and the hidden door slid open with a soft hiss, revealing a dimly lit passage beyond. The flickering light inside cast long, eerie shadows. All right, now who doesn't want to explore a creepy hallway in a spaceship full of hostiles? His heart beat faster in anticipation. He stepped forward, leaving the semi-polished corridors of the ship behind, and entered the heart of the garbage chamber.

Instead of calling up his ball of fire, Ari turned on the light fixture of his handheld. Its narrow beam was just wide enough to see where to go.

"I'm in," he told Morgan, keeping his voice low. The sharp nefarious stench burned the back of his throat. He sucked in a breath, which only made it worse. His eyes teared up. Thankfully, Morgan had given him a small device that hung inside his nostrils. Once in place, he took a breath of cool, clean air. Damn, he should've put that in before he stepped one foot inside this disgusting place.

He did his best to ignore the thick, viscous streams of dark sludge oozing down the walls he could see out of the corner of his eye. Probably a toxic cocktail of alien chemicals and decaying organic matter.

The muck glistened in the dim light, leaving a trail of iridescent residue that clung stubbornly to the corroded metal.

He took in a grateful, clean breath. Thank the goddess, he didn't have to continue to breathe more of that nasty stuff.

A faint purplish light up ahead caught his attention. He frowned. Was that there before? To get a better look, he switched off the handheld light. The deeper he ventured into the darkness, the brighter the purple glow grew.

"I see a purple light ahead. Is there something that should do that?" he whispered.

"Purple light?" Confusion laced Morgan's animated voice. "There is no way there should be a light like that there." A pause.

Woman must be studying the schematics on her computer.

"You're almost to the main chamber where there's a heavy concentration of that crystalline mixture. It's to your left when you enter. Tell me if you see anything."

"Yes, missy bossy ma'am," he snarked. The daydream of her bossing him around in the bedroom came back. Whoa, slow down, boy. Pay attention to the purple menace first, bedroom Olympics later. Maybe. Hopefully.

When Ari reached the end of the narrow, grimy hallway, the space opened into a vast chamber, dimly lit by flickering orange lights. Mountains of garbage rose in chaotic heaps, filling the cavernous room. A wave of oppressive heat gave him the crazy idea that the chamber was alive and breathing.

On his right, a massive machine dominated the place. Its mechanical arms moved with relentless, rhythmic precision. The device grabbed piles of refuse, compressing them with a deafening crunch before depositing the compacted blocks into a gaping chute below. The machine's gears groaned under the strain, sending vibrations through the floor.

Wow, good thing that hadn't been on when he was there before. He might have gotten caught up in that mechanical monster's deadly grasp. His to-do list didn't include getting mushed into a cube.

A glowing purple light attracted his eye to a narrow path along the edge of the chamber. It was just wide enough for him to skirt around the machine's reach. Going sideways, he squeezed away from the main chamber and found himself in a small room. His breath caught. There, in a crude, makeshift cage fashioned from bent metal bars, stood a figure unlike anything he'd ever seen before. The man, if he could be called a man, consisted entirely of crystalline purple. The guy's body refracted the dim light into shards of amethyst hues that danced across the filthy walls. His faceted skin glimmered, and his eyes, deep and mysterious, met Ari's with a mix of fear and desperation. The cage seemed almost too small for the being, confining him to a hunched position, yet the crystal man's presence was undeniably powerful, radiating a strange, silent energy.

"Uh, Morgan?" he rasped.

"Yeah?"

"Good news! I think I know what is making that crystalline stuff." Ari reported with a wry grin. "Bad news... it's glaring at me like I owe it money."

Ari didn't wait for Morgan's reply as he eyed the crystalline creature in the cage, fascinated by its faceted form glinting under the harsh overhead lights. The weight of its gaze—confused and utterly alien made Ari's heart pound. He stood frozen, feet glued to the metallic floor. The confusing fight-or-flight instinct warred inside him.

"As'ni *sooo* hungry." The purple crystal's voice was masculine, but soft and hesitant. "You bring As'ni food? As'ni hungry," he whimpered. "Furry, furry won't feed. Furry, furry won't let me out!"

Ari relaxed at the childlike cry and cocked his head. "Morgan, did you hear that? Is this guy saying he's hungry?" he asked. "How is it I understand him and not the Ozevroc?"

"You must have some kind of translator device implanted in you that could pick up his language," she chuckled. "I think I'm glad it doesn't work with the Ozevroc. No telling how they'd react to your less than funny humor."

Not so. He was as funny as hell. Looks like a conversation he had to have with the obviously clueless woman later. Aiming the handheld to the humanoid creature, he ran the scanner over the purple crystals, mirrors, and glass.

"Morgan, are you getting this?" He kept his voice low.

"Oh, the poor thing," Morgan crooned. "Look how sad he is." She cleared her throat. "Get a little closer so I can scan him better."

Oh, sure. Get closer to the behemoth stuffed in a cage. Exactly what he'd been dreaming about doing his whole life.

When Morgan gave an impatient hum in his ear, his shoulders slumped. Well, crud. No getting around it. He shuffled closer to the cage, but kept an eye on the large, ah, thing. "Hey, guy. How ya doing?" Ari winced. Wow, that was lame. He cleared his throat. "I'm Ari. You say you're hungry, eh?"

The purple crystal man nodded, then tilted his head. He gripped the bars of the cage in one massive hand while holding out the other. "I know you?"

Now it was Ari's turn to frown. This thing knew him? Impossible. "I don't think so."

The behemoth didn't like that answer. The crystals around his wide mouth pursed. He shook the cage. "As'ni need food!"

If Ari wasn't mistaken, the guy's clear, purple eyes fixated on his handheld. When he raised it, the creature's eyes followed as the prominent ridge above his eyes furrowed. "No, more. Not enough!" As'ni made a fist from his thick, three-fingered hand. With a sudden, deliberate motion, he lifted his massive arm, each crystalline joint shifting with a grating sound, like boulders scraping against one another.

His fist slammed down with brutal force, knocking Ari off balance.

The impact hit with a power Ari never imagined was possible as the metal floor buckled and rippled like lake water when a stone was thrown in. The resulting shockwave traveled outward, making him stumble again, his hands instinctively reaching for the wall as the ground shifted beneath him.

A deep, resonating hum filled the air, vibrating through Ari's bones, as the ship groaned in protest. The walls shuddered, and overhead, the lights flickered. His pulse quickened, matching the erratic thrum of the lights as he fought to stay upright, his fingers digging into the cold metal for stability.

Then, as quickly as it began, the quake subsided. The ripples in the floor stilled, leaving the surface warped and uneven, a permanent scar from the creature's wrath.

Ari's chest heaved as he forced himself to breathe, adrenaline rushing. He glanced at the creature, its crystalline form unshaken but somehow diminished.

The temperature in the room dropped. Puffs of cold air came out of Ari with each exhalation.

The creature put his hands over the side of his head and moaned. "Hungry. So hungry." He shook his head back-and-forth.

"Did you shine the multicorder light on him?" Morgan asked, her voice in his ear.

"Yeah. I think that's what made him mad." Ari made sure the beam was away from the creature.

"The readings I'm getting from your handheld confirm he's made of the same materials that crystals and glass are on Earth. Of course, with a few alien variations mixed in." She continued. "If that's so, I think I know something that will help feed him."

Ari's eyebrows rose. "You want to feed this thing?" A bunch of crazy scenarios swarmed in his mind. And most of them ending with him suffering excruciating pain.

"Yes." Her voice was excited. "If we can get him to trust us, we can make sure he doesn't go around killing more Ozevroc or sabotaging our systems."

Watching the alien with its arms around its knees, rocking and groaning, Ari voiced his concerns. "I don't think he's smart enough to create the system problems we've been having." He didn't want to voice his suspicions this was the guy who killed the two Ozevroc. From what he could see, the blocky teeth from the creature fit the indentation on the last furry body they'd found.

"Of course not," Morgan admonished. "But he can help us find the Ozevroc who are trying to overthrow Welozz. And that kind of revolt will get us killed before we fix *Elemi* and escape."

Good point. "Okay," Ari said. "What do you want me to do?"

"See if you can generate that ball of fire again. Then take it close to the creature and see how he reacts to it."

"Reacts?" He didn't like the sound of that. "In what way?"

"I'm hoping that kind of heat and energy is what he needs."

Her calm statement sent a dull throb through his temples.

"So, what do you want me to do? Toss it at him?" Then run like hell.

"Perfect! Yeah, do that!" she exclaimed.

Ari swore to the goddess...if that was her clapping in the background...

With one last look at the simpering crystal giant, Ari put out his hand, palm up. Hey, look at that. He brought the fireball up with barely a thought. His fingers tingled with raw energy as the psychic fireball coalesced in his palm, its heat licking at his skin without burning him.

The ball pulsed with a fierce inner light, swirling and rolling like a contained storm.

Ari focused, shaping the fiery orb with his will. He stepped closer to the cage. "Hey, As'ni? That your name? As'ni?"

The alien's crystalline body reflected the chaotic glow of the fireball. The bulky creature stopped moaning and looked up, his huge palms falling to his sides. "As'ni. Yes." He nodded. Then his eyes fixated on the bright ball Ari carried. "Food?"

Ari raised his hand. "Is this what you need, As'ni?" Please let this be what the guy needed. He'd sure hate for him to lose his shizzle again. No telling if the ship could handle another tantrum like that.

As'ni jumped up, hitting his head on the top bars. Not that he seemed to care. He hunched and threw out his massive paw, his fingers opening and closing.

The look of sheer hunger stamped on his face made Ari take a step back. Damn, he'd hate for that creature to look at him like that. But no, the guy remained fixated on the ball of fire.

"Gimme." As'ni's voice wavered. "Give to As'ni."

No way was Ari going to get close enough for the mammoth creature to grab him. Tossing it might be the chickenshit way to go, but at least it'd give him a chance to survive. His jaw tightened. Okay, let's see if this worked.

"Okay, As'ni. Catch!" Leaning on one leg, he pulled back his arm, the psychic flames flaring brighter in response. With one a swift motion, he hurled the ball of fire at As'ni.

It soared through the air, leaving a trail of searing light in its wake.

As the fireball struck As'ni's chest, something unexpected happened.

The flames didn't explode on impact. Instead, they paused, hesitating for a fraction of a second before an unseen force sucked them into his body. Then the fireballs of wild energy flowed inward, absorbed into the countless facets of As'ni's crystalline form.

Ari sucked in a breath. Wow, that was the weirdest thing he'd ever seen.

As the fiery light spread through As'ni's body, it moved like liquid fire. The creature's translucent surface glowed brighter, the fireball's energy becoming one with it, refracting and scattering in brilliant patterns. A dazzling light danced within, illuminating every edge and angle until it radiated a steady, blinding gleam.

Ari blinked in disbelief as As'ni's crystalline form shimmered with an almost joyous glow, the remnants of the fireball casting playful patterns of light across the room. The creature shifted, his massive head tilting to one side, and for a moment, Ari could swear he saw something like a smile in the way the crystals curved at the edges of what passed for a mouth.

As'ni's body pulsed with a soft, contented hum, the sound vibrating through the floor.

Then, just as suddenly, the light dimmed. The fireball extinguished—completely absorbed, leaving no trace. As'ni's body returned to its usual cool gleam, the flames snuffed out within its depths, as if they had never existed.

Ari clenched his fists. Hopefully, he didn't just help that creature become more erratic.

"So good. Yes, food," As'ni rumbled, patting his tummy. His voice resonated like stones rolling together. The creature's tone was warm, almost affectionate. Happy like a puppy getting a treat.

Ari swallowed, nerves still taut, but he forced a small, cautious smile. "Yeah, food. We're... friends now, right?"

As'ni's head bobbed in a slow, deliberate nod. "Friends. Better than bad furries." His purple head tilted with a frown. "Don't like furries."

"What's a furry?" Ari whispered to Morgan.

"He must be talking about the Ozevroc holding him hostage," she replied.

Well, that made sense.

"Good." Ari stepped closer to the cage. "As'ni feel better?"

"Yes, yes!" As'ni clapped. "Go with friend?" The creature's unibrow scrunched together as he gripped the cage bars. "As'ni want."

"Okay, As'ni. But you've got to be real quiet so the furries don't find us," Ari warned. "Think you can do that?"

"Yes! Yes!" The giant grinned, showing his blocky, lilac teeth. "As'ni be real quiet." He made a shushing noise. "Okay if As'ni bring toy?"

Toy? "What kind of toy?" Ari asked.

His eyes widened when As'ni reached behind him and pulled out something that looked like a curved claw.

The object appeared to be crafted from a blend of precious metals and crystalline materials. Etched on its surface were elaborate carvings and symbols pulsating with a soft, ethereal blue glow.

If Ari wasn't mistaken, that thing had to be the ancient relic the Ozevroc were looking for. Goddess, Ari hoped this wasn't a mistake—letting this guy bring that. But maybe it would give him and Morgan an advantage somehow. "Sure, bring it." He nodded.

As'ni gave a happy chirp and clutched the relic like a favorite stuffed animal against his wide chest. His crystalline face creased in a childlike grin.

Keeping As'ni in his sights, Ari walked around the cage, looking for a latch of some kind that held the door shut. Ah, there. Reaching over, he flipped it open and took a careful step back. With a flourish, he gestured to the open doorway. "Come on, buddy, time to get out of there. Follow me."

As'ni hesitated only for a second before lurching forward with surprising eagerness. The heavy thuds of his steps were like an excited child eager to follow his new best friend.

"Hey, Morgan"—Ari headed back to the dingy hallway out of the garbage chamber with the lumbering steps of his new friend close behind—"hope you're ready for a sleepover. But I gotta warn you, he's not exactly a chatterbox, but I swear he's bringing a gift that will just keep on giving."

Morgan couldn't remember the last time she was this nervous. Which was just ridiculous. Not like she wasn't in constant contact with Ari, so she had no reason to worry about him traipsing around a hostile spaceship with a strange alien. Yep, he was just fine. The man was clever enough not to get caught. Even without his memories, he was a confident, smart guy. Okay, she should keep that in mind. Maybe the reason for her edginess was the *gift* he promised to bring. He had such a goofy sense of humor, there was no telling what it could be.

Besides, she had a little surprise of her own. She glanced at the worktable. Fingers crossed, that last, final touch was the only thing needed.

Rubbing her sweaty palms down the sides of her overalls, she jumped when she heard low murmurs and less-than-stealthy, clumping footsteps. She rushed to the engine room doorway, gripping the multicorder a little harder than she should have.

"In here, buddy."

The sound of Ari's voice made her tense muscles relax. They made it.

"More food! Yes?"

That gravelly deep voice had to be the crystal creature's.

The lilting tone of his grinding, childlike voice was a surprise. Even though she heard and saw much of their exchange on her own handheld, she suspected seeing him in person would turn out different.

When Ari slid in first, she sucked in a breath, examining him with her eyes wild. Just to make sure he was okay. No reason to linger on parts of him she enjoyed the most. No siree. Keeping it professional here.

Then the loud thumps of the lumbering giant when he came into the room made her take a step back. Holy goddess, he was big. Not necessarily tall, but stretched wide as all get-out. His humanoid form maintained proper proportions while striking an intimidating chord all the same. But when she checked his blocky face, she relaxed. The child-like eagerness when he looked back at her made her smile.

"Oh, pretty lady!" The creature trudged to her before dropping to his knees with his arms wide. "I like pretty lady." He looked back at Ari. "Can I play?"

"No, As'ni." Ari smiled. "She's mine to play with. I promise we'll find you something even better."

Morgan shivered as thoughts of what playtime with Ari would entail. Sensual, enjoyable explorations for two consulting adults to enjoy. Not that she'd admit that to him. Crossing her arms, she gave her full attention to the crystal man.

The giant's shoulders slumped and his lower lip pouted. "Okay, Ari friend. As'ni be good." He stood and looked around, clapping his hands. The echo of his crystal palms hitting together made a unique musical timbre. Like something a caveman would do with two re-sounding rocks. "As'ni go over here." The crystalline alien moved with an odd, clumsy grace, his multifaceted form glinting under the harsh overhead lights. He stopped in front of a sprawling heap of discarded tools, metals, and assorted junk. A collection of the ship's many repairs and mishaps that hadn't made it to the incinerator yet.

"Remember, As'ni," Ari's voice was smooth but firm. "Don't go out of this room or the furries will find you. Okay?"

As'ni's bulky head nodded vigorously. "No leave. Stay with Ari." The glint of the discarded metallic pile grabbed the creature's attention.

It was then Morgan noticed the swinging object hanging from a protruding crystal at As'ni's waist. "Is that..." She moved toward the crystal man, but Ari stopped her with a firm-but-gentle grip on her upper arm.

She glanced at him.

"Yeah, I believe that's the Talon thingy the Ozevroc are looking for." He nodded to her multicorder. "Why don't you scan it first, just to make sure."

Heart pounding, Morgan aimed her handheld at the swinging device as As'ni moved from object to object. He'd pick one up, then discard it over his shoulder before moving to another. With his back to them, he sang a simple ditty and appeared absorbed in finding his new favorite toy.

Morgan hummed to herself, and it only took a moment to examine the readings before she decided. "Yes, that's definitely the Talon of Ancients." She pursed her lips. "But that gives us a bigger problem."

Ari tilted his head. "How so?"

"How are we going to give it back to the Ozevroc without them blasting us into extinction because they think we stole it?"

"Well, first things first." Ari studied As'ni. "We've got to get it away from him before we do anything else. Trust me"—he eyed the busy alien—"you don't want him throwing a tantrum." With his lips pressed into a thin line, he sauntered over to the crystal man and crouched next to him. "Have you found a new toy yet?" He gestured to the pile.

As'ni's glassy eyes flickered with interest as he studied the debris.

Morgan moved to stand next to Ari. Goddess, she sure hoped As'ni wouldn't choose anything sharp or dangerous.

With an exclamation of joy, the crystal man reached out with surprising gentleness and plucked a small, twisted coil of metal from the pile. It was a simple thing, once part of some now-defunct mechanism, with an intricate spiral design that caught the light in a dozen different ways.

It reminded her of an old Slinky toy made popular several decades ago in the human world.

As'ni held it up, turning it slowly in his hand, the metal reflecting off his crystalline skin creating a dazzling display of colors. He seemed mesmerized by how the light played through the coil, creating shifting patterns on the walls. There was a childlike wonder in the way he examined it, as if he'd discovered something truly magical from a pile of junk.

Morgan exchanged a glance with Ari, who raised an eyebrow and shrugged. "Guess he's into shiny, bouncy things," he muttered with a note of unexpected softness in his tone.

She agreed. How interesting that the giant found one of the simplest of things in the pile to hold his attention.

"As'ni—" Ari placed a hand on the creature's shoulder. "—is this what you want?"

As'ni's smile was wide as he nodded. "As'ni keep."

"Okay, buddy." He patted the purple crystalline shoulder. "But where are you going to keep it?" He pointed to the artifact dangling from his waist. "Looks like that would be the perfect place for it. Would you like to trade me so you can keep your new treasure with you?"

The alien's nod turned vigorous. "Yes, yes! You keep." He took the artifact off the hook at his side and handed it to Ari between his finger and thumb. "I no want now." He dropped it, not even looking to see if Ari grabbed it or not.

When he did, Morgan breathed a sigh of relief.

"As'ni—" Ari stood. "—you stay here and play with your new toy. Morgan and I will be right over there." He pointed to the workstation.

The creature nodded, singing to his new toy, and ignored them.

When she and Ari reached the workstation, she leaned to him and kept her voice low. "Now, what?" They had to get rid of the artifact before Welozz made another unscheduled appearance.

"Well—" Ari scratched the side of his scruffy jaw. "—I think the only thing we can do is put it back where it belongs."

Morgan put her hands on her hips. "And just how do you propose we do that without getting caught?"

"Yo... Wrench Queen," an unfamiliar, male mechanical voice piped up from the table. "Good thing I'm here to save the day."

Morgan jumped. She'd totally forgotten her own surprise for Ari.

"What's this?" Ari leaned down with his hands on the top of his thighs and glanced at Morgan. "You got it to work?"

"Hey, Captain Obvious! Of course I'm working." The gold-and-silver spider bot on the table jumped up and down. "And I ain't no 'it', buddy!" The droid poked a slim, golden foreleg in Ari's direction. "You better mind your manners, or I'll tell everybody about that sexbot you took just before we left."

Ari straightened. "Huh?" His golden brows furrowed. "What's a sexbot? And why would I want one?"

Morgan glowered at Ari and crossed her arms. A sexbot? One of those monstrous sex toys that looked like a metallic Barbie and held her prisoner on FiPan? She knew damn good and well why he'd steal one of those. Especially if he got it to work.

"Jeez, Arakiba," the spider-bot complained. "If I have to explain that to you, why did you insist on taking one?"

"Arakiba?" Ari's hands fisted at his sides. "Is that my name?" He looked away with a blank expression.

Morgan turned to the small droid. "Is that his name?" She pulled up her multicorder and typed it in. It didn't take long for the device to spew out various scenarios until the last paragraph. There it stated that Arakiba was one of the original *Adamou* created after the Titans. It stated that he and his four "brothers" perished in the great flood thousands of years ago.

She looked up at Ari who was still lost in his thoughts. That couldn't be him. Could it?

The bot dropped onto his bulbous butt, like a dog with his back four legs spread out. "Hey, what's going on here?" His spider head swiveled between her and Ari. "If you didn't know that's his name, what've you been calling him? Blondie?"

She ignored the droid and put a gentle hand on Ari's forearm. "Does that name sound familiar to you?"

He blinked before focusing on her. "No." He shook his head, rubbing the back of his neck. "It doesn't."

Morgan turned her attention back to the small bot. "Are your memories intact? Do you have total recollection?" Hopefully, this droid had the key to not only help Ari, but it might have the info they needed to speed up the repairs on *Elemi*. "Do you know what your designation is?"

"Designation? Get a load of you, Missy!" The bot stood on all eight legs. "My *name* is JR12. But you can just call me Starchaser." His metallic undertones had a slight whirring sound.

"Look, Zippy." Ari addressed the droid. "Answer her question. Are your memories intact or not?"

"What?" JR12 cocked his head. "Yours aren't?"

"JR12..."

Morgan hid her smile behind her fingers at the exasperated tone in Ari's voice.

"Down boy! Dang, if it was any more obvious, it'd be written in neon." JR12 groused. "Of course I do." His multifaceted eyes glinted in the low light of the room. "But then I wouldn't know if I didn't, now would I, Einstein?"

Cheeky little bot. Morgan snickered.

"Believe me, you'd know." Ari's jawline hardened. "Okay, let's try this another way." He turned and faced her. "Morgan..."

"Morgan?" JR12 jumped up and down. "Are you Morgan Elara Jackson from Atlanta, Georgia?"

Startled, she took a moment before she answered. She'd forgotten she'd told the Zerin when she'd joined their exchange program she was from that place in America. Being undercover, she hadn't divulged her true origins from Aethralis. But how did this droid know her fake profile?

"No," Ari answered before she could. "She's from..."

"Yes, that's right." She interrupted before he finished. "I'm Morgan Jackson from Atlanta." She pursed her lips. "How'd you know that?"

"Holy cosmic craziness! I don't believe it." JR12's excited tone matched the quivering of his small gold-and-silver metallic body. "Look at us, completing our mission without even trying. Didn't we show them stupid naysayers we had what it took? Finding her that fast in this big, wide galaxy!" He snapped his front chelicera together. "Boy, Sue Fitzmaurice sure was right when she said, *'You must go on an adventure to find out where you truly belong'*. And boy, oh boy, was she ever right! Ain't we's da bomb, A-Man?"

Ari chuckled.

A-Man? Morgan eyed the man, who had a stupid grin on his face. What a dumb nickname. Did he want to be called that? Or should she now call him Arakiba? She gave the muscular, handsome man a quick once-over. Nah. He'd always be Ari to her.

Back to business. "What do you mean you found me?" Morgan quizzed the bot. "Were you looking for me?" She glanced at Ari, who shrugged.

"Yes!" JR12 replied. "The Chancellor of the Federation Consortium, D'zia E'etu, sent us to find the missing human women kidnapped from the exchange program."

She couldn't help it. His little hops made her grin.

"And we were lucky enough to score *Elemi* to take our journey with." The bot stopped moving and glanced around. "And just where is the divine diva?"

Before Morgan pointed the prone ship out, JR12 slumped. His body turned to the vessel in the corner of the large engine room. "Oh no. That purple ass did more damage to her than I thought."

"Purple..." Ari began.

"Pretty toy!" As'ni stomped over to them, his hands outstretched, fingers clenching and unclenching with an eager childlike rhythm as he focused on JR12. "As'ni want!" The spring he'd coveted swung on the hook from his side, apparently forgotten.

"As'ni, no!" Ari stepped in front of the crystal alien before he crashed into the table.

As'ni skidded to a stop. He stood rigid, his enormous fists clenched at his sides. His lower lip quivered, jutting out as his breath came out quicker, shallower. The unibrow over his deep-set eyes furrowed, casting shadows over his wide eyes, which were rapidly filling with clear crystal tears. He glanced from Ari to Morgan, and his wide chest rose and fell as a soft, high-pitched whimper escaped his lips.

"As'ni no play?" His voice quivered.

"Ack! It's him!" JR12 squeaked and jumped high enough to land on Ari's shoulder to nestle under his long blond hair. "Don't let him get me!"

What in the world? Morgan watched the bot quiver and shake as if the crystal man scared him.

"No, As'ni." Ari patted the alien's shoulder. "JR12 not good for you, very boring."

"Hey!" JR12 chirped from Ari's shoulder.

"See, you like this better." Ari picked up a small penlight from the tabletop. "Lookie how pretty."

"Ooh, pretty."

Ari successfully diverted As'ni's attention.

The giant played with the light after Ari showed him how to click it on and off.

"Now, be a good boy and sit over there to play with your new toys. Okay?" Ari gave him a couple more pats before nudging him with an open palm between his crystalline purple shoulders. "And if you stay there and behave, I'll make you some more food."

"Food?" As'ni looked up with a wide grin. "As'ni like food."

"Good. Go on, then." Ari gestured to the small pile of discarded metal the creature had played with earlier.

With a cheerful hum, As'ni did as he was told. When he reached the edge of the metallic hump, he dropped his butt onto the floor with a loud thump.

"Jumping galactic glory." JR12 announced in a calmer tone from Ari's shoulder as he scratched the side of his bulbous head with one of his spindly forelegs. "Who'd have thunk?"

"Thought what?" Morgan asked, watching As'ni play with this new collection. The alien shined the penlight on his metallic spring as he bounced the coils over and under the light.

JR12 grunted. "That the very creature that blew up *Elemi* is now as docile as a cat pretending it didn't just eat your pet mouse."

CHAPTER NINE

A rakiba? Aah-raack-kee-bah? A-rack-kha-bah?

Ari rolled out the strange name around his tongue, trying it on for size. "Arakiba." He closed his eyes and let the sound float in the air. No matter how many times he said it, it didn't feel right. He was Ari.

"Do you want me to call you that now?"

He opened his eyes and focused on Morgan.

She tilted her head and gave him a steady stare with one eyebrow lifted.

Her concern made him smile.

"You can always call him A-Man, like I do," JR12 helpfully stated from Ari's shoulder.

Time to nip that annoying suggestion in the bud right now. "No, I like it when you call me Ari." He grinned at her and ignored the bot. "Less of a mouthful."

She frowned. "Okay... *Ari*."

The sweet sound of her voice with the slight rolling of the "r" in his name made him itchy. In a good way.

"So, Terra Twins," JR12 didn't move from his perch on Ari's shoulder. Even though the bot didn't weigh a damn thing, having that mechanical voice right in his ear took some getting used to. "Now that we've cleared up this *muy importante* agenda... *A-Man*," the bot's slight snicker made Ari's eye twitch. "Why don't you clue me in on what's going on here?"

"Well, first off, what did you mean by saying he blew up *Elemi*?" Morgan insisted. She thumbed over her shoulder at As'ni. Before the bot answered, she put up her hands. "Hang on. I'd better hook you up to my multicorder first. That way you'll get up-to-date on what's going on here and give us access to your stored memory bank." She pulled up her handheld and typed something in it. "Jump to the table and I'll sync you to it."

The back panels on JR12's silver-gold body parted and iridescent wings flickered out. He buzzed to land on the table and sat on his butt, his back legs fanned out. "Ready."

"Okay, here we go." Morgan placed the multicorder next to the spider bot. "After this is done, maybe you can advise us the best way to help *Elemi* heal so she can get us out of here." Pushing on the top of the screen, she stepped back.

The droid became still, nary a twitch from his legs or eyes. A few seconds passed before his multifaceted eyes reflected different colors before settling on the shiny black orbs they were before. "Well, as the great George Washington said, *'The harder the conflict, the greater the triumph.'* And that's what we got here, boys and girls. An impossible task and nothing to work with." JR12 eyed Ari. "Unless we can get you to use your powers for good once again."

"Huh?" Ari scratched his jaw. "What do you mean?"

"Well, slap me sideways and call me Sally! So, it's true, then? You don't remember anything?" JR12's head tilted like an inquisitive hound dog's.

Ari closed his eyes to capture the fleeting images that refused to stay. The harder he strained to grab them, the more elusive they became. His mind remained a fog—a dense barrier that refused to yield any details of his past. Frustration rose like an uncontrollable tide and bubbled inside him, leaving an acidic aftertaste. He shook his head.

"Dang, A-Man. Nothing? You sure?"

With a growl, Ari opened his eyes. "Of course I'm sure. I can't remember a *fruking* thing!" He slammed his fist on the workstation tabletop.

The air rippled with energy, causing loose objects to vibrate and lift off the floor.

With a selfish grin, he welcomed the chaos, feeling a twisted sort of satisfaction as the surroundings mirrored the turmoil in his mind.

The sound of As'ni's laughter and clapping hands snapped him out of his brief outburst and brought everything down. His head spun as his mouth soured. Rubbing his eyes with the heel of his palms, he then dropped his arms to his side. Acting like a child wasn't helpful. No matter what he did, nothing filled the void of forgotten memories. Emptiness gnawed a burning pit in his gut. He was more lost and alone than ever before.

"You okay?"

Morgan's soft whisper was a balm to his bruised soul. She put her hand on his arm and gave him a gentle squeeze.

He placed his hand over hers, grasping it like a lifeline.

"Don't know what you're so upset about, A-Man." JR12 twirled his golden foreleg around the room. The small bot shrugged, making his upper abdomen shake his four front legs. "Looks like you still got your powers and all."

"Yeah, well, it'd be nice if I could figure out how to use them." Ari couldn't help the bitter tone in his voice. What was the good of having any so-called powers if he couldn't remember how to use them?

"Maybe you should go up against the purple mental giant over there again," JR12 offered. "Who knows? Doing the same thing might reboot your brain."

Morgan's pretty brows furrowed. "What does that mean, doing the same thing? What did they do?"

JR12 gave a mischievous chuckle. "Why don't I show you?"

Ari stilled and studied the bot.

In the dimly lit room, the long shadows made the gold and silver of JR12's body gleam with a metallic sheen. The small spider-like AI crawled to the center of the table, his legs clicking softly against the surface as he found a stable spot. A single lens on his body blinked to life, projecting a vivid holographic image, small enough for just him and Morgan to watch.

Ari glanced over his shoulder to make sure As'ni was still distracted by his toys.

The crystal man hummed happily as he swished the penlight over the spiral curls.

Looking back at JR12, dread curled in the pit of Ari's stomach. Not that he'd regained any memories, but did he really want to know what made him lose them? His fists clenched at his sides, knuckles whitening as the scene unfolded.

In the projection, a vast, empty chamber appeared, the walls an ominous hue that seemed to swallow light.

Ari saw himself standing at the far end, his expression one of fierce concentration. He barely recognized his own face, the tension pulling the muscles taut, his eyes burning with an intensity he hadn't felt since... ever.

As'ni loomed before him in the image. A maniacal twist on his features translated into crass determination that had now been replaced by his simple, childlike expression. The purple crystals that made up his body shimmered and reflected the flickering light of the chamber. Each movement the alien made sent ripples through his crystalline form, distorting his figure momentarily before it reformed into a thousand sharp-edged mirrors.

It took a moment for Ari to recognize the place as the inside of the ship *Elemi*.

The battle began without prelude, a silent war of psychic wills.

Ari watched himself raise a hand, his palm outstretched and his face twisted as if he summoned every ounce of his psionic strength. The surrounding air wavered and vibrated from an invisible energy, a force that Ari pushed against As'ni, trying to penetrate the alien's crystalline defense.

But As'ni was relentless.

And Ari saw the struggle on his own face—how the veins on his temple pulsed, how the sweat beaded and dripped down his brow. Every effort he made seemed to falter against As'ni's sheer presence.

The crystal alien wasn't just deflecting his attacks; he was feeding off them, growing stronger, his faceted body glowing with a sickening, ethereal light.

Ari's breath hitched as he watched the moment he dreaded—the precise instant everything went wrong. In the hologram, his doppelgänger's stance wavered, his knees buckling slightly. A flash of panic crossed his eyes, something subtle but unmistakable.

As'ni seized that weakness, his crystalline fist slamming into the ground. The chamber shuddered, and the walls rippled like water.

Ari staggered, his psychic defenses crumbling.

A final surge from As'ni, and the scene froze—the last frame capturing Ari mid-fall, his eyes wide, a scream of agony caught in his throat. His body twisted as if every bone shattered at once, and then the image dissolved into static.

Ari exhaled a breath he hadn't realized he'd been holding. A tight iron band wrapped around his ribs made his chest tight. His heart pounded—each beat sending an icy burn through his veins. The image of his own broken form seared into his mind, echoing with the familiar-yet-fragmented memories of that battle.

He felt Morgan's eyes on him, but he couldn't meet her gaze. Shame, anger, fear—emotions hard to distinguish churned inside him, threatening to overwhelm the fragile calm he desperately tried to hold. The memory loss had spared him by wrapping him in blissful ignorance. But now... now the truth hit him like a punch to the gut, stripping him bare and leaving him exposed. He stood there, the weight of his failure crashing down, sharp and relentless. No more hiding, no more excuses—just the harsh reality that he hadn't been enough.

Just an utter failure.

JR12 clicked softly, and the hologram faded, leaving behind a heavy silence. As the AI's lens blinked off, he retreated a few steps, as if sensing Ari's humiliation.

Ari's fingers slowly loosened, the residual pain from clenching them so tight grounded him to the here and now. To gather his thoughts, he took in a deep breath and tried to make sense of the chaos clouding his mind. Yet the image of that final, failed moment clung to him, a ghost that refused to go away.

He couldn't say anything. He turned around, his shoulders sagging as he slipped into the shadows on the far side of the chamber. He struggled to outrun the nightmare he'd just seen—one that shattered everything he thought he knew about himself.

Instead of finding himself alone, he discovered Morgan had followed close behind.

"Ari."

He barely heard her soft voice.

"This is a good thing."

Ari refused to look at her behind him. "Oh? And how's that?" he croaked. "Now we know for sure what a total failure I was when I had my memories." His laugh was hollow. "So what good am I when I can't remember a damn thing?"

"As'ni here. As'ni help Ari!"

Ari spun around.

There was the purple alien he'd battled and lost to bouncing the coil in one hand and doing a little dance.

Standing next to him was the beautiful Morgan, holding JR12 in her upturned palm.

"Don't you see?" Morgan stepped close. "The four of us now have a better chance at fixing your lost memories so we can repair *Elemi* and escape."

"As the great Einstein said, 'In the middle of difficulty lies opportunity'." JR12 gave a quick, self-satisfied nod. "So, let's stop dicking' around and dive right in. Ooh whee! Just imagine the sensational story we'll have to tell when it's all said and done!"

Morgan's heart ached for Ari. She hated seeing the defeat shadow his face, especially when his alluring lips pressed into a tight, unhappy line. It didn't look like he was willing to dive into what they should do now. Honestly, she could relate. All her life, she'd felt like she didn't measure up to her friends and family. Living in a world of powerful psychics had been tough when she wasn't like them.

Especially after her parents died unexpectedly when she was sixteen.

The shield holding the Titans had wavered and cracked. Since they were part of the guardian elites, her grandfather called in her parents to join the team to contain the breach.

Morgan's father, Kai, had strong telepathic shielding abilities that were crucial in containing and repelling any invasive psychic force.

Her mother, Lily, was a psionic amplifier who could increase Kai's capabilities twofold. She'd also been a strong influencer, one who could control minds, making the Titan susceptible to containment.

Morgan's breath caught as the memory of that fateful day flashed before her eyes—the dark, twisted tendrils of the psychic entity of a Titan that ripped through the city's defenses, its glowing eyes as it fought burned into her soul. She could still hear the sharp crackle of energy in the air, feel the tremor beneath her feet as the icy ground shook with each pulse of its power. Her parents' faces, etched with pain and fear, haunted her—her mother's hand outstretched toward her, her father's last, desperate glance as the entity's relentless force engulfed them.

The world had crumbled over and around them, leaving nothing behind but the suffocating silence of their absence.

A warm hand on her shoulder made her jump.

"Hey, you okay?" Concern laced Ari's smooth baritone.

Putting a hand over her racing heart, Morgan gave him a wan smile. "Yeah, sorry. Zoned out for a moment." She threw her shoulders back. "So, what do you say we go back to the workstation and plan on what to tackle first?" She concentrated on making her smile wide and looked him in the eyes. "Especially the Talon of Ancients. We've got to hide that somewhere before the High Chieftain comes back."

The tense brackets at the side of Ari's mouth softened. "Yeah, that's a good idea."

Grabbing the jewel-encrusted object, she called up the replicron and set it inside a drawer. Satisfied the artifact was as snug as possible, she demanded the machine disappear again.

"As'ni hungry." The purple giant grumbled as he lumbered behind them. "Ari food?"

"Oh, hey!" Morgan snapped her fingers. "I did a little research to see what we have here for him to eat." She pulled out a suitcase-shaped device from under the workstation. Something she'd created with a little help from the replicron. "It's an electromagnetic device that draws unused power from the free-floating magnetic fields the ship emits. As'ni, sit here." She pointed to the floor and placed the matte-silver device on the floor in front of him.

The soft, pulsing glow from the resonator reflected off his crystalline purple form.

The alien's lavender eyes widened with curiosity, and his blocky fingers traced the glowing nodes on the surface with childlike fascination. "Pretty lights," he murmured, tilting his head as if listening to the hum of the energy coming off the gadget.

"I promise, you're going to love this, As'ni," Morgan said gently, kneeling to meet his gaze. "Whenever you're hungry, all you have to do is sit close to it and do this." She tapped a stubby metal knob, and the device responded with a soft hum. Various energy lights on the surface glowed. "Feel the energy? It's like the sun, but safer. Just let it wash over you."

As'ni nodded, his hand hovered over it. "Food... As'ni. Safe... not hurt?"

Morgan smiled, making sure her voice remained calm and reassuring. "That's right. It's safe. You're in control." She watched As'ni inch closer.

As his body absorbed the energy, the once-dim crystals and mirrors on his body brightened. His eyes and mouth widened with wonder, and the usual blank confusion in his eyes melted away.

"Good, As'ni. Just like that." She patted his hefty shoulder, surprised by the unexpected warmth radiating from him. "You okay now?"

As'ni's full smile showcased his chunky, lilac-colored teeth. "As'ni like!" He turned back to the resonator with his coil toy in one hand and introduced them to one other.

"He's not going to OD on that thing, is he?" JR12 asked from his perch on Ari's shoulder.

Morgan snorted. "Of course not. I made it so it would analyze the input As'ni got from it and turn off when it reaches an optimum level."

"That's amazing," Ari praised. "Now if only we could solve *Elemi's* problem that easily."

"Just so you know—" JR12's wings expanded, and he flew back to the tabletop. "—I tried to communicate with your family back home, but the shields around the *Nebula Viper* are blocking me." His wings buzzed before sliding back into the exoskeleton covering his back. "So I guess we're on our own."

The pensive expression on Ari's face made her step in. She'd make sure they'd look into Ari's family later. Like when they were safely away in *Elemi*. "Now that you know what we're up against"—she addressed the bot—"can you come up with a way for us to help speed *Elemi's* healing process?"

"Well..." The spider-bot scratched the side of his round head. "If A-Man was up and running like normal, I'd tell him to use his psychic mojo and heal her. That would be the fastest way."

Ari's eyebrows rose. "I can do that?"

"That and more, big guy." JR 12 humphed. "So, without the psychic amplification Ari could provide, we only have two other choices." The bot sat on his hindquarters, allowing his back four legs to spread out. "One, regenerative bioengineering. This would aid in reweaving her organic tissue to regrow the cells she needs. Or two symbiotic nanobots. If we don't have the time for the bioengineering, we can create nanobots to open communication with Elemi so we can determine the best way to help her. Of course, we'd have to be careful not to interfere with her primary consciousness functions."

Well, damn. Morgan's shoulders slumped. Neither one of those were good options. It'd take weeks, if not months, to get either of those things going. She fought the tears threatening to grow. She pursed her lips. Crying wouldn't get things done.

"*Fruk* me front and back," Ari cussed. "There's got to be..."

A bright surge of light blazed, making her blind before complete darkness blanketed the room.

"Light gone!" As'ni's cry echoed in the large room. "Bad furries come back!"

"Goddess, I hope he's wrong," Ari stated as his steady arm wrapped around her shoulders.

For a moment, she let herself fall into this comforting embrace. With a resigned sigh, she pulled back. "I'm afraid he's right." She fumbled around the tabletop to find her multicorder. There. She grabbed it and turned the screen light on. In the hazy glow it provided, she looked into Ari's steady gray eyes. "It's another system shutdown that puts us in danger. I doubt Welozz will listen to anything we have to say to defend ourselves."

"Danger? Ha, ha, ha! I laugh at danger!" JR12 exclaimed.

Morgan blinked as she aimed her multicorder at the spider-bot. "I can't believe you just quoted Simba from *The Lion King*."

JR12 gave a quick hop on his eight legs. "Okay, then. How 'bout these cookies? *Danger is my middle name!*"

Morgan couldn't help it. Her lips quirked into a smirk. She loved the Austin Powers movies. "Well, considering what we're up against, it seems a quote from the movie *Jaws* fits this situation better."

"Oh yeah?" JR12's head cocked. "What's that?"

"We're gonna need a bigger boat."

The distant sound of Ozevroc claws clicking on the metal floor in the hallway made Morgan tense. With deft fingers, she called up the ship's data to get a quick reading on why the lights went out since the ship's computer wasn't working either.

Let's see... life support, engine functions, and gravity all within normal parameters. Oh wait. Navigation. Not only was it sucking in extra power for no good reason, it was making the ship go way off course. Instead of skirting around Federation Consortium space, the Ozevroc ship now headed straight for the heart of that galactic seat. A place full of patrols and bounty hunters eager to get their hands on any Ozevroc smugglers... dead or alive.

If that happened, she and her new friends had zero chance of survival.

"Someone bypassed navigation to make this ship head straight for Consortium space." She narrowed her eyes on the handheld as she tried to find a way into the system so she could countermand the current orders. So far, the pathway eluded her.

"And that's a bad thing?" Ari looked over her shoulder.

"Yeah, A-Man." JR12 scuttled under the glow of her handheld, his metal legs clicking with purpose. "Our hosts have bounties on their head across every corner of Federation Consortium space. So, if we're really lucky, we'll get blasted to bits instead of getting hauled in and arrested."

Morgan nodded. "That about sums it up." Heat crept up her neck as she continued to search for a way to fix the problem before the high chieftain and his horde burst in. She glanced at the purple crystal man with his hands over his head, whimpering. His figure was on the outskirts of the glow of her handheld, but she saw enough to know his agitation might get out of hand.

"Quick." She nudged Ari to look in As'ni's direction. "Take him to a dark corner so the Ozevroc doesn't see him."

Too late.

Before Ari could move, a group of Ozevroc rushed in. First the sharp smell of their unwashed bodies filled the room, then the clacking of their hard stomping claws echoed on the unforgiving floor. Each one carried pole-shaped weapons in their upper arms that had a glowing tip, giving them plenty of light to see from.

"Human. Today you die!"

And there he was, the high chieftain Welozz of the Ozevroc. Looked like he was in a fine tizzy. Angrier than she'd ever seen him before. His four beady eyes glowered in slashes of red while spittle flew out of his snout and exposed his yellowed sharp upper and lower incisors. Dang, he might even mean his greeting this time.

Putting her shoulders back, she gripped her handheld and faced him, eyes averted. "Not today, High Chief. Lots to fix." Boy, that was true now more than ever. "Ship headed to forbidden void. Must stop." She'd learned early on to never utter the words Federation Consortium. The Ozevroc refused to acknowledge anything beyond their little slice of existence. Especially since they blatantly robbed and smuggled whatever they could from the established galactic systems.

"You die! Then stop ship."

Morgan blinked. Her brain scrambled to see if she'd heard him wrong. Nope, that's what he said.

"Oh, great and mighty High Chieftain—" She gave a slight bow, watching him out of the corner of her eye. "—I cannot fix if dead." She straightened. "If the ship goes into the forbidden void, all Ozevroc will perish from foul foes."

With a shrill cry, Welozz swung his staff and lashed out at the smaller guard next to him, making him fly across the room. The smaller alien landed with a clanking thud into a pile of discarded metals.

"You fix! Now!" Welozz pointed his glowing stick in her face, its hot tip mere inches from her eyes.

One of his guards gripped her from behind and trapped her in a tight hold.

With a cry of rage, Ari jumped in front of her, pushing Welozz's stick away as he shoved the Ozevroc on his ass.

Pandemonium followed.

The other Ozevroc swarmed Ari, slamming him to the floor and pinning him under their crushing weight.

JR12 jumped on her shoulder and shouted at Ari, waving one of his front legs like a tiny fist. "Yo, Ari! If you're aiming for an exit plan, might I suggest *up*? Cause getting flattened under all that rubble isn't winning you any man-card awards!"

From the other side of the room, As'ni roared and barreled into the smaller aliens attacking Ari.

Furry bodies flew, most pinwheeling in the air with cries and hisses of pain and surprise.

"Is it a bird? Is it a plane? Nope, it's As'ni launching fuzzballs into orbit!" JR12 whooped. "Woo-hoo... alien pinball!"

Instead of stopping JR12's asinine commentary, Morgan took advantage of the interruption to study her handheld again. She ran an anti-virus app, and it didn't take long for her system to highlight the problem. A couple of clicks here and there. Almost got it...

"Come on, A-Man! I've seen you take down tougher piles than this!" JR12 switched his commentary back to Ari. "Staying buried under aliens isn't a long-term plan, dude!"

There. The lights came back on. With a hard wave of her hand, she called up her ship's computer screen. The clear monitor flashed on and displayed the system schematics she'd been working on. Just need to input a couple more...

Hard hands gripped her arm and yanked her away.

JR12 went flying.

She could only hope he had enough time to pull his wings out to keep himself from getting trampled in the melee.

"Hey!" She jerked her arm, but couldn't free herself from the hard hold Grozzik had on her. He stopped, and she almost ran into him. "I'm not done yet!"

Grozzik jerked her close enough to his snout that his putrid breath made her eyes water.

"I don't want you to fix it, *human*." His grip tightened and cut her circulation off.

Morgan's eyes widened when he spoke in perfect English. She never imagined they could speak in any tongue but their own. "I don't understand..."

He hauled her close enough to hear his insidious whisper. "I don't care if you understand." He tugged her back-and-forth. "The only thing I want you to do is die."

He pulled his top paw back, holding the burning tip of his pole-weapon to drive it into her eyes.

With a gasp, she raised her hands and ducked.

Rage.

Unmitigated, blinding vehemence took over Ari.

His pulse thundered in his ears as the Ozevroc swarmed and covered him, their coarse fur scratching against his skin. Each one was powerful and relentless, pressing him down with their six arms, keeping him pinned to the cold metal floor. The acrid smell of burning circuits filled the air, mingled with the rancid scent of the aliens' sweat. He could barely breathe under the weight of their bodies, and his ribs strained with every shallow gasp.

But the pain didn't matter. Nothing mattered except Morgan, trapped by a brutal creature who aimed his glowing pole between her eyes. He had it pulled back as if ready to thrust the radiating sheen of his weapon into her. Her life hung by a thread, and there he was, powerless—a stark reminder of his own crushing failure. Buried beneath a relentless pile of smelly aliens who threatened to drown him in pain and blood as they punched and poked him with their sharp objects.

Thrashing beneath the pile, he strained to break free, but there were too many of them. Their hands—so many hands—grabbed at his arms, his legs, and his neck, dragging him down with inhuman strength. The suffocating press of bodies on top of him threatened to overtake him. In the chaos of the oppressive weight of the Ozevroc, Ari's world narrowed to a singular, piercing sound: Morgan's cry.

It cut through the din like a blade, sharp and clear. The sound of her despair sliced through the thick fog of rage and desperation clouding his mind. That cry, laced with pain or fear, shattered him. Her plea was an echoing expression of vulnerability he had never heard from her before. A shiver of dread rooted him to stillness for a heartbeat too long.

It was as if the universe came to a standstill and forced him to confront a terrifying reality of what mattered most.

Morgan.

Every one of his muscles tensed and shoved against the weight of the Ozevroc. He thrashed harder, frantic. The panic of losing Morgan ignited something primal and deadly within him. That she could suffer, hurt, just a few feet away as he lay here pinned and useless was unthinkable. A true nightmare come to life. Everything dimmed around him. His vision tunneled as his mind fixated on that cry, replaying it over and over. Unable to dislodge his snarling captors, he felt a knife of helplessness cut deep into his heart. He screamed in rage and anguish.

Then, just as fear threatened to paralyze Ari, something stirred deep within. His desperation morphed into something dark. Something strong and sinister. It went far beyond mere anger. It was an all-encompassing violence so intense it burned the fear away and left a singular, savage determination.

Save Morgan.

Then, a familiar sense of internal power struggled to awaken. The overwhelming urge to protect his woman, the woman he needed more than life itself, took over. She was the one person who defined who he was. He had to save her. Nothing else mattered.

That cry—Morgan's cry—was the catalyst that ignited the storm, a raw spark that shattered every restraint and unleased the binding chaos inside him, waiting to erupt.

Something snapped.

His fury and love, fear and desperation, collided and merged, exploding into a torrent of energy that shattered the chains holding his memories—and his powers. Ari let out a primal roar, the sound more animal than human, as the dam within him burst with the psychic power he had long forgotten. With it came something ancient and powerful that was an intricate part of him. Freedom wrapped around him as memories, distant and yet achingly familiar, surfaced, thrusting him savagely back to a time when he had been more than just a man. More than just flesh and bone. A part of something greater than himself.

Time stood still as those memories rushed back in blinding detail.

CHAPTER TEN

O *n board the spaceship* Elemi, *heading to the edge of Federation* *Consortium space, one month prior*

"That is just about the ugliest thing I've ever seen in my life."

The mechanical undertone of JR12's observation about the bright-pink sexbot Arakiba saved from FiPan made him chuckle. "Sparky, you've only been alive for less than two months. I hardly think you're some kind of expert in beauty."

He concentrated on the CPU inside the android and ignored the bot skirting around the workstation.

The sharp tips of the spider-shaped gold-and-silver bot's eight legs made a light clicking sound.

Squinting, Arakiba made some final adjustments.

"Oh, my darling," the sentient sultry, wispy voice of the spaceship, *Elemi*, piped in. "While I may not have the bright, youthful eyes of your cute little spybot, it saddens me to say I agree with the thing."

"Him." JR12's tone was sharp. The two of them had had this conversation more than once since their crazy journey began. "I'm a him, missy. Stretch your circuits and try to remember that, hmm?"

"Well"—the coy feminine voice had a trace of laugher in it. Like an adult patting a clueless child on the head—"I'll endeavor to give it a try."

"'*Do or do not, there is no try*'—I'd appreciate it if you take the great Yoda's words to heart." JR12 huffed.

Arakiba studied his handiwork. Yes, it looked like everything should work. Now he'd find out if it was worth having taken the time to teleport it back to *Elemi* with him before they left FiPan. In the short time he'd enjoyed his freedom from slavery, Arakiba found he had an affinity for all things mechanical. His brothers might have thought he was only interested in the services the droid might provide, but that was the furthest thing from the truth. He couldn't wait to get his hands on the pink android to see if he could make it work. It was a challenge just calling out to him.

Okay, the moment of truth. He pushed the circuit at the back of the droid's neck to get it fired up. Nothing happened. "*Fruk* Tiamat's titties!" He fisted his hand on his hips. What was he missing?

"So sorry to interrupt you, my love." Elemi cooed. "But we have a potential hostile heading straight for us."

Arakiba jerked around to face the main viewscreen. He clicked a button on the side of the workstation to make it disappear into the wall and keep the android secure. He'd worry about it later.

"What kind of hostile?" He plopped onto the captain's chair to study the schematics *Elemi* brought up. There, in the distance, was a definite outline of a small ship headed in their direction.

"Why, I believe it's comprised of the same crystalline properties your brother Abalim provided us before we left."

Arakiba's stomach dropped. He wasn't anywhere near finding the human woman Morgan yet. All this time, he'd been relying on the brief vision he'd had of her when he was on FiPan. There he'd been able to tune into her psychic energy. Which, if he was honest, was quite exciting. Most human women lacked any trace of psychic ability. But finding one who had it? That opened endless possibilities he couldn't wait to explore.

He squirmed in his seat at the memory of that vision. There she stood, at the edge of the dimly lit prison cell, her silhouette sharp against the blurred scene surrounding her. For a moment, everything else had faded—the low hum of his brother's voices, the distant chatter of JR12 on his shoulder. It all became background noise as his gaze locked onto hers.

Morgan moved with a fluid grace, her every step purposeful, as if she was unconcerned about being held a prisoner.

Ari's pulse quickened, and his heart thudded like a drumbeat. On their own, his eyes traced the curve of her shoulders, and the way her golden curls cascaded over them. The confident tilt of her chin. The curves of her body showcased in the worn and torn clothing she had on. He swallowed hard, feeling a sudden dryness in his throat. She'd stolen the very air from his lungs.

A strange warmth spread through him, a mixture of heat and electricity, making his skin tingle with an unfamiliar sensation. He couldn't tear his eyes away. It was as if his body recognized something his mind hadn't caught up to yet—an undeniable pull, a magnetic force drawing him in. His muscles tightened, the tension coiling in his chest, urging him to step forward, to bridge the distance between them.

But he hesitated. What in the world was happening to him? This was only a vision, after all. His mind raced as he ignored the flood of emotions that crashed over him. Instead, he forced himself to maintain a sharp clarity of her, to burn into his mind everything he could about her. Like how the light played off the warm glow of the smooth, caramel color of her features. How the subtle curve of her lips and the way her bright golden-green eyes, even from a distance, held a depth that beckoned him to dive in and drown.

For a fleeting moment, the only thing he was capable of was to stand there, rooted in place, as the vision faded back to reality. Only one truth remained—her grip was irresistible and absolute.

And now, before he found her, this threat was coming to stop him from saving this unique treasure of a woman.

Confident in his abilities, Arakiba lowered his sight on the ship's readouts with a sinister grin. *Bring it on, asshole. I've got you.*

"How do you know that ship is coming for us?" JR12's bulbous head tilted as he focused on Arakiba from the main console. "Maybe it's just passing by. As the great Jack Sparrow said, 'The world doesn't revolve around you, or anyone else'. It's a big galaxy, ya know."

Arakiba ignored the bot. With every fiber of his being, he knew the ship was coming for him. Or rather, the creature inside it was. The malevolence from the incoming alien shot at him in psychic waves, solidly intent on capturing him. This guy had to be a Krystalii Abalim had warned them about. But this one wasn't looking for only a human female. He was searching for any human, now overjoyed when he thought he found one.

Yeah, Arakiba couldn't wait to show this guy his prey was anything but human.

The conference room in the hidden moon city of Azadi - a month and a half prior

"We appreciate you taking on this important task," the chancellor of the Federation Consortium, D'zia E'etu, announced.

His sincere expression made Arakiba relax. Since the Zerin was in holographic form, he couldn't psychically scan the fellow to see what his intentions were. He glanced at his older brother, Adapa, to make sure he didn't have any problem with what the galactic government asked them to do.

Nope, Adapa's swarthy skin had a healthy brown glow with nary a flush to darken his cheeks.

Arakiba checked out his other brothers.

Abalim's steady gaze on the image in the middle of the table was unflinching, as was their serene brother, Azazel's. Not that anything fazed Azazel out of his picture-perfect, *I'm always calm. Nothing bothers me* annoying attitude. The only way to find out what the guy was really thinking or feeling was to meld their minds together.

Arakiba shuddered. The one time he did that, he swore he'd never do it again. His brother seethed with an amalgamation of hidden depths, best left buried.

That left Asmodel. The copper tone of his brother's near-perfect features turned pale, his eyes locked on something faraway. Like he wasn't paying attention to what was going on in the room.

Not that Arakiba blamed him. This shit was boring as hell. Crossing an ankle over one knee, he balanced his hand in the crook of his bent leg. Couldn't they just get on with it? The lure of a space adventure called to him.

"And, as I'm sure you're aware, we must keep this mission as quiet as possible," D'zia continued.

"It would be an honor to assist in locating the missing women from the Zerin exchange program." Azazel spoke in his soothing, steady tone. "We admit we have little to contribute to the restoration of modern Earth after the Akurn invasion and subsequent almost annihilation from one of their ships crashing out of control there."

He gave a slight bow, causing the curtain of his long hair to fall over his shoulders and pool on his lap.

Arakiba resisted the urge to roll his eyes. *By the horned crown of Enlil. Blah, blah, blah.* Did his brother have to talk like he thought he was the smartest guy in the room? It's not like Azazel was the one who reached into space and pulled that stupid ship out of the sky to stop it from destroying Earth. Arakiba did, thank you very much. Talk about an extinction event if that had happened...

On board the starship Zikia - two months ago

"Who are these guys?"

The strange sound of a woman's whisper made Arakiba jerk his head in her direction. She had to be an Akurn, with her white hair and pale skin. But she was wearing something no female would ever put on. Dressed in form-fitting black pants with a short jacket over some kind of shirt with round things holding the fabric together. The word "buttons" flashed. Oh, those were called buttons.

She was speaking to another Akrun in a strange language. It took him a moment to translate what she said in his head. Interesting. He wasn't sure if the man she spoke to was an Akurn or not. He was tall and pale like one, but had pointed ears like Azazel's.

Both Arakiba's eyebrows rose as his lips pursed when the male spoke utter nonsense.

"If I'm not mistaken, they are my father's brothers who perished in the great flood."

His father? Who was his father?

The woman's mouth dropped open. "How..."

"Hang on."

Finally, a familiar face.

Princess Inanna approached the duo.

He growled when the man put his arms around her. That male had no right to touch Adapa's woman!

Before he ripped the guy's arm out of his socket, she continued. "I think Azazel is about to tell us."

Azazel?

"Well," Azazel said in that same strange language, tugging his ear-lobe.

Oh no. When the guy did that with a sheepish grin, he was about to confess something. Usually something he was uncomfortable to confess.

"I was desperate to get us to Adapa before the Akurns destroyed Earth." He shrugged with his hands wide in supplication. "I never planned on taking us to the future."

Arakiba's eyebrows flew up.

"The future? What nonsense are you talking about?" Asmodel growled. "That wall of water is almost upon us..."

"How many years have passed, brother?" Abalim's quiet tone was firm. "Fill us in on the current danger."

An earthquake rumbled and everybody stumbled, their arms pin-wheeling. It only lasted a few seconds, but it was enough for the metallic frame of the *Zikia* to groan under the stress.

"We'll talk about the passing years later, my brothers," Adapa commanded with his fists clenched. "Our immediate danger is an out-of-control Akurn ship headed for the middle of the planet."

Abalim's frown deepened. "Do you have any way of showing us this vessel?"

"I have it on screen here." A man with an unusual shade of rus-set-red hair and beard declared. He headed to the bank of monitors displaying the massive spaceship racing toward Earth. "We don't have a way to stop it."

Adapa glanced at each one of them. The psychic information he sent them lasted only a second. The plan was for them to combine their immense psychic powers to halt the ship before it hit the atmosphere.

Since Arakiba had the strongest telekinetic ability, he'd be the one to grab the ship. He nodded at the others.

Adapa turned to the tall, white-haired man and nodded. "Everybody stand back. My brothers and I will take care of this."

Without a word, Arakiba joined his mind with his brothers'. They created their own circle with eyes closed, their heads tilted back, and open palms at their sides. Even without his physical sight, the bright light they created blazed between them, a violent whirlwind of iridescent energy ribbons that centered on their small group. He ignored his long blond hair whipping around his face and body. Keeping his eyes closed, he felt the sizzling force of the storm pushing into him, making his back bow.

The sensation of his body flying apart allowed him to join with the very fabric of the universe, making it easy to find the out-of-control ship. He reached out, whipping his translucent hand into a grip to capture the ship before he solidified again.

Abruptly, the psychic energies stopped. He was once again whole.

Opening his eyes with a mischievous smirk, he couldn't resist opening his clenched hand and raising it so everyone could see. In the center of his palm was the metallic spaceship, no bigger than a child's toy. "Is this what you're looking for?"

Earth 7,000 years ago - Akurn scientific mining colony

"Now here is the youngest of the group."

Arakiba glared at the Akurn who was introducing him and his brothers to the visiting princess. Thoth's smug smile made him clench his hands into fists.

"This is Arakiba, and a more likable young man you'll never meet." The shorter man reached over and patted Arakiba on the shoulder. "He's polite, well-spoken, and rarely gives anyone any trouble." He gripped the shoulder harder. "And a hard worker! Even with these puny muscles!"

Yeah. He'd show the *shep-sin* how puny his muscles were when he ripped the bastard's face off with one swipe. Arakiba forced himself to keep his false image intact. The image made him look like a small and underdeveloped child. Even though he was the youngest, his bulk overshadowed the build of his brothers. Not that he worked hard to keep it that way.

"Good man, good man."

The annoying ass had the temerity to laugh at him. Good thing the jerk turned his attention to Arakiba's eldest brother, Adapa. If he had to suffer one more minute of Thoth's attention, no telling what he'd do.

Swallowing his humiliation, Arakiba concentrated on the first female he'd ever seen. Princess Inanna from Akurn was beyond anything he'd imagined a female to look like. Her skin was so pale it glowed under the low light of the chamber. Her hair, a strange blend of reddish-blond strands, framed an alabaster face that was both serene and mysterious. But her eyes were the most striking—a bright turquoise that contrasted against the stark whiteness of her features.

She dressed simply, but her gown accentuated her royal presence.

He couldn't help but acknowledge her beauty, but her appearance was more a curiosity than a draw. Like appreciating a golden sunrise.

But then, something shifted.

Arakiba watched her posture stiffen.

Her gaze flickered with a new light.

He followed her line of sight to his brother, Adapa, standing beside him, his dark eyes centered on the woman. The transformation between the two of them was subtle, yet undeniable.

Her previously calm demeanor sparkled with a warmth that flooded into her eyes as she took in Adapa's appearance. Her lips curved into a soft, almost involuntary, shy smile. A blush of color touched her cheeks.

Arakiba became engulfed as a crackle of electricity sizzled between her and his brother.

Then came a subtle shift in her aura, and the way her body leaned ever so slightly toward Adapa was telling.

When Adapa reached for Inanna with his psychic imprint, the room narrowed down to just the two of them.

Taking a step back, Arakiba let the past go.

The echo of Morgan's painful cry brought him back to the present. Now whole, saving her became his battle cry.

And nothing—not the Ozevroc, not the universe itself—would keep him from her.

They say when you're facing death, your life flashes before you like some bad movie reel. Well, Morgan was convinced whoever came up with that stupid scenario should stand in her shoes right now. The only thing flashing in her brain was the life-ending promise filling her vision from a humongous pointed, burning weapon now ready to sear through her eyes.

With every ounce of useless strength she had, she ducked with her hands raised. Not that she was far enough away to make a difference. Squeezing her eyes shut, she braced herself for the killing blow.

Which... didn't happen.

Pursing her lips, she peeked through her arms to see what Grozzik was doing. Grozzik wasn't doing anything but getting choked to death by a massive, purple-crystal hand wrapped around his furry neck. The little alien dropped his weapon, trying to dislodge As'ni's grip on him. All six hands fumbled at the crystal hold while he kicked, his legs held several feet off the ground.

"No hurt pretty lady!" As'ni shook Grozzik and snarled in his face. "Bad furry!" He shook him again.

Grozzik's four eyes bulged as his black tongue hung out the side of his snout. His low breath sputtered little bubbles that drooled in sporadic lines to the floor.

"Enough!"

Everyone froze at the booming male voice. They were all still and lifeless as statues made of hard clay.

Morgan whipped around to face the speaker. It was Ari. Her heart raced. The man she knew was there—the familiar shape of his broad shoulders, the way his hair fell just so across his brow—but there was something more now.

He seemed taller, not in stature, but in presence. His very being filled the space, commanding attention with an effortless ease that hadn't been there before.

The light caught his steely-gray eyes with an unfamiliar intensity. Now, there was a depth to him that pulled her in, like the mesmerizing expanse of the cosmos. His gaze, when it met hers, held a quiet power, a certainty that made her breath catch. Ari had always been confident, but now it was as if he had a quiet mastery that radiated from him, tangible and magnetic, overshadowing everything around him.

Ari moved toward her, each step measured and purposeful. There was a grace to him now, a controlled energy that spoke of a man who had not only accepted his abilities, but had woven them into the very fabric of his being.

Even the most powerful psychics she'd grown up with, those deemed formidable beyond comprehension, paled compared to the effortless magnitude of the man headed toward her.

Morgan's chest tightened with an unfamiliar emotion as she studied the lines of his face, the way his lips curved into a faint, knowing smile. With trembling fists at her side, she stood rooted to the spot, unable to tear her eyes away. Ari was more than just a man. He was a force of nature that drew her into his pulsating orbit.

She prided herself on being truthful with herself. No matter how hard or ridiculous that truth was. And now she couldn't continue denying the obvious—she experienced more than mere attraction to the man who stopped in front of her. Something deeper wove into the very fabric of her being. It was that quiet, still smile that solidified the obvious—she'd fallen hard for him. Oh, not just for who he had been, but for the man he truly was.

Any doubts she harbored melted away. Morgan was irrevocably his.

"Are you okay?" His large palm caressed her cheek. "They didn't hurt you, did they?"

She leaned into his warmth, her lids half-masted. The sense of peace and belonging that swept through her left her entire body languid. "I'm just fine." She nodded to the still form of As'ni gripping Grozzik by the neck. "As'ni saved me just in time."

A sour look crossed Ari's face, making his full lips twist into a grimace.

She giggled.

"I wanted to be the one to save you," he grumbled.

Morgan stroked his prickly jawline with her fingertip. "You already have," she assured him.

In the dimly lit room, the soft hum of the ship's engines was the only sound as Morgan moved in closer to Ari, their eyes locked in a silent conversation. The tension between them was electric, a palpable force that was unspoken but undeniable. Nestled in the heat of his body, she bathed in the warmth of his masculine scent as it mingled with hers in the small space between them.

Morgan's heart pounded as she gazed up at him. Her breath caught at the intensity of his gaze. There was something in the way he looked at her now—an unguarded vulnerability mixed with a powerful resolve.

Ari's hand drifted across her cheek. His fingers traced the curve of her jaw with a gentleness that sent shivers down her spine. The touch was tender, yet with an undercurrent of something more—a promise of the depth of his feelings. Emotions no longer hidden.

"Morgan," he whispered, her name a breathless claim.

She got the crazy idea he was testing the weight of her name in this new, charged moment.

Not wanting to spoil what was happening between them with mere words, she nodded and leaned into his touch. Her eyes fluttered closed as the world faded away. The only thing that mattered was *him*. This man had become everything to her.

Ari's hand slid to the back of her neck, drawing her closer, and then his lips were on hers—tentative at first, as if he were afraid to break the fragile spell woven between them.

But the moment their lips touched, a spark ignited like wildfire.

Morgan responded instantly, her hands finding their way to his shoulders, pulling him closer as she surrendered to the kiss. It was slow and searching, each movement deliberate, as if they were both mesmerized by the feel of each other. A heady rush of conflicting emotions flooded through her—desire, need, and then something deeper. Something she was afraid to name.

Ari's other hand slid around her waist, and he pulled her against him.

The kiss turned urgent, more demanding. It was as if they tried to pour everything they had into that single connection, to say with their lips what words could never fully express.

When they finally broke apart, Morgan gulped to control her breathing. Resting her forehead against his solid chest, she did her best to steady herself. Struggling to take a deep breath, she licked her lips and savored the taste Ari had left behind. Lifting her head, she let her eyes flutter open to meet his smoldering gaze. In their depths, she saw the same fire, the same overwhelming need reflected at her.

His full lips creased into a wicked grin. "Hi, I'm Arakiba. Pleased to meet you."

Her answering smirk was just as mischievous. "Hello, Arakiba. I'm Morgan." She tilted her head and brushed a strand of his loose blond hair from his eyes. "May I still call you Ari?" He would always be Ari to her.

"You can call me anything you'd like," he whispered close to her ear. She quivered as he laved the shell of her ear with his tongue.

Her inner vixen urged her to stake her claim.

"Then I'm going to call you mine."

Morgan grimaced. Seriously? Could she say anything cornier? Jeez, Ari must be growing on her. Throwing her shoulders back, she gave him a winsome smile, hoping he took what she said in the serious manner she meant.

"Ah, Morgan"—his voice deepened—"I've always been yours."

The pounding of his heart under her hands backed his calm statement. Growing up around powerful psychics, she'd quickly learned to rely on body language since she couldn't read their minds. People could say or do anything, but their bodies always told the truth.

Ari held himself with confidence, but there was a hint of vulnerability in his bearing. Holding her in his arms, his shoulders were relaxed, his stance open.

The corners of his mouth curved into a gentle, almost shy smile that made her feel cherished. His hands pressed her close to him, and his warmth seeped into her very soul. The tenderness in his eyes and the subtle way he wrapped himself around her spoke louder than any words ever could.

The realization that Ari loved her sent a warm, dizzying rush through her entire being. Any trepidation she had melted away.

"What Ari want As'ni do with bad furry?" The purple behemoth shook the unconscious Ozevroc.

Morgan started at the sound of his gravelly voice. She glanced at Ari with a raised eyebrow. "I thought you froze everyone."

Ari shrugged. "I guess As'ni's psychic powers are getting stronger." He turned to address As'ni. "Go ahead and put him down. Gently!"

As'ni raised his arm and held the alien above his head, then dropped the Ozevroc like a stone.

The sound of snapping bones as Grozzik hit the hard floor on his side echoed. Being held in a frozen psychic state, he didn't utter a word.

Morgan was certain he'd make plenty of noise once Ari released his psychic hold.

"Well, I wouldn't call that gentle." Ari chuckled.

"Oopsie." As'ni snickered behind his hand. "As'ni hurt bad furry." The crystals and mirrors on his body reflected in the low light as he shrugged. "Oh's well."

Morgan frowned at the immobile Ozevroc. "You know, he said something to me just before he tried to kill me." She stepped away from Ari and toed the prone alien to his back. A thin trail of blackish blood seeped out of his snout. She glanced back at Ari. "He stopped me from fixing the navigational system. And he said it in English."

"That's because he's been the one sabotaging the ship." Ari crossed his arms as he glared at Grozzik. "At first he had some help, but once he had the Talon of Ancients, he made As'ni kill his co-conspirators."

"As'ni no want." The crystals on the purple giant's broad cheeks darkened. "Bad furry promise As'ni food if he hurt other furries."

"We get it, big guy." Morgan patted As'ni's arm. "No one is mad at you for that." She turned to Ari. "I guess you know all that because your memory has returned, and with it you can access your psychic abilities."

Ari gave her a sheepish grin as he scratched his scruffy jawline. "Yeah. Well, when that asshat threatened to kill you, it broke something inside me."

She couldn't resist placing her hand on his forearm. "How do you feel?"

"I feel great!"

Without warning, he swooped her into his arms, giving her no choice but to wrap her legs around his taut waist and her arms around his thick neck. Just to hang on, of course.

"Especially now that I don't have any doubts about you loving me."

The low tone of his evil whisper made her shiver all over again. "Hey!" Morgan lightly slapped his shoulder and gave him a mock frown. "No fair using your mojo to read my mind, buster."

"I don't have to read your mind to know that." After a quick peck on her lips, he set her down. "But, first things first. Business before sexy times, *irnini*."

She stuttered, unable to separate what to say first. He was the one... she never... aargh! She popped her fists on her hips and gave him a narrow glare, resisting the urge to stomp her foot. Damn it!

Ari's wicked smirk didn't fool her one bit. The man loved to tease her. She crossed her arms. No worries. She'd spent years honing her mental security features to keep psychics out, and she'd have no trouble building barriers against him. It might take some time, but she was confident she could do it.

"What should we do first?" He looked around at the frozen Ozevroc. "Should we use the *Nebula Viper* to head into Federation Consortium space while I've got them contained like this?"

"Ozevroc ship, stand down!"

Morgan jumped. The booming sound of someone speaking over the ship's external communication array had startled her.

"Comply within the next five clicks, or we will fire upon you with full force."

Ari snorted. "Well, I guess that answers what we should do first."

Morgan nodded at Ari's dry tone. "While I stop the ship, why don't you find out what bossy voice wants?" She brought up her working floating monitor. "I've opened a channel for you." She gave him an absent wave, her attention focused on the information scrolling in front of her as she slowed, then stopped the ship.

"Um, okay." Ari raised his eyes to the ceiling. As if that would help him see who he was talking to. "Hello, disembodied voice. What do you want?"

He grinned at the telling silence.

Morgan couldn't help but grin back.

"*Nebula Viper*"—the harsh, masculine voice continued—"prepare to be boarded."

The sound of the communication clicking off echoed.

A loud shudder made the ship jerk.

"Guess we have uninvited visitors," Ari quipped. "Shall we take out the fine china, dust the place off, and spritz something sweet to eliminate the Ozevroc stench?"

Morgan eyed him. "You seem awfully chipper about an unknown fraction boarding our ship." Her eyes narrowed. "What do you know?"

Ari spread his arms wide. "Why, nothing, my *irnini*!"

"Did you psychically scan them?" His innocent expression didn't fool her one bit.

His guffaw was short. "Now, darlin'. What fun would that be?"

CHAPTER
ELEVEN

A ri hadn't lied to Morgan. Just because he'd gotten his psychic abilities back didn't mean he should put himself in a vulnerable position if he didn't have to. Look how opening his senses turned out when he first encountered As'ni aboard *Elemi*. Luckily, his arrogance only cost him a temporary memory loss.

Speaking of As'ni, he checked on the crystal being.

The guy was happily playing with his coil toy as he hummed, his back against the wall.

Case in point... As'ni was now a much different person than before they combated. The crystal alien had once been a vastly intelligent creature with an immovable determination to capture Ari at all costs and was as formidable an opponent as he'd ever met. His intent to take Ari to his Krystalii master from another dimension, Lord Baelon, was all-encompassing, and drove him to extremes.

Not that Ari had the faintest idea why the Krystalii wanted a human, any human, for some sort of breeding purpose. That wasn't gonna happen to this boy. He'd rather die than suffer at the hands of some perverted dictator again.

The intense psychic fight with As'ni ended in a draw, with neither one of them overpowering the other. The only thing they'd accomplished was blasting the ship, JR12, as well as themselves, into unconsciousness. Which left them afloat in the galaxy to be picked up easily enough by the Ozevroc. When he'd finally come to, he'd lost all his memories and a huge part of who he was at a fundamental level.

While he watched As'ni hold the Ozevroc in a death grip, Ari ran an encompassing psychic scan on him. The prior intellect As'ni had before was gone. It's as if their battle left a permanent scar on his brain, leaving him with the limited intelligence of a child. A happy and contented child, but a simple one nevertheless.

"Can you take this off first?" Morgan interrupted Ari's musings. She confronted him, gripping the *nutesh* snare around her lovely neck. "Otherwise, I can't leave this room without getting my head blown off."

Ari cupped her precious face in his hands. "This crass material doesn't deserve to touch your lovely skin, my *irnini*." He made the leather collar disappear, casting its molecules into the very fabric of space. With her reddened skin exposed, he placed a light kiss on the side of her neck and smiled when she shivered.

She gripped his hands, her eyes smoldering. "Thank you."

Not one to fight such a powerful urge, he leaned in and pressed a soft, lingering kiss to her full lips. "Let's greet our guests, hmm?"

Morgan stepped back with a warm smile that reached the golden-green of her eyes. "I can't wait to get to know the real you when we're done with all this chaos."

His stomach tightened. Stepping closer to her, he brushed one of her golden curls behind her ear. "I'd like that, Morgan. I only hope I'm worth the wait."

Her grin was mischievous. "We'll see." She turned and exited the engine room, bypassing several prone Ozevroc frozen in place.

Mesmerized by the sensual sway of her hips, it took her leaving his sight to jolt him back to reality. From the corner of his eye, he noticed JR12 prone on the workstation table. "Come on, Zippy." With a light tendril of power, he finger-waved at the bot and psychically lifted him to rest on his shoulder. The action juddered the spybot awake. "No time to sleep on the job. We've got work to do!"

"First, you shut me down for no good reason, and then you act like it's my fault?" JR12 groused. "I'm mad as hell, Ari, and I'm not going to take this anymore!" The bot huffed, stomping his front two legs. "It'd serve you right if I just stayed here and let you flounder on your own."

"Quoting old movies won't get you out of things, Sparky." Ari was light as a feather as he rushed out of the room to follow Morgan. "Besides, it'd piss you off more if I left you behind. Right?" He picked up the pace when he spied her turning at one of the branching corridors.

"Fine." JR12 huffed. "You're lucky I like havoc as much as you do, A-Man." The little bot poked him in the neck with one of his pointed forelegs. "Now, keep up, or I'll quote something really annoying to make you move faster."

It didn't take Ari long to catch up with Morgan since the docking station was close to the engine room. The low hum of machinery grew louder as they entered the immense chamber. The stark lighting from the ceiling cast long shadows over the floor, giving the place an eerie atmosphere. A groan of metal on metal fixated him on the main bay doors, which took their sweet time sliding open.

Morgan stood beside him, her arms crossed, her expression revealing nothing.

The ship that emerged from the darkness of space was unlike anything Ari had seen before.

Sleek and angular, it was almost predatory in its design. The matte-black hull absorbed the light rather than reflected it. No insignia or identifying marks adorned its surface, leaving its origins and intentions a mystery. The vessel hovered silently for a moment before descending with a controlled grace that belied its size, touching down with a hiss.

Ari's gaze swept over the ship, taking in the subtle curves of its wings, the way its thrusters cooled with an eerie blue glow. Something about it set his instincts on edge. The hairs on the back of his neck prickled. He hated this—the unnatural silence of the ship, its windows blacked out, concealing whoever—or whatever, waited inside.

"Ever seen a ship like that before?" Morgan's voice was low, barely above a whisper, but with a sharp edge to it.

"No. How about you?" Ari addressed JR12. "Anything like that in your database?" He kept his eyes on the hatch on the ship's underside as it slid open with a smooth, almost mechanical precision.

"That looks like an AoA ship," JR12 supplied. "My dad worked with some of them before." His two-pronged silver-gold body gleamed in the light as the matte-black bottom of his eight legs remained muted. "Wouldn't that be great if it were them?"

The longing in the spider-bot's voice was a surprise.

Sending out a tendril of psychic exploration, Ari took a chance and scanned the inside of the ship. So far... it was hard to tell. There wasn't any malevolence. But then again, he barely sensed anything at all.

"Well, let's keep our guard up." Morgan interjected. "At least until we know who they are."

Nodding, Ari watched as the ship's ramp extended in slow motion. That's when he sensed a surge of unease.

The bay's lights reflected off the glossy black surface of the ramp as it touched the floor with a soft thud. A hiss of pressurized air escaped from within the ship.

For a moment, the silence was so absolute that Ari could hear his own heartbeat thudding in his chest.

Then, a massive humanoid figure appeared at the top of the ramp—tall and shrouded in a flowing, dark cloak and cowl that obscured their features. They paused, as if surveying the bay, before taking a single step forward.

The tension in the air was palpable, thick enough to cut with a knife.

Before the figure finished coming down the ramp, a much-shorter figure raced down the ramp. Instead of being shrouded in mystery, this one was clearly a human. A human female who rushed to Morgan with open arms.

"Chloe, stop!" The shrouded figure reached out an arm as black as midnight. "*Diofokyo*, female! I told you to stay on the ship."

The male's thundering shout didn't stop the female.

Ari relaxed when he read the woman's intent. She was overjoyed and excited to see Morgan.

While shocked, Morgan returned the feelings.

"Morgan, girl!" The shorter female rammed into Morgan and wrapped her in a hard hug.

From her accent, Ari deemed her an African-American from America on Earth.

She pulled back, keeping her hands on the other woman's upper arms. Her dark eyes studied Morgan from head to toe. "I can't believe it's you!"

Morgan pulled the newcomer back into a hug. "Is it really you, Chloe?"

She let go, giving Ari a clear view of her tears rolling down her cheeks.

"I'm so happy to see you." She glanced up at the humongous male who now stood behind her friend and towered over the females.

"And who is this?" Morgan stepped back.

Ari pulled her back to his front. Any excuse to keep her close was a good one.

The woman's face glowed as she tugged the male closer.

Ari smiled as he absorbed the sheer joy Chloe had for the male.

"This is Aylzrunth, my, er, husband." Chloe patted the male's side. "Damn, gargantuan man. Take your stupid cloak off. You look like a pathetic imitation of Darth Vader."

"Female, you must allow me to ascertain the situation before you continue to put yourself in danger." At first, the male's overtly male voice came out muffled, but the words became clear when he pulled the hood of the cloak back and revealed his features.

Ari's eyebrows rose at the guy's appearance.

The guy definitely wasn't a human. His skin was blacker than midnight, with an opulent sheen. His full lips were a deep purplish-black now set in a hard line while the alabaster white of his hair could rival any Akurn's. The strands rested on his shoulders in a straight line, nary a wave or curl in sight.

But it was the neon-blue pupilless eyes framed by platinum-white eyebrows and lashes that gave Ari pause. The intelligence shining from them was obvious. Here was a formidable male. To be safe, Ari sent a tendril of psychic power to him, just to make sure he wasn't a threat. What he found wasn't a big surprise. The male's mind was a formidable one, not that easy to penetrate. For now, Ari pulled back to keep his options open.

"Oh, Ay," Chloe turned her back on the male and waved his admonishment away. "Please. As if I'd be in danger with Morgan, here." She narrowed one eye at Morgan. "Right, sista?"

"More than right." Morgan's smile was wide. "If you came an hour ago, things would have been much different."

Chloe gawked around the docking the bay. "We thought we caught a criminal Ozevroc ship in Federation Consortium space." Her attention came back to Morgan. "So why are you here and not them?"

Morgan chuckled. "Well, they are here," she thumbed over her shoulder at Ari plastered to her back. "But my friend here has them in a psychic freeze."

Chloe's dark eyes bore into Ari. "Is that right?" She hummed, tapping a finger against her lips until her eyes widened on JR12. "Oh my god!"

Her squeal made Ari wince.

"Is that JR10?" Chloe leaned to get a closer look at the droid on Ari's shoulder. "Wait, you're not JR10." She straightened with a frown.

"No." JR12 gave a little dance. "I'm his son, JR12!"

"How can..." Chloe frowned.

"Are you still with the AoA?" JR12 bounced. "Are there some of them on board? Can I meet them?"

"I don't..." Chloe started.

"*Aruu*—" Aylzrunth placed a large palm on Chloe's shoulder. "—I think there is much to discuss."

"I believe he's right," Ari agreed with the male. "Isn't there a better place for us to get acquainted, Morgan?"

Morgan sighed. "This entire ship is a cesspool of Ozevroc, ah, stuff. It's either here or back to the engine room." She looked up at him. "What do you think?"

Ari smiled with a nod. "I think here is just fine."

With little effort, he generated a large cushioned sectional couch that the four of them could relax on. "How 'bout you all get comfortable and I'll go back to the replicron and grab the consumable-maker so we can have some food and drinks."

He laughed at their wide eyes and open-mouthed gapes before teleporting away.

The small group gathered on the sectional Ari had made for them in the cargo bay.

Whenever she got a chance, Morgan studied Ari out of the corner of her eye. She couldn't believe how strong his psychic ability was. Especially after he teleported to get the consumable-maker from the replicron and brought it back so the four of them could get whatever they wanted to eat once she programmed their requests.

It seemed easy enough for Ari to conjure things up while keeping the Ozevroc frozen. She couldn't imagine the energy drain it took to do that. Keeping a close eye on him was becoming second nature as the four of them enjoyed the most relaxing hour she'd had since leaving Aethralis. Like four friends getting acquainted at dinner rather than being on a hostile alien ship.

Now that the light meal was long gone, the four of them relaxed with drinks in hand.

Morgan smiled when Chloe laughed at something Ari said. While she hadn't been in the same group as Chloe on the *StarChance* during the exchange program, they'd become fast friends during the meal breaks. It was nice to reconnect with her.

Chloe preened when Morgan commented on the unusual tiara her friend wore.

Aylzrunth called it a *Qabhuth-Kun*, something he'd been born with.

The thin circlet looked like silver with a gleaming, diamond-shaped blue gem at its center.

Hard to believe every part of it was living tissue.

He explained that, on his home planet Runihura, a male placed this circlet on the head of his *aruu*, his eternal mate. Instinctively, the *Qabhuth-Kun* merged into her skin, signaling to everyone they belonged together.

Morgan wasn't sure she'd want to wear a body part from someone else. But at least Chloe didn't have to worry about ever losing it.

"I always wondered why I hadn't seen you after the first week," Chloe said to Morgan with a sigh. She sipped the Mojito Morgan had given her, smacking her lips with a grin.

"Yeah, that's what I got for snooping around where I wasn't supposed to," Morgan admitted. She'd just told them the tale of how she ended up on the Ozevroc ship. Instead of confessing the real reason she'd been at the exchange, she kept her cover story as being from Atlanta, Georgia, rather than being from a hidden city under the Antarctic. She just wasn't ready to confess how she wasn't fully human. She glanced at the male sitting next to Chloe. Not that she thought for a second the other woman would mind her hybrid status.

Chloe snorted. "Those gray little pissants, the fibber-mcgee somethings, tried to get me too." She patted her companion's beefy arm. "But Ay here took care of 'em. Didn't ya, snuggle bunny?"

"Friebbigh, not fibber-mcgee, *aruu*." Aylzrunth pulled Chloe onto his lap and massaged her neck with his strong-looking fingers and thumb.

Her eyes lowered to half-mast with her mouth slightly agape.

"And don't call me snuggle bunny. I am not a small, Earth mammal in the Leporidae family."

"Yeah, 'k. Whatever you say, you sly foxy snookums." Chloe moaned.

Her behemoth companion's thick, alabaster eyebrows rose as he frowned.

Morgan stifled a laugh. The guy might not be much of a conversationalist, but by God, Ay's expressive face said it all. It was clear he knew arguing with Chloe was a lost cause.

"Anyhoo," Chloe continued. "I can't wait to meet this purple guy you've got stashed somewhere. Never seen a crystal dude before." She gave Ari a narrow eye. "You've got him under wraps, right?"

Ari sat with his hands laced behind his head and his feet up, ankles crossed, on the ottoman he'd generated. "I've got everything under control." He kicked the footrest away and put his feet on the floor. Resting his arms on his thighs, he leaned forward. "But it's important we take him to Earth as soon as we can. Once there, we'll work with our family and the Federation Consortium on the best way to stop the Krystalii from invading this dimension." He narrowed his steely-gray eyes at them. "Can you help?"

"Are you asking us to assist you in returning to your home world?" Aylzrunth asked in his rumbling voice. "Or join in your endeavor in stopping the invasion?"

"Well—" Ari drawled, sitting back. "—you should probably stick to your original plan with the Ozevroc. That way, we won't have to worry about them coming after us when we leave."

"Leave?" Morgan swung to Ari with a hard stare. "How in the heck are we going to do that? We don't have a ship." She had no trouble fixing the *Nebula Viper's* engines, but piloting the damn thing was far beyond her capabilities. She gave the guy next to her a narrow-eyed consideration. They hadn't a chance to talk about it.

Don't worry. Ari spoke in her mind. *Now that I've got my abilities back, I can fix* Elemi.

Startled, Morgan narrowed her eyes on Ari. Good thing she was used to psychics poking into her brain without an invitation. *Are you sure?* Since he'd opened the path between them, she now had a mental way to reply to him.

Of course.

Morgan mentally humphed. Hopefully, he wasn't being too overly optimistic.

"That's good, since there isn't enough room on our ship to take all the Ozevroc," Chloe piped in. "We'd planned on towing their happy asses."

"My *aruu* is correct." Aylzrunth confirmed. "It would be unwise to let the Ozevroc free to interfere. Should the Krystalii become the major ruling party in this galaxy, the Ozevroc would surely strive to ally with them, aiding in identifying the systems that benefit the crystal race the most."

He stopped massaging Chloe's neck, and she rested her head against his massive chest.

"I believe it would be prudent to take them to the AoA headquarters to be dealt with there. While there, we will inform AoA of the upcoming difficulties the Krystalii bring. They will be an invaluable resource in defeating this new threat. However—" He shrugged his massive shoulders. "—their base is in the opposite direction of the Chancellor's palace. Thus, we cannot be of assistance in ensuring your safety on your journey back."

Morgan was glad Chloe had previously explained what AoA meant... the Alliance of Assassins, of all things. Mercenaries, among other talents for hire. Looked like her friend had been a busy woman since leaving Earth.

"Eh, it's all good. We'll be fine." Ari stood. "I agree. You should take the Ozevroc back to the AoA to keep them out of the way. If you don't mind, we've got a ship inside the engine room that needs to be repaired before you go." He glanced at the spider-bot on his shoulder. "You ready to fix *Elemi*, JR12?"

Wow, she'd forgotten all about the spybot. He'd been uncharacteristically quiet while the four of them got to know one another.

Chloe sat up, eyes wide. "*Elemi*? You got *Elemi*?"

"Oh, that's right," the spybot piped up. "When you worked with Dad, you worked with *Elemi* too, eh?"

Chloe scooted off Aylzrunth's lap and rubbed her hands down her pants.

For the first time, Morgan admired the simple, black, wide-leg pants topped with a long, sleeveless vest over a bright, multi-colored knit sweater. She sighed. She'd give anything to wear something besides the mechanic's coveralls. Back home, she kept up on all the latest trends and was a bit of a fashionista.

"Yes!" Chloe exclaimed. "Wait!" Her dark eyes narrowed. "Are you tellin' me she's hurt?" She put her fist on her hip while she wagged a chastising finger with the other hand. "You'd better take me to her right now!"

"Come on." Morgan thumbed over her shoulder to the entryway. "I'll lead you to her."

Chloe looped her arm through Morgan's and tugged them to the door. "Let's go, then. No time to waste."

Morgan couldn't agree more.

Morgan led Chloe and Aylzrunth out of the docking bay while Ari used his telekinetic ability to make the furniture disappear before following them. As they approached the engine room, they passed the area in the corridor that suffered the blast.

Chloe whistled and looked at Morgan with an eyebrow raised. "That's new." She sniffed. "I can still smell the burnt circuits and metal."

"Yeah." Morgan snickered. "The high chieftain here has employee problems."

Chloe snorted and kept walking.

Once they entered the engine room, they stopped and surveyed the frozen Ozevroc stuck in several poses.

Which was creepy at best and nerve-wracking at worst. Even given her experience with a multitude of psychics in her lifetime, Morgan didn't know anyone who had abilities similar to Ari's. She glanced sideways at him. The man hadn't broken a sweat with everything he'd done so far. And now he claimed he could fix *Elemi* at the same time? She couldn't imagine how he'd complete that momentous task all by himself.

"Pee-ew!" Chloe waved a hand over her face. "What in the hell is that smell?"

"What?" Ari chuckled. "You don't like eau du smelly alien parfum? It's all the rage this side of the galaxy."

Chloe narrowed an eye at him. "Boy, you are one sick mofo if you think this stinky shit is something I want to continue breathing."

"Then it is a good thing we will not be transporting the Ozevroc on the same ship as us," Aylzrunth deadpanned.

Morgan chuckled. She'd gotten used to the Ozevroc odor and hardly noticed it anymore.

"Oh, lordy, two gargantuan smart-asses. Just what the universe needs." Chloe shook her head.

"As'ni happy Ari back!" As'ni lumbered to them through the Ozevroc, causing some of them to fall to the floor or crash into one of their comrades. He clutched his springy coil toy. "Look what As'ni did!" With a wide smile showing his blocky lilac teeth, he held up an identical coil in his other hand as he bounced it up and down. He stopped in front of them, his crystalline body swaying to a tune only he could hear.

"Dah-yam!" Chloe took a step back with her hand over her heart. "There're three gargantuan men!"

"As'ni," Ari said. "These are our new friends, Chloe and Aylzrunth."

As'ni nodded vigorously. "As'ni like new friends." Clutching his treasures, he held the coil high. "See? As'ni make pretty!"

Chills ran up and down Morgan's spine. He psychically created something out of nothing? "Do you think he's getting stronger?" She pursed her lips and glanced at Ari.

His comforting smile made her feel better. "No." He shrugged. "I'm afraid our little, ah, altercation damaged him beyond repair. But—" He patted As'ni's shoulder. "—deep down, he has no love for the other Krystalii, especially Lord Baelon. Isn't that right, big guy?"

The mirror and crystals on As'ni's purple face creased into a scowl. "I no like icky Lord Bay-lon. He bad man."

I don't have time to explain, but I've scanned him and he is just what he appears to be. A simple creature with basic needs. Ari mentally told her. *But I want to take him with us. I think my brothers can uncover distinct memories from him on how to defeat the Krystalii better than I can.*

Morgan eyed their childish companion. *Okay. If you're sure.*

Ari turned to Aylzrunth and Chloe. He thumbed to the other side of the large room. "Come on. *Elemi* is this way."

As'ni joined them as they weaved between the group of frozen Ozevroc guards. This time, the hulking crystal giant avoided bumping into the unmoving furry aliens. Soon, the dominant bulk of *Elemi* nestled in the corner became clear.

Chloe squealed. "OMG! Look at her!" She ran the rest of the way to the ship. Petting the dull outside hull with both hands, she crooned at it. "Sista, you in there?" She spied the open doorway. "I gotta get inside." She sprinted through the dark entryway.

"Chloe, wait!" Morgan rushed in after her. Damn. If her friend didn't like the outside, no telling how she'd react to the devastation of the inside.

The keening wail from Chloe was answer enough.

Who would have guessed that the woman's tough demeanor hinted at her having a soft heart? Especially for a ship.

"Oh, baby girl! What did they do to you?" Chloe twirled around with her arms raised. "Can you hear me?"

The only response was silence.

"I thought this ship annoyed you, my *aruu*." Aylzrunth put one of his massive palms on her shoulder.

Chloe wiped a tear from her eye. "Yeah, but she didn't deserve this." She turned her dark gaze to Ari. "How can you possibly fix this?" Dropping her arms, she studied the room. "*Elemi's* very soul is gone. It's nothing but an empty shell now."

"She's not dead, Chloe." Ari assured her. "It might take me some doing, but I've got everything I need to make her whole again. Trust me, she'll be better than a hyperdrive held together with duct tape."

"Well, ain't you a hope in hell." She rolled her eyes. "I don' understand how you can do that." She gestured with a hand wave.

"Time to confess, A-Man," JR12 interjected. "To quote the British SAS motto, 'He who dares, wins.'"

Ari scratched the side of his temple. "Thanks, JR12. That's real helpful." He shrugged with a sheepish grin. "Well, I've, ah, put her someplace safe."

Now it was Morgan's turn to frown. "What do you mean, you put her someplace safe?" She crossed her arms.

"Okay, I'll show you." Ari put his hand up. "But you've got to promise me you won't freak out."

Morgan's eyebrows rose, pretty sure her expression mirrored Chloe's. "I don't like the sound of that."

"Morgan, I mean it." Ari put his fists on his trim hips. "You've got to keep your cool when I show where I put *Elemi*. Just remember, I did this way before I knew you."

She pursed her lips and looked first at Chloe, then Aylzrunth, and finally As'ni. What choice did she have? None. That's what. Besides, she trusted Ari down to her core. Steeling herself, she nodded. "Okay. I promise. Show us what you've got."

Ari stared at her before a warm smile pulled his full lips up. "Good. Okay, then." He took a step and grasped her upper arms, pulling her into a brief kiss. "You won't regret it, I promise."

Face hot from his show of affection, she humphed and pulled away. Crazy man.

Ari went to the middle of the opposite wall, closed his eyes, and placed his palm on it. The organic material of the panel parted, then widened. He opened his eyes and stepped back to reveal a tray holding a still figure with its eyes closed.

It was a sexbot. A bright-pink, freakin' sexbot from the gangster planet FiPan.

One of those hated jailers she and the other human women endured while trapped in a cramped cell no bigger than her bathroom at home. Just the sight of the prone robot burned her blood. Good thing Ari made her promise not to "freak out" because it took everything she had to swallow the scream threatening to erupt. She clutched her hands into tight fists.

"You have a fucking sexbot?" Her voice was low as she glared at him. "Care to explain why?"

"It's a good thing I had it!" Ari held his palms up in defense. "It was the perfect place to put *Elemi* just before I lost it." He let his hands drop and went to the still robot. With a flourish, he placed his hand on the side of its bald head and pressed. "Wake up, Elemi. Time to get to work."

Ever so slowly, the android's eyes fluttered open. Her eyes, the color of flamingo pink, widened. "Arakiba?"

"Yes, darlin'." He reached out and took her hand to pull her up. "Time for you to wake up."

If Morgan's eyebrows rose any higher, she'd lose them in her hair. Darlin'? She'd show him who his *darlin'* was...

"What took you so long?"

The whine in the female voice stopped Morgan. The shrill tone made her wince.

"Honestly, Arakiba. I expected more from you." The droid yanked her hand out of his and sat straight. She narrowed her gaze at him. "Perhaps I overestimated your abilities."

"And there she is," Chloe announced with a grin. "The diva herself is back. Just in case any of ya'll forgot who was really in charge."

CHAPTER TWELVE

"**N**o, I refuse." Elemi the sexbot narrowed her pink gaze at Ari. "I enjoy being mobile and there's nothing you can say that will change my mind."

Ari couldn't believe he'd been arguing with the stubborn AI for the last twenty minutes. Chloe had warned him she was stubborn, but Elemi's attitude went beyond stubborn. He fought the urge to shove her consciousness back into the ship where she belonged.

"Listen—" Ari tried for the umpteenth time. "—if I don't put you back into the ship, it won't heal." He crossed his arms and glared right back at her. "And if the ship doesn't heal, then we can't get off this bucket of smelly bolts and head back to the Federation Consortium. And if we can't do that, we won't be there to help my family stop the invasion from an extra-dimensional threat. And if that happens, your stupid metal body will cease to exist just as much as any organic being's." He turned to the purple crystal giant who entered *Elemi* with the rest of them. "Isn't that right, As'ni?"

The simpleminded beast fingered a ragged section of the ship and didn't answer. His grip on the springy coil in his other hand tightened.

"As'ni?"

The creature jumped like a child caught doing something he shouldn't. "Wha?"

"If Lord Baelon and his troops come through, everything will die, including someone like her." Ari thumbed to the pink sexbot. "Right?"

As'ni's lavender eyes widened as he vigorously nodded. "Bad. Lord Bay-lon bad. All die. Even shiny bug." He jiggled a finger in JR12's direction.

"Hey, now!" JR12 sprang from Ari's shoulder to hover over it. "Let's all take a deep breath—and I'm talkin' to you who breathe—so we can reset this stupid conversation." He flew to face Elemi, who stared at the small bot as it came closer.

For the first time, Ari noticed the android didn't blink.

"You, sexbot-ship on steroids." JR12 addressed Elemi. "What if he put you back into the robot body once things got settled? Maybe even find something better looking. Cause I gotta tell you, I've seen vending machines with more class."

Ari chuckled when Elemi's metallic jaw dropped.

"Well, I never..."

"And you ain't never gonna until you let the blond superman here put you back!" Chloe stomped her foot.

Ari raised an eyebrow. Superman? Well, didn't that just put a damper on everything? The sheer weight of that expectation was a burden far heavier than anything he'd ever experienced before. Talking himself into pulling off this gargantuan task was challenging enough. Not that he'd admit that to anyone. Especially to this stubborn, pain-in-the ass excuse for an android...

"And we's don't have time to get another ship here to take ya'll to the other side of the galaxy!" Chloe continued with a huff. "Elemi, you always claimed how much better you were than us emotional creatures. Looks like you're worse than any of us." The woman crossed her arms and turned her back on the android. "I'm ashamed of you."

"My *aruu*—" Aylzrunth said to Chloe in a soft tone. "—that was a bit harsh."

"I don't care." Chloe nodded over her shoulder to the pink droid. "She's being selfish, and she knows it."

"Chloe, dearest!" Elemi wailed.

"Do you think you can put her into another android body when this is over?" Morgan placed her soft hand on Ari's arm.

He scratched the side of his head. Honesty or guesswork? He glanced at her bright golden-green eyes, studying him. Did he really have a choice? No, no, he didn't. Okay, honesty it was.

"I'm pretty sure I can. Yeah, I think so," Ari hedged his confession. "But, understand when I did it the first time, I was desperate to save her because things went sideways real fast with our friend here." He patted the bulk of As'ni's shoulder.

As'ni beamed at Ari's show of affection.

Ari turned to Elemi. "But I can promise I'll do my best."

Elemi's fuchsia eyes widened as she swung her intense, pleading gaze to Chloe, silently begging for understanding. Her lips parted as her metallic hands clenched tightly together. At Chloe's mulish frown, Elemi threw her metallic shoulders back and lifted her chin. "Fine. For you, I'll agree, Chloe dearest." Her metallic lips pursed. "I just hope this blundering fool knows what he's doing."

Chloe turned back to Elemi, then swung her attention in Ari's direction. "You know, she brings up somethin' I've been meaning to ask you." Her dark gaze narrowed. "How did you do all this mumbo-jumbo stuff in the first place? Not only taking Elemi from the ship and putting her into a sleaze-bot, but creating that couch and stuff back there." She thumbed over her shoulder. "You never explained how you did that. What? You a magician or somethin'."

Ari tilted his head with his hands behind his back.

Morgan frowned at his mischievous grin.

"Yeah, something."

Didn't look like his innocent act fooled Chloe one bit.

"Now, what does that mean?" Chloe fisted her hands on her hips. Lowering her head, she stared at Ari through hooded lids.

"Chloe, my *aruu*. He is not a human." Aylzrunth rubbed her back.

"Huh?" She glanced at him before swinging her attention to Ari with an up-and-down perusal. "What do you mean he ain't human?"

Great. How did Aylzrunth know that? He didn't sense any psychic abilities from the Runihura. Maybe now wasn't the time to address that question. Better to keep things simple. "You know how some people have mixed heritage?" He directed his question at Chloe.

She nodded with a guarded expression.

"Well, mine's just... *really* mixed. Like, muddled out-of-this-world mixed."

"Say again?" Chloe's dark brows rose.

"He is telling us that his genetic makeup is a combination of human and alien." Aylzrunth explained. "He is a hybrid."

"Yep, that's me." Ari spread his arms wide. "My DNA is just one big galactic smoothie."

Morgan bit her bottom lip as her eyes twinkled.

Chloe frowned and studied Ari again. "Figures. Ain't no way a human guy could do all that and be so good-looking." She humphed and grabbed Aylzrunth's large hand in hers. "Just like my man here, no one on Earth is anywhere near as beautiful."

"Female," Aylzrunth grumbled. "Do not describe me as beautiful."

The sound of Morgan's giggle made Ari smile. Especially when the onyx man's cheeks flushed darker.

Aylzrunth turned his neon-blue eyes to look at Ari. "How much time do you need before you are ready to depart?"

Ari rested with one of his arms across his waist and plunked his elbow on it. Tapping his forefinger on his chin, he looked away as he tried to figure out the best answer. He let a moment pass before he looked at the alien taller than himself. Again, he had to be honest. It's not like he'd gone around fixing organic spaceships all the time. "I'm not really sure, but hopefully not too long. But I think it'd be best if you remove your ship, so when *Elemi* is ready, I'll be able to put her in the docking bay so we can launch from here." Goddess willing.

Ari braced himself under Aylzrunth's glowing, wide-eyed stare. "If that is so, what an impressive feat it would be. I have never seen the like." Now his pupilless eyes narrowed. "When we have finished this situation satisfactorily, I would appreciate the opportunity to ascertain your background."

"What my man is trying to say, in his own convoluted way," Chloe piped in. "Is we'd like to get together again. Okay?"

Morgan's smile widened. "I'd really like that. Wouldn't you?" She turned to Ari.

"Ab-so-frigging-lutely," he returned her grin. He'd rather do anything than delve into his background right now. Especially since he wasn't sure if he could pull this momentous task off successfully. It was going to stretch his limitations, transferring *Elemi's* consciousness then rebuilding her ship body. Not to mention keeping the Ozevroc frozen at the same time. At least if he failed, he wouldn't have to worry about his brothers finding out. Because if this didn't work, he'd probably end up blowing them all to hell.

"It's a date." Ari widened his grin and rubbed his hands together. "So, whaddya say we pretend it's another Tuesday and save the universe, people?

Tension melted from Ari's shoulders as Morgan volunteered to lead Chloe and Aylzrunth back to the docking bay. He'd almost expected her to dig in, determined to stay by his side no matter the danger. As if he'd let that happen. The last thing he wanted was to risk her safety while he focused on the impossible. Damn, he was sure lucky the universe cut him a break for once. He didn't have time to deal with battling her relentless stubbornness to make sure she remained as far away as possible in case everything went south.

So, he'd take advantage of Morgan being gone for now. The quicker the better. He turned to JR12, As'ni, and the android Elemi inside the empty ship.

"You know," JR12 said from his shoulder. "I didn't want to say anything in front of the other organics, but I have an idea about merging Elemi with, ah, *Elemi*."

Ari glanced at the small gold-and-silver bot looking up at him with his multifaceted eyes. "I'm listening." Anything would help at this point.

"All right, A-Man," JR12 began. "It's like this. Instead of fully extracting Elemi from the android unit, consider a more efficient solution—allow her to share her consciousness between the ship and the android body, creating a dual interface where she controls both simultaneously. After all, as Da Vinci once said, 'Simplicity is the ultimate sophistication. '"

Hmm, maybe that'd work. Ari turned to Elemi. "What do you think?"

In a sultry tone, Elemi said, "Darling, that would be fabulous. Why should I settle for one form when I can be magnificent in two? Imagine me—gracing the ship with my brilliance while still keeping this fabulous body. It's perfection, really."

"Okay, that's doable." Ari pointed to the pulverized navigation console. "Stand there and put your hands here." He motioned to a broken protrusion that used to be part of the command station. "I'll set up a station where you can plug in, so stay calm."

Thankfully, she did as he asked, putting her palms on the withered material without making some mind-numbing comment.

"As'ni." He turned to the purple crystal giant sitting on the floor with his legs splayed.

The purple entity was playing with his coils, bouncing them up and down while singing a repeating ditty.

"As'ni, pay attention."

As'ni looked up. "Ari?"

"I'll need your help to fix this pretty ship. Okay?"

As'ni bounced to his feet, still clutching his toy. "Yes! As'ni help! Yes, yes!" His head bobbed with each word.

Ari put a hand on the crystal creature's shoulder and steered him to the opposite wall. "Put your back against the wall. I'd like if you could share some of your energy with her without hurting yourself." He eyed the simple creature. "You think you could do that?"

"Yes! As'ni do." He clutched both toys in one hand to his chest and didn't let go. "No problem, Ari." As'ni thumped his back against the wall.

"Good," Ari nodded. "If it hurts, you move away, okay?"

"Yes, Ari. As'ni do."

"As for you," Ari addressed the spider-bot on his shoulder. "I want you out of here." He nodded to the open entryway. "Leave the engine room altogether so you don't get caught up in anything happening here. Also, I need you to keep Morgan out." The muscles in his neck tensed. "Make sure she doesn't come anywhere near this room while I work. I swear, if she gets one scratch…" He left the threat hanging.

"Like the great Issac Asimov once wrote, 'Violence is the last refuge of the incompetent.' Fortunately for you, I'm highly competent, so I can ignore your absurd threat." With a parting snort, the spider-droid pulled his wings out and hovered before zipping over the frozen Ozevroc to speed out the entryway. Hopefully, JR12 would catch up with Morgan before she headed back.

Returning inside the dim interior of the prone ship, he double-checked that his two companions were where he wanted them. Satisfied all was ready as could be, he closed his eyes. The stillness in the room weighed heavily on him. Pressed in on him. As if the universe held its breath while it waited.

Ari pressed his hands, strong and steady, where the ship's navigation controls used to be. He might not be a healer in the traditional sense, but the energies he carried were all-encompassing. The drive to repair the ship's core grew stronger as he searched for *Elemi's* essence within the android, reaching to grasp her ethos. To give him more leverage, he shifted his focus inward and shut off his external senses. The organic mesh of *Elemi's* living body, her threads of consciousness, of memory, housed in the android, stretched out before him. As he gathered who she was, he healed some of the tangled and frayed bits of the ship caused by the damage.

Slowing his breath, Ari deepened each inhale until he filled his chest with the energy he needed. With no hesitation, he reached toward the core of her—not physically—but with something else entirely. Something within him that was unique to him hummed beneath his skin. It wasn't light, not exactly, but it was warm. It pulsed at his fingertips, invisible but undeniable, answering a universal call he'd never make out loud.

Elemi's overall consciousness brushed against his, tentative at first, as if she was testing him after being burned.

There was resistance—pain, fear—a tense emotion telling him she didn't want to be split. Didn't want to risk breaking what she had even more. He didn't force her. Steadily he waited, holding the connection open for her to complete the invitation to join with the ship, her original form. For this to work, it had to be her choice.

Thankfully, her hesitation dissipated as the warmth of her consciousness spread out from him.

Her tendrils of energy slipped through the cracks in the damaged threads of the ship.

Together, they stitched and mended, piecing the broken fragments back together.

Elemi's essence shifted from the shadows into the stronger dual light he controlled.

The process wasn't quick. It wasn't smooth. It was chaotic, fragments of her mind scattered, only to return when he guided them with gentle, controlling intent.

His heart pounded, not in fear, but in rhythm with hers as she and the ship slowly healed.

When the power within Ari drained, As'ni's psionic energy joined in, bringing with it a sense of joy and playfulness.

That's when the faintest hum within the ship's hull broke the silence. The connection deepened, stronger now, until it wasn't just him reaching into the ship. *Elemi* reached back, allowing him to join her fully with her android body and the ship.

Then, with one last thrust, Ari rearranged the damage done to the ship in a microscopic speck of time and space, and he rebuilt the ship to her former glory.

Stretching out his consciousness, he followed *Elemi's* thread of awareness, now split in two. Instead of one being cut in half, she was a sentient being with two forms. Whole—alive, aware, and unique as only *Elemi* could be.

Nostalgia washed over Morgan as Chloe stepped through the airlock, Aylzrunth's towering onyx form by her side. Though she and Chloe came from completely different worlds on Earth, their shared experiences aboard the *StarChance* brought them together. It'd be nice if she and Chloe could explore a closer friendship when everything settled down.

Better yet, she'd love to bring her friend to Aethralis. Wouldn't that be something? Now, all she had to do was figure out a way to get the High Guardian to agree to it. Maybe she could introduce Chloe as a representative of that mercenary group, the AoA, to be on call if that shield holding the Titans got weaker. Yeah, that might...

"Yo, Wrench Queen."

Morgan jumped when JR12 buzzed in front of her.

"You stuck or something?"

Morgan blinked. "Stuck?"

"Yeah, you're just standing there with a blank look on your face like a downed sexbot." JR12 zipped to her right shoulder and landed. "Did the other organics leave yet?"

Morgan checked out the closed bay doors. "Yes, they're gone." Glancing at the droid on her shoulder, she asked, "What are you doing here?" Looking around, it was easy to see he was alone. "Where's Ari?" Annoying little guy rarely strayed far from him.

"He's busy fixing *Elemi*."

"What?" she exclaimed, spinning around to head out the door. "Without me?"

"Hey, hang on, Gizmo Guru!" JR12 buzzed in her face.

She halted to avoid smacking into him.

"He told me to keep you away until he gives the okay to return."

Morgan thumped her fists on her hips. That was the stupidest thing she'd ever heard. "What? Why?"

"Because, you clueless organic female, it would be dangerous for him to split his concentration between watching you and fixing the ship. Stupid man can't take his eyes off you when you're around." The hovering bot humphed. "He'd probably end up blowing us all to hell."

Morgan's lips curled into a soft smile. The thought of Ari unable to tear his gaze from her sent her pulse into hyper-drive. A warm dose of satisfaction bloomed in her chest. Someone as strong and intriguing as Ari, captivated by her, left her both flattered and relieved. She dreaded thinking his feelings for her weren't as strong as those she had for him.

Too bad things were so chaotic they hadn't had a chance to explore their attraction in person. And not just in a Dreamwalk.

Throwing her shoulders back, she glared at the bot. "Okay, *Flash*. What do you propose we do in the meantime?" She raised her hand palm up to invite him to land there. She didn't like talking to him when she couldn't face him. Looking over her shoulder as they talked made her cross-eyed.

"Glad you asked. First, let me pose a quandary to you." The bot twisted his head to look at her sideways. "Tell me, have you seen any female Ozevroc?"

Female Ozevroc? What in the world brought that on? She stared at the ceiling as she searched her memories. "No," she drawled. "Hmm, now that you bring it up, I don't think I've ever seen any female Ozevroc." She focused on JR12.

His multifaceted eyes gleamed in the low light.

"Why do you ask?"

"I think you're going to want to see this." He lifted his right foreleg and pointed to the door. "Come on, let's go this way."

JR12 winged off her palm, leaving Morgan no choice but to follow. As they took a mobile elevator, they headed to the lower levels.

When the doors swished open, Morgan's steps slowed as she followed JR12 deeper into the ship's underbelly.

The small droid's metallic wings buzzed like a rotund bumblebee's, spinning the thick, soured air layered with the scent of decay and filth.

Her stomach churned.

Dim lighting flickered in the hallway, casting eerie shadows that danced against the rusting walls.

Why would their females be down here? This couldn't be right. Her breath hitched as they approached a sealed door.

"Here we are, Wrench Queen. But I warn you. Prepare yourself." JR12 said, his voice bittersweet. "This won't be pretty."

Morgan hesitated. Something in JR12's rigid posture made her tense. Taking in a deep breath, she hesitated and studied the dull, faded surface of the metal door layered with corrosion streaks before pushing on it. As it moved it created a high-pitched screech that ended with a final dull thud when it stopped. As she walked through, a blast of foul air hit her. She turned her head with eyes closed, trying to hold her breath. Wheezing, she took a chance and opened her eyes. Her heart slammed against her ribs at the sight before her.

Cages. Dozens of them, stacked haphazardly, filled with matted, filthy shapes huddled in the corners.

It took a heartbeat moment before the horror sank in, chilling her to the core. These were Ozevroc females. Their long snouts pressed to the cold metal of their enclosures, eyes black and lifeless. Patchy, tangled fur covered their gaunt bodies, ranging from dull gold to a ghastly shade of blue. Some huddled around tiny shapes—young, barely moving, mewling weakly. A constant low whimper from the huddled bodies filled the air like an endless, mournful drone.

The nearest caged female lifted her head, her gaze heavy with exhaustion. Her coarse fur clung to her bony frame, ribs sharp against her skin, as if she hadn't eaten in days. She pressed her face against the bars, and her tongue flicked out to catch moisture from a filthy trough.

A knot tightened in Morgan's throat, her chest heavy. She couldn't look away. Not just confined—their spirits lay crushed beneath years of neglect and cruelty. Tiny shapes wriggled at the edges of her vision, babies clinging to their weakened mothers.

Behind her, JR12's sensors hummed. "As the great Gandhi said, 'The measure of a society is how it treats its weakest members'. I do not understand how organics can behave in this neglectful manner to their own. At the very least, this level of disregard does not align with efficient biological output. The probability of survival for these females and their offspring is practically zero unless something changes immediately."

Morgan's stomach lurched at that understatement. Reduced to mere vessels, these females were nothing more than a grim production line to produce offspring. The cages, the damp stench of unwashed bodies, the groans of hunger and pain—all screamed of something far worse than mere captivity.

She clenched her fists at her sides, knuckles turning white. Forcing herself to step closer, she walked past cages filled with emaciated forms barely clinging to life, past trembling creatures too weak to stand. One baby, no larger than a house cat, let out a weak, rasping cry as it pressed against its mother, who didn't move.

Morgan knelt, her heart breaking in her chest. "This... this isn't right." Her voice came out hoarse, barely a whisper. She glanced at JR12. "What can we do?"

"I'm glad you asked." JR12 words came out in a playful, sing-song cadence. "I have an idea you're just gonna love."

Morgan glanced at the floating bot with a faint spark of hope. "Really? Tell me." Anything was better than the suffering those poor creatures endured.

"Two things." JR12 landed on her shoulder. "First, did you notice these females aren't frozen from Ari's mojo?"

Morgan stilled. Eyes wide, she took in the alarming scene. Damn! How'd she miss that?

"Good thing he didn't know about them, because we need to talk to at least one." JR12 continued. "Second, we need that Talon of Ancients."

Morgan's mouth dropped open. Never, in her wildest dreams, did she think the bot knew about the missing artifact. Much less that these females were here. "Wait... how do you know what that is?" She cocked her head.

"Oh, please." JR12 rasped. "Interfacing with this ridiculously simple ship took less time than to tell you about it."

She crossed her arms. "Okay, Inspector Bug-Eyes, why do we need the Talon of Ancients?"

"See, this is why you organics need me." JR12 snorted. "The Talon of Ancients isn't just a pretty bauble. I'm sure you realize it's the seat of Ozevroc power. By their own traditions and laws, whoever has the artifact is automatically their leader." She watched JR12 look up at her from her shoulder where he once again perched. "So, if we give that to a female, she can take over from the males. The only hard part is finding one of them coherent enough to understand what we're proposing."

Morgan's gaze swept over the suffering Ozevroc in the dim light. She sucked on the side of her lower lip. Finding one of these females awake and strong enough for their plan to work was a long shot. Good thing she spoke their language. She stood in the narrow corridor between cages so most of them could hear her.

Ignoring the stench of neglect in the air, she swallowed hard and glanced at JR12 as he rose from her and hovered beside her. She could hear his sensors flickering faintly. He must be scanning the area.

Morgan threw her shoulders back, making sure her voice remained soft but steady. "Can any of you speak? Anyone well enough to talk?"

The silence was deafening. Only the soft sound of labored breathing filled the space.

She scanned the rows of cages, eyes catching on a few who stirred weakly, blinking their beady eyes in her direction. But none moved. None responded.

Then, farther down, a flicker of motion caught her eye.

One female slowly raised her head. Her fur, that once might have been dark and sleek, now hung in matted clumps. She struggled to lift herself, using the bars of the cage to steady her trembling limbs. Her eyes, dull but aware, locked on Morgan.

JR12 buzzed quietly. "Look over there. That one looks like she understood you. Let's go."

Morgan exhaled and went to the female's cage and lowered herself to meet the alien at eye level. "We want to help." Her voice was soft but clear. "Can you... can you talk?"

The female's throat quivered as if unsure of how to speak. When she did, her voice came out as a rough, rasping croak. She swallowed, and her four eyes darted to look at the others around her as if gathering strength to speak.

Morgan leaned in, her chest tight, waiting. This was their only chance.

The female Ozevroc blinked, her button-like eyes narrowed with an intensity that didn't match her frail form. She shifted again, her limbs trembling as she pulled herself closer to the edge of the cage, her long snout pressed against the cold bars. "I can speak," the female rasped, her voice hoarse but fierce. Her determined spirit came through like a smoldering flame beneath layers of ash. She glanced at the other females, then back to Morgan. "We... are dying. Can you help us, strange one with the gold-eyes?"

Morgan whooshed a surge of relief. This one sounded strong and aware. She checked JR12, who hovered silently just outside the cage, his sensors scanning the female.

She knelt and rested her bum on her heels, her hands resting on her thighs. With a firm but gentle tone, she asked, "What's your name?"

The female stared at her, unblinking. "We are not allowed names." Bitter contempt laced her words. Her body, despite its weakened state, tensed with defiance.

Son of a bitch! Morgan's heart squeezed. These poor females had been stripped of their dignity, their very identities. They were nothing more than discarded tools. It was unthinkable what they suffered. She shook her head. "No. That bullshit ends now." She took in the female's potent gaze, the determination clear behind her gaunt features. "I'm going to give you a name right now. How about... Zara?" A small smile tugged the corner of her mouth. "It means 'princess,' and I think you deserve that profound name."

The female blinked, her expression unreadable for a moment, as if she was processing the idea. Then, slowly, she nodded. "Zara..." Her voice was low, as if testing the name on her tongue for the first time. Her eyes met Morgan's again, this time with a flicker of something deeper. Hope. "I accept this name." Her voice became stronger now. "I ask for your help. Not just for me... but for all of us." She glanced at the other cages, where several females were watching with wide, cautious eyes.

Morgan's chest tightened for a different reason. Now there was less fear, more purpose in the atmosphere. She reached out, gripping the bars of Zara's cage. "We'll get you out of here, all of you," she promised. "But we'll have to work together in order for us to do that."

Zara lifted her chin, the fire in her gaze burning brighter. "Tell me what to do," she said firmly. "And I will see it is done."

JR12's sensors flickered as he addressed the Ozevroc in their language. "If we get you the Talon of Ancients, will you accept the mantle of leadership?"

Morgan watched as the words hung in the air between them, heavy with meaning.

Zara's eyes, dark and deep, flicked up from staring at the floor of the cage to meet hers. For a moment, the Ozevroc female was still, her emaciated form unmoving except for the faint rise and fall of her chest.

The ship's low hum filled the silence, but Morgan's focus was entirely on the being in front of her.

Zara's three sets of hands, once trembling and weak, tightened around the bars of the cage, her knuckles pale beneath her matted fur. Her gaze was no longer clouded by exhaustion or fear. Instead, it burned with something stronger—resolve. Her body trembled as she pulled herself upright, her movements deliberate, despite the obvious strain.

There was no hesitation as she spoke, her voice stronger now, more certain. "I have been denied a name, freedom, and hope. If leading means freeing my sisters, our children, and myself, then I accept." Her four eyes gleamed with a determined glimmer of hope. "I vow not to fail them."

Morgan felt a shiver run down her spine. The frail creature in front of her had transformed—no longer a victim of her circumstances, but a force to be reckoned with.

Zara straightened as much as her body allowed, a presence far larger than her physical form could convey.

"Okay, now on to task number two." Morgan smirked at JR12. "Let's hand over that Talon of Ancients to them. You with me?"

"Well, since it was my idea..." JR12 admonished. "Of course I am."

How silly of her. Of course he was. "Well, then." She turned to Zara. "Let's get started."

CHAPTER THIRTEEN

"A s'ni done now," the purple crystal giant stated. "I nap." He lumbered to the edge of the room and slumped onto his butt with his back to the wall. With an enormous yawn that showed his blocky lilac teeth, he rubbed his eyes, then leaned back, eyes closed, and started snoring.

Ari stared at him for a moment, amazed a creature made of glass, crystals, and mirrors would snore. He shook his head. Feeling the weight of *Elemi's* consciousness, he let his hold on her go, bringing his psychic sense back to himself. He stretched, his back and neck popping like old floorboards. Dropping his arms, he glanced around with a satisfied smirk. Yep, the organic ship was back to her former glory—hearty and whole, as they say. A job damn well done, if he said so himself.

The pink spybot sat motionless in a restored console chair, her metallic fingers on her lap with her fingers wide. Elemi's metallic body appeared to be rebooting itself while the ship glowed with internal health.

Time to check in with Morgan. He debated before taking the chance to meld a small part of his mind with hers. Their relationship was still so new, he didn't want to come across as being too pushy. Especially since psychics raised her. From what little she'd shared, she didn't appreciate someone like him poking around in her mind without permission.

Morgan? He kept his mental voice light, the connection soft. What he got back was astonishing.

She grabbed his psychic tendril and held it with an iron grip.

I need you down here right now. She cut the connection, but left enough of herself for him to teleport to where she was.

Ari frowned. It didn't seem like Morgan faced any danger, but she sure acted pissed off about something. No telling what kind of mess she and JR12 had gotten tangled up in.

Ari took a moment to glance at the sleeping form of As'ni, then the android body of Elemi.

The fingers on her right hand were twitching, but otherwise, she was unresponsive. The interior of the ship was still making some repairs, but all in all, it looked like it would be ready as soon as she synced herself between the mobile and ship's body.

Closing his eyes, he gripped the psychic thread Morgan left behind and teleported to her. When he reformed, the stench choked him, making his eyes burn. He coughed, then took a chance to see what made the place smell worse than the garbage chamber he'd stumbled into before.

The scene before him was something out of a perverted nightmare. Standing behind Morgan, he looked over her shoulder at the rows and rows of small creatures he presumed were Ozevroc imprisoned in tiny cages. Like something out of a madman's science lab.

With an inward hiss, he focused on his woman. Licking his lips, he made a quick examination of her, just to make sure she was okay. He expanded his senses to see if there were any hidden threats around. As nothing hostile came back, the tension in his gut loosened, allowing him to focus on Morgan. After everything he'd been through, she was the one constant that grounded him, the only thing that truly made sense. She was his, undeniably, as no one else ever could be.

Her back was to him, and he noticed JR12 perched on her right shoulder as she talked to someone on her handheld. "Yeah, I'm just waiting for Ari to show up so we can switch the males with these females."

"You sure they can take care of themselves before we get to Runi-hura?"

The image of Chloe on Morgan's device confirmed the voice Ari heard.

"I think once we get them out of these cages and into a better environment, we'll find out what we're dealing with better."

Ari leaned over Morgan's shoulder to watch the interaction between them.

"Okay, let us know when they're ready to go. If you need help, just let us know. In the meantime, we'll stand by." Chloe's image blacked out and shifted to some schematics.

Morgan glanced at him over her shoulder.

Ari smirked when she didn't appear to be surprised he was there. For a non-psychic, she was truly impressive. He couldn't resist placing a hand on her left shoulder and drawing her close, making JR12 yelp as he jumped off her and extended his wings.

JR12 buzzed to hover in front of Ari, making his eyes cross.

"Dang, A-Man! Warn a person next time." The small bot snorted and zoomed to land on Ari's shoulder.

"I'll see what I can do." Ari non-promised. "So, what's going on here?" He waved to the moaning creatures in the small cages. "Are these Ozevroc prisoners?" From the stench, filth, and obvious neglect, that's what made sense.

"No, these are female Ozevroc," JR12 supplied. "As far as we can tell, they're kept like this to service the whims of any Ozevroc male who wants to get their doinky-doink on."

"JR12!" Morgan put her fingers against her mouth and unsuccessfully hid her trembling grin. "I can't believe you even know what that is."

"Yeah, so what?" The bot shrugged the upper part of his small body. "I'm right, aren't I?"

Ari frowned. From the small forays he'd made on the Ozevroc leader's mind, he never got that the male enjoyed making others suffer. But, then again, the alien thought little beyond his own needs and interests. He glanced at Morgan's profile. "I gather you have something in mind."

Morgan nodded. "Oh, you bet I do." She turned to face him with arms crossed, as if bracing herself for him to argue with her.

Ha! Little did she know, he'd do just about anything she asked to erase that scowling frown from her beautiful face.

"I want you to switch the male Ozevroc with these females. Give the assholes a taste of their own medicine."

Ari's brows rose. "Really?" He dragged his eyes from her to survey the room. There didn't seem to be much movement from the females in their small cages. "Are they strong enough to be taken out of where they are?"

"Come here. I want you to meet someone." Morgan grasped his forearm and stopped in front of a cage. "This is Zara." She proudly introduced the small Ozevroc.

The small creature blinked her four black eyes at him with a look that was clear, direct, and unafraid. Her painfully thin body made it easy to see she was breathing hard. Her three sets of skeletal arms did little to hide her protruding ribs.

Ari crouched to meet the Ozevroc eye to eye. "Hello, Zara. I'm Ari." He had to swallow the roar of anger that threatened to escape at the pitiful sight of the abused female. "Would you like me to take you out of there?"

Morgan stood next to him and translated for him in the Ozevroc guttural language.

Moving the Ozevroc around would take some doing since he'd just expended a lot of energy healing *Elemi.* But at least he won't have to create something new.

Zara tilted her snout up and replied.

He didn't need the translation to know she was more than willing.

"One other thing, A-Man." JR12 poked his neck with this needle-like front leg. "Think you can get us the Talon of Ancients from its place in the replicron drawer?"

"I can." He glanced at the bot. "Why?"

"Once Zara has that in her possession, she'll assume all Ozevroc authority as high chieftain." Morgan helpfully supplied. "That'll demote Welozz to a common male."

"What's stopping him from fighting her for it?"

Morgan's full lips twitched into a sardonic smile. "See, that's the best part." She stood straight with her arms crossed. Ah, there she stood in his favorite pose, putting those plump breasts on the shelf of her arms.

He dragged his eyes from her chest as he stood. It took everything he had to zero in on excited expression on her face instead.

"Did you know Aylzrunth comes from a tight matriarchal society? The females there rule with an iron fist. What better place for these females to learn how to rule than from them?" She lifted her handheld. "I spoke to Chloe, and they both agree to take these females to his planet, Runihura, where a place for them has already been set up." Morgan nodded to Zara, who was still watching them with avid eyes. "They'll receive excellent care, while the Federation Consortium takes custody of the males for the galactic crimes they've committed."

Ari whistled under his breath. His woman was formidable as hell.

JR12 hopped. "To quote the great Hannibal Smith from The A-Team, 'I love it when a plan comes together!'"

What surprised Morgan was most of the females in their cramped cages still lived. Best of all, she was happy to find out several of their mewling young were alive and in pretty good health as well.

But by the time Ari finished teleporting the females to the common eating room, then locked the males into those cramped cages, Morgan's stomach tightened with worry.

His face had paled, shadows gathered under his eyes, and his movements had lost their usual steadiness. He lingered, taking a labored breath, as his shoulders slumped a bit more with each step.

Morgan hesitated at first, not wanting to leave him. But the females needed food, and she didn't want to ask him to teleport the consumable-food making machine when she could just run to the engine room and grab it. Giving him one last look, she darted out and hurried there while leaving Ari to finish switching the Ozevroc.

By the time she returned, the females had settled in and silently watched her enter. Taking the machine to Zara, she showed her how to use it. Then she and Ari handed out shredded meat on platters to the starving females. Soon the sounds of happy murmurs filled the air as the females ate and consumed cups of clean precious water.

Morgan promised herself that before they left, she'd show them how to use the replicron to make anything else they'd need.

Now her worry over Ari deepened, almost more than she could bear. The weight of exhaustion etched into his features was sharp, making his cheeks hollow. His clenched jaw sent a ripple of unease through her as he continued to work as if nothing was wrong with him. She didn't need to be a psychic to see he was on the verge of collapse. Someone had to look after this stubborn ass—a job she was more than ready to take on.

"Ari—" Morgan approached him with a soft smile. "—JR12 and I can take it from here." She rubbed his arm and nodded to the spybot next to her. "I want to show Zara and some others how to use the replicron and the communication console so they can talk to Chloe and Aylzrunth on their journey to Runihura. Why don't you rest in *Elemi*? That way, we can enjoy some alone time on our trip back." Tilting her head, she gave him a sultry glance through half-lidded eyes.

The gunmetal color of Ari's eyes darkened as his full lips curved into an alluring grin. "*Irnini*," he bent down to meet her face-to-face. His tense expression smoothed as he whispered against her lips. "I look forward to having lots of 'alone time' with you."

Morgan's face heated as unbidden memories of their Dreamwalk rushed back. Waiting to be with this incredible man might be tough, but she wanted him to be ready for her... not exhausted. She sucked in a shuddering breath and reached up to give him a light kiss. Placing her lips over his, she wrapped a hand behind his head to bring him in closer. She fused her lips to his, joining their tongues and turning the kiss into a passionate foray, intent on revealing to him how much she craved him. That way, he'd never consider she'd reject him.

When Ari pulled back, she swallowed her mewl of disappointment and looked up at him. She squirmed with desire as she absorbed his rugged handsomeness. How amazing was it someone like him noticed someone like her? Much less aimed such a direct, intense look in her direction. She licked her lips, savoring the flavor he left behind.

His eyes narrowed. "You're playing with fire, *irnini*." Wrapping her in his firm embrace, he whispered in her ear. "And I love playing with hot things."

Morgan giggled. Oh lordy, trust him to make a hokey statement to break the mood. "You nut." She pulled back and playfully swatted his firm pecs. "Go on, now." She gave him a mock shove. "I promise you, you're going to need your strength later, mister."

"As my lady commands." Ari stepped back and put his hand over his heart, then disappeared.

His amorous grin made her lighter than air. With a sigh, she turned back to the group of Ozevroc females.

JR12 landed on her shoulder. "Okay, miss Wrench Queen." The bot settled, folding his iridescent wings under the smooth golden elytra over his back. "What's first?"

Morgan surveyed the females getting comfortable. Some moved more than others. Pulling out her multicorder, she adjusted it to a medical level. "First thing, I'd better double-check each one of them and see if any are in critical condition. Once that's done, we'll hand Zara the Talon of Ancients and adjust the ship's logs to show the transfer of leadership to Zara. Then I'll let Chloe know where we stand so they can head out to Runihura."

"I wonder if Ari left those males frozen." JR12 huffed. "I hope he didn't since it'd serve them right to experience life in those cages."

Morgan smirked. "Oh, I don't think he was nice enough to leave them frozen." With Ari's tendency for orneriness, she bet anything he woke them up. "But it wouldn't hurt to ask him when we're done."

Taking another glance around the room, she sighed. "Okay, we've got lots to do. Let's finish this up so we can go home."

Done. It was finally done.

It'd taken longer than Morgan hoped to get everything settled. JR12 proved invaluable since he learned how to communicate with the Ozevroc as well as she did.

After the initial surprise of his unusual appearance wore off, the females warmed to him with surprising ease. Especially the younger ones.

The spybot had to dodge several grasping young hands to avoid being played with like a toy.

While he dodged the little one's hands, the older females told JR12 what they needed, and he'd bring their orders to Morgan so she could show Zara how to use the consumable-maker and the replicron. It was a pleasant surprise, how intelligent the female Ozevroc was.

It didn't take Zara long to catch on to the intricacies of the machinery, and she quickly chose other females to help her.

Morgan was more than satisfied the Ozevroc were in excellent hands. "Okay, JR12," she said to the spybot on her shoulder. "Let's head back to *Elemi*. Hopefully Ari got some sleep."

"Yeah, he's not the only one. Running around an obstacle course from all those younglings wore me out," JR12 complained. "I swear if I was there any longer, I'd have to hide under your hairline just to save myself."

"Oh, you big baby." No sympathy from her. The bot had to be the most exciting thing those young ones ever saw in their brief, hard lives. The look of sheer joy in their eyes was well worth any inconvenience the droid experienced. "I bet you enjoyed every minute."

"Yeah, well. I'm too young for this..." the bot muttered.

Morgan ignored him and stepped into the engine room where *Elemi* was. She sucked in a breath when there was nary a male Ozevroc in sight. The empty place made her smile, knowing they were now tucked safely away in the females' cages. Which they deserved, thank you very much. With each step, her grin widened as her boots clicked in soft rhythm on the now-pristine floor. Her breath caught as she stopped short when her eyes landed on the previously decimated vessel *Elemi*.

The spaceship sat in the same corner she'd always been in, but was now no longer a crumpled, lifeless husk but something else entirely. The smooth curves of her hull gleamed under the bright lights, like polished stones. There were thin veins of light pulsing just beneath the surface, weaving intricate patterns along her organic skin.

It reminded Morgan of a magnificent creature breathing softly in the stillness. The once-jagged scars and scorched metal were gone, replaced by a seamless blend of organic and metallic textures, like muscle fused to bone in perfect harmony.

As she drew closer, a soft hum of energy filled the air, a faint but undeniable gentle thrum of a heartbeat.

The ship's bioluminescence shimmered along *Elemi's* sides, casting faint reflections that danced across the floor. For the first time in weeks, the ship looked whole—no, not just whole—but *alive*.

Morgan's hand hovered near the surface of the ship, tracing the faint glow of the veins that pulsed gently beneath her fingertips. She hesitated. Would the ship respond to her touch in a good way?

The answer came as a soft ripple passed along the ship's hull. The glow intensified for a moment. Then, with a slight audible hiss, a section of *Elemi's* smooth exterior shifted. The lines of the hull peeled back, not mechanically, but fluidly, as though *Elemi* herself was stretching open. The organic material folded in on itself, curling gracefully to form an arched doorway.

Morgan inhaled a sigh of wonder as the pulse of energy brightened.

The opening widened, revealing a soft, glowing interior. Warm, inviting air rushed out.

She swore she heard the faintest sigh, like *Elemi* herself beckoned her inside. Without a word, Morgan stepped through the archway. Inside, the air maintained its constant, comforting warmth. A soft, rhythmic hum vibrated from the floor and seeped through her boots.

The organic walls shimmered with a translucent sheen, almost like a lustrous pearl. The colors shifted from deep blues to silvery whites as the light moved through them.

The floor beneath her had the faintest give, responsive, yet solid enough to support her weight.

Veins of bioluminescence threaded throughout, winding like roots beneath the surface.

Her every step made them flicker and dance, as though the ship hugged every move she made.

"Well, well, darling," *Elemi* purred, her feminine voice smooth like silk, a soft, sultry tone laced with just enough arrogance to remind

Morgan whose space she was in. "It's about time you graced me with your presence. Took your sweet time, didn't you?"

Morgan glanced around, half expecting to see Elemi's android form, but it was just the ship speaking to her directly now. "Oh, so sorry. I was a little busy, you know," she muttered, studying the undulating curves of the walls, trying to make sense of how something like this could be so... alive.

The ship let out a delicate, almost amused hum. "I will let your tardiness slide this time, my dear. But do remember I have my standards and do not appreciate being ignored. However, since your absence allowed my precious Arakiba to get the rest he needed, I suspect you and I will get along fabulously."

Morgan snorted softly as a slight smile tugged her lips as she put a hand over her heart. "I'll do my best to deserve your continued support." Freaking diva.

As she ventured deeper, she exclaimed at how the central control station grew from the floor like a living thing. No cold metal or glass met her gaze; instead, the station arched gracefully, its controls woven organically into the ship's tissue, pulsing faintly with life. The entire structure seemed to shift and breathe, as if emphasizing it was a sentient creature.

"Touch nothing without asking, love," *Elemi* said with a hint of superiority. "I've just regained my health, and I'm far too pristine for rough handling."

Morgan's fingers hovered above the glowing surface, resisting the temptation to explore further. She curled her fingers to stop herself. "Wouldn't dream of it." Ha! She was such a liar. She'd give anything to explore the intricacies of *Elemi* at the mechanical level.

"See that you keep that in mind," *Elemi* purred again. "I like you, Morgan, truly. But let's not forget who's in charge here."

"Oh, please." JR12 chimed from his perch on Morgan's shoulder. "You act like we're in the presence of galactic royalty. Should we bow, or will a sarcastic clap do?"

"Droid." *Elemi* responded in a huff. "I don't need validation from something that's barely more than a glorified calculator."

"You..."

"Okay, JR12, that's enough." Morgan admonished the bot. "Let's not start something that has no ending. *Elemi*"—she addressed the ship, keeping her voice steady but respectful—"we'd better leave the Ozevroc ship and head out for the Federation Consortium palatial space station as soon as possible."

For a moment, the ship was silent, as if contemplating the request. Then *Elemi* responded in a voice smooth and rich, with the familiar undercurrent of sass. "Oh, darling, you want to go *there*? The Consortium is so..." A fake sigh. "*Dull*. All those regulations. Hardly the place for a ship of my elegance."

It was hard, but Morgan resisted rolling her eyes. Not that it would make much difference. "It's not like we have a choice. Chloe and Aylzrunth are ready to take this ship to Runihura, and they can't do that while we're here. We've got to put some distance between us and them so they can take those female Ozevroc to a safe place." She paused. "You wouldn't want them to suffer any more than they already have, would you?" Who said guilt wasn't a useful tool?

The lights in the cockpit dimmed for just a second, as if the ship was pouting. "Fine."

"Wait!" JR12 exclaimed. "Are Ari and As'ni secure?"

"Of course they are, you underdeveloped bug," *Elemi* responded in a condescending tone.

Morgan smirked, but quickly made her face bland. No need to encourage this budding rivalry. "Good. When Ari wakes up, I'll tell him how accommodating you've been. I'm sure that'll absolutely thrill him."

A simpering giggle from the ship erupted. "Oh, thank you!" *Elemi* said with a playful lilt. "I'd do anything to make that *gorgeous* man happy."

While Morgan had the same inclination, she let that statement go. Instead, she watched as the soft pulse of light rippled across the controls as *Elemi's* systems hummed to life. The ship's engines purred beneath her feet with faint vibrations that increased as she powered up.

"Plotting the course now," Elemi continued, her tone chipper. "And no worries, darling. I'll have all of you there safer than any of those rust buckets they call ships in the Consortium. Honestly, I don't know why that beautiful Chancellor D'zia doesn't beg *me* to join their fleet."

Morgan shook her head. "You're way too important to be part of some fleet." She hid her grin behind her fingers. "But if it'll make you feel better, I'll ask him when I see him. Just get us there in one piece first, okay?"

"Of course, darling girl."

The ship shifted slightly as the platform it was on lowered to the hanger deck beneath the engine room.

Morgan sat on the pilot's chair with JR12 safely settled on her shoulder and watched the change from one section to another on the vid screen in front of her.

The hangar doors opened to reveal a vast stretch of star-filled space before *Elemi* detached from the dock.

A subtle shift told Morgan they were in motion as *Elemi* glided smoothly from the Ozevroc ship.

The engines whispered, yet pulsed with a powerful, restrained energy that hummed through the floor and walls.

"Heading into the stars, darling."

Straps crisscrossed over Morgan's shoulders and held her safely against the secure chair.

"Hang on, JR12." She spoke to the small android on her shoulder. A small tickle of pain where his feet dug in told her he didn't waste time taking her literally.

"Sit back and relax," *Elemi* purred. "You're in excellent hands, my dear. *Very* excellent, if I do say so myself."

Morgan sank back into the pilot's seat, savoring the subtle thrill of acceleration as *Elemi* carried them forward, slipping smoothly into the boundless darkness of space.

Morgan watched on the vid screen of the command deck as Chloe's ever dwindling ship, the *Nightshade* towing the *Nebula Viper*, sailed farther and farther away.

In her last communication, Chloe assured her all the Ozevroc were snug and happy. "Well, not *all* of 'em are happy-clappy." She smirked on the screen of her multicorder. "Here's my parting gift to you. It's a vid of Zara displaying their gemstone encrusted, claw-looking thingy to the former high chieftain. It's funnier than hell to watch the m'fer bellow and cry like a whiny little brat." Her chuckle made her dark curls dance around her smiling face. "Once we get those females settled on Runihura, we'll contact the authorities at the Consortium and dump the male assholes off. Then we'll get in touch with you so we can kick some crystal-ass back to where they come from." She glanced away from the screen. "Come on, gargantuan man, let's go. Let's get this done so's we can get our buds from the AoA to come and join the fun." Her attention came back to Morgan. "Girl, try not to start shit before we get there, 'k? See ya soon!"

Chloe's live communication ended, and a short vid displayed the former High Chieftain Welozz losing his shizzle as Zara haughtily declared herself high chieftain and that he and his males were now under her total control. She raised the Talon of Ancients high above her bony head, causing the males in the cages to drop to their knees, wailing and roaring the whole time.

Morgan sat back with a satisfied grin when the vid ended. Yeah, karma was a bitch and she didn't take prisoners. Served the hubristic clods right. Maybe the Ozevroc as a species now had a chance for a better life. If nothing else, at least the females and their children would survive. Maybe if they were so inclined, they'd show their males a way better way of life that benefited the species.

Speaking of males. "*Elemi*, how do I take these straps off?" Morgan tugged at the immovable soft material covering her chest. They were warm, like smooth skin. She gasped when they slid off her and merged with the material on the chair. Sitting up, she checked on JR12, who was resting on her shoulder with his needle-like legs tucked under his bulbous body.

"*Elemi*, where's Ari?"

A brief silence.

Morgan was afraid the ship wouldn't respond at first.

"My starshine is asleep in the slumber chamber I created for him." *Elemi* didn't elaborate.

Morgan crossed her arms. "And how do I get there?" Nothing was going to keep her away from a warm and drowsy man she itched to wake up.

Again, silence. Morgan tapped her foot in time with her forefinger on her arm.

"All right, fine." *Elemi* grunted. "Just follow the blinking yellow light on the floor. It'll lead you to him."

Morgan glanced at JR12. "You stay here and watch her," she whispered and lifted her eyes to indicate the ship. "Make sure she stays on course and doesn't get the bright idea she wants to go someplace else."

"No worries, Gizmo Guru." JR12 stood and saluted her with one of his forelegs. "When the going gets tough, the tough call in their favorite JR. I'm on it!" His wings slid out of his back, and he lifted off, humming as he buzzed away.

Good. Now was her chance to show Ari reality was way better than some damn Dreamwalk.

CHAPTER FOURTEEN

Ari had to be dreaming. Reality was never this good, and Dreamwalking couldn't come close to the vivid fantasy his mind created from wishful thinking. He clung to the lavish sensation of Morgan's soft lips suckling his neck. Chill bumps broke out, causing his flat nipples to harden. No, this had to be real. Never in his wildest imagination could he dream up the languid feelings consuming him. This sensation of sheer wantonness drove him to search for more. He couldn't let it all disappear into the empty spaces of his mind.

Now her tongue traced a spellbinding path over his ear.

He moaned and tightened his hold around the soft, silky skin of her upper arms.

"Soft, silky skin?" he murmured, keeping his eyes shut. He didn't dare open them in case the woman of his dreams wasn't really there. "Yes, my..."

"Hush," came her command. "Just lay back and let me explore you." Morgan's sweet voice hummed. "Ahh, look at you. Being so thoughtful to sleep with no clothes on." She nuzzled his neck with a soft breath that bathed his skin.

A whiff of her natural feminine musk, along with a faint hint of an earthy balsamic note of soft sandalwood, covered him. Taking in a deep breath, he gloried in her tempting allure.

"*Irnini.*" was the only coherent thought he had when one of her velvety palms caressed his upper chest and stopped to tease one of his hard nipples.

She pinched and tweaked it before her scorching mouth surrounded it. Nipping the puckered skin with her blunt teeth, she then scoured it with the flat of her tongue. Not to be outdone, her wandering hand crossed his quivering stomach before reaching the curls surrounding his cock.

Ari groaned as lightning excitement blazed through him when she scratched through the curls above his dick, which strained for attention.

Morgan's mouth moved from one nipple to the other while her tormenting touch lowered. Now she cupped his tight balls, a gentle rolling action between her fingers.

He had to see. His eyes flew open. Catching himself on his elbows, he watched his beautiful woman travel down his chest. Her deft fingers still caressed his taut sac while the tip of his neglected cock seeped pre-cum.

Her succulent mouth lifted from his stomach as her head bobbed over his crotch.

For a split second, Ari was terrified she wouldn't fulfill this particular fantasy he had about her. Fortunately, that notion vanished when her sweet tongue swept glorious friction to the underside of his member before she sucked his entire shaft into the furnace of her mouth.

A small, rational part of his brain poked at him, chastising him for this being so one-sided. He should be the one who gave pleasure to her before he achieved his. But the unwavering action of her mouth, tongue, and teeth sucking and massaging his eager cock muddled his ability to think beyond what she was doing to his mailable flesh. He had to touch her in some way that wouldn't interrupt the magic she created. So, the only thing he dared to do was stroke his lover's corkscrew blond hair, reveling as the springy curls coiled around and between his fingers. He gasped, his hips bucking in time with her mouth as she suckled him in a firm, wet, up-and-down motion. His grip on her tightened.

Morgan didn't miss a beat.

She ramped up her fellatio efforts that drove Ari completely lost in lust. His elbows turned to rubber, and he fell back, his head lolling back and forth on the soft bed. His world had turned into one of hedonistic, all-consuming pleasure that her talented mouth created for him. A surge of brutal rapture roared to life. He arched his neck as an uncontrolled stream of his sperm erupted and spewed down her throat.

He roared his completion.

Morgan moaned and swallowed.

She continued her gentle suction until Ari lay motionless on the bed. With a satisfied mewl, she finally released his half-erect cock.

When Ari could open his eyes, he groaned as she licked her lips.

As she crawled up his torso, her golden-green eyes flared with intent. And with blatant determination, she didn't stop until she'd melded them flush together. Naked front to naked front.

"*Kashshapta*... witch of my dreams." Ari's eyes went half-lidded as the color of Morgan's stunning eyes became eclipsed by her dilated pupils. His whole being settled at the purpose in her gaze. He lingered, and in that moment, something shifted deep inside him—like pieces of himself, long scattered and forgotten, finally aligned. Even with his memories returned, he'd suspected something was still missing from his life.

But when he looked at Morgan, he saw more than a brilliant mind or the fierce tenacity she carried in every fiber of her being. She was someone who saw him, the *real* him, even when he didn't. His pulse quickened, not out of fear or the chaos that usually accompanied his psychic visions, but from something heavier, warmer. A connection that went beyond the physical, beyond the pull of attraction.

As she met his gaze, a curious spark lit her eyes and a sense of clarity hit him. It wasn't just that he wanted her, but that with *her*, he was finally complete. And in a way he hadn't realized was empty. For the first time, he didn't have to hide behind the façade he'd fabricated—the jester, the carefree soul who created laughter and jokes to conceal who he was inside. It was humiliating to admit, but he needed Morgan to become the person he was always meant to be.

Yeah, time to show her how much she meant to him. With a wicked grin, he grabbed her slender hips and raised her until her sultry core was in line with his watering mouth. His eyes burned at the tempting female flesh above him.

"Now it's my turn."

Morgan gasped when Ari grabbed her by the waist and put her throbbing, slick channel over his mouth. She braced her hands on his shoulders and hissed when he lightly kissed her hardened clit as it peeked through her slick folds. Then his hungry tongue delved deep inside her. Blistering streaks of steamy joy rumbled from within her inner core, a prelude to what was coming.

"Oh my God!" She threw her head back. "Ari..."

As he ramped up his efforts, she craved every touch as her passion turned into an addiction that only got stronger the more he licked and suckled. As Ari tasted her, his tongue pressed into her narrow slit, making her cry out as a tidal wave of ecstasy ripped through her. He acted like a starving man devouring a succulent meal. The efforts of his devastating mouth caused her to pull away, dreading that once she let loose, nothing would ever hold it back again.

"Ari... it's too much." She groaned. "I can't..."

"Yes, *irnini*. You will."

And just like that, her will evaporated. In its place, a shameless creature she never dreamed was part of her came alive. A sensual beast that clawed its way through to take over.

Ari's tormenting tongue pushed in hard and deep, retreating, then pushing in again while his diabolical fingers found purchase on her straining nub. First a quick pinch, then a circular motion that made her head swim. And just before she reached her goal, the tune his fingers played on her clit stopped. She whimpered, but moaned when those fingers began their symphony again, while his other hand reached for one of her breasts and tweaked the hard nipple.

That's all it took. She came on his tongue. Waves and waves of release roared through her, unraveling her, as she came apart in a boneless mass of glory.

She hardly noticed Ari's chuckle as he rolled her underneath his solid body, his thighs settling and widening her splayed legs.

He pushed inside, hard and deep. He lowered his head and engulfed her lips with his, his tongue plundering inside her mouth.

The combination of her taste mingling with his masculine flavor created a sensual dance for her to savor. A contest was born between their joined mouths and sexes until Ari broke off the kiss. His slumberous, heavy-lidded gaze held hers spellbound.

Watching his clear-eyed intent made everything right. This... this is what she longed for. Someone who recognized the real person beneath all the masks and bluster put on for others.

Not taking his eyes off her, he sped up each of his forceful strokes. He paused and lifted her legs with his wide hands, pushing them back before relentlessly diving into her.

"Love you, Morgan." His strangled confession came out in a low growl, but never wavered, never hesitated.

Tears filled her eyes. For this man to confess his feelings at this point of vulnerability meant more to her than she could say. Swallowing hard, she declared her feelings as well.

"And I, you, Ari." The freedom of her confession drove her release to fly free. It wasn't just the physical deliverance that tore through her, but an emotional one as well. Her soul recognized his, craving to merge with him, unable to deny they were one.

Ari's face contorted as she tightened around him in her climax. He drove into her repeatedly, all the while groaning her name. Then, with one last solid stroke, he buried his full length into the gripping depths of her body, filling her with himself. As his hot seed erupted, his glistening emotional gaze never left hers.

When the last shudders of release rippled through her, he wrapped his arms around her and rolled them to their sides, snuggling her head under his chin.

"I will never leave you, *irnini*," Ari claimed, whispering over her head. "I go where you go." He kissed the top of her curls. "Even if it's to Aethralis."

A fear she didn't realize she carried loosened inside her. Deep down, she worried what would happen between them once the looming disaster passed.

"You'd do that?" She spoke in a tight, low tone as she fingered the solid furrow in his muscular chest. "Live away from your family?" Now that he had his memories back, maybe he didn't want to leave them.

"You're my family," Ari declared, then shrugged. "Besides, since my brothers are all powerful psychics, there's no distance that can keep us apart." His deep sigh rumbled in his chest. "Speaking of which, they're bugging the hell out of me right now." He chuckled. "It seems with me having amnesia, they didn't know if I was dead or alive."

Morgan smiled and pushed back to face him.

His face held no tension, but his mouth had a light smirk on his full lips.

"Maybe you should take some time and fill them in on what we've discovered." She told him. Introducing them to a harmless As'ni might give their side some much needed intel.

Ari rolled onto his back, pulling her with him. Nudging her with his palm, he rested her head on his chest. "Nope, they can just wait." He put a finger under her chin and lowered his mouth to hers. "I've got better things to do," he whispered before claiming her lips with his.

EPILOGUE

A ri stretched his arms overhead, muscles loosening as the remnants of sleep clung to him. All tension unraveled with each satisfying pull. The warmth of the bed still lingered on his skin, and for the first time in what felt like ages, he was rested and clearheaded. His limbs remained heavy, but in the best possible way. Like he'd finally shaken off the weight of endless battles and worries.

With a yawn, he reached out, seeking the warmth of Morgan beside him. His fingers brushed cool sheets where a whiff of her feminine scent still lingered and teased him with her absence. His chest tightened with an unexpected pang of disappointment. The space beside him felt too vast, too empty. He closed his hand into a fist against the empty spot. The fleeting peace from the restful night slipped away with the realization she wasn't there.

"Why does this ludicrous ship inform me you've been asleep for over ten hours, Arakiba?"

Ari jerked his head at the foot of the bed at the harsh derisive sound of a familiar masculine voice. Adapa. His eldest brother. Standing there with his arms crossed and a stern, narrow-eyed expression of disapproval with his fists clenched under his arms. It wasn't until then he noticed his brother wasn't talking to him in a psychic sense. The man was actually standing at the foot of his bed. In the flesh. Which meant he had to be close enough to teleport.

"Have you done anything while you were gone besides cater to your own pursuits?" Adapa snorted.

"I..."

"Did you even bother to find that woman you were supposed to?" Adapa looked around the compact room. "I gather you didn't, because if you had, she'd probably be in bed with you right now."

One moment, his brother stood in front of him, arms crossed, casting a familiar shadow of authority, and the next, there was a shift in the air. It wasn't until he caught a subtle movement over Adapa's shoulder that he realized Morgan had slipped into the room—silent as a predator stalking its prey.

Before he could react, Morgan was behind Adapa, her movements fluid and precise. In an instant, he glimpsed her pressing a small, sleek cylinder to the back of his brother's neck, just below the base of his skull.

The device hummed faintly, its deadly potential unmistakable.

Ari's breath hitched. How did she get behind Adapa so quickly, so quietly? Even his brother, one of the most seasoned psychic fighters he knew, hadn't noticed her until it was too late.

"Don't move," Morgan's voice was low, almost a whisper, laced with a band of steel.

Adapa froze. His body tensed at the sudden contact. He didn't turn, didn't react—only his eyes flicked toward Ari, a glint of surprise flashing across their dark depths.

Ari watched, his heart pounding. He'd seen Morgan's intelligence, her strength, but this—this was something different. She had slipped past his brother's defenses effortlessly, and now had him at her mercy.

"Morgan," Ari began, his voice strained, unsure whether to be more shocked or impressed. His eyes flicked between the two, feeling the weight of the tension in the room. The way she handled herself, the way she moved—it was as if she'd been preparing for this moment her entire life. And he realized just how dangerous she could be when she needed to.

Adapa's lips twisted into a smirk, though Ari could see the strain beneath his calm façade.

"Ah, so you did find her," he said, the words slow, deliberate. "And surprise, surprise. Here she is in your bedchamber."

Morgan didn't move. "I warn you." Her voice dripped with disdain. "Growing up around psychics like you taught me early on how to defend myself. I can react before you even realize I'm there."

Adapa's eyebrows rose.

"So, whoever you are, apologize to Ari. He's been through a lot and doesn't need shit from some asshole. What he needs is time to regain his strength, and he can't do that with you bullying him."

Ari guessed Morgan had pushed the weapon harder when Adapa flinched.

"Now."

Adapa chuckled under his breath, but stayed perfectly still. "Damn, she's a fierce one, Arakiba."

A surge of pride mixed with disbelief consumed Ari. "Well, let's not put her to the test on you." He kept his voice calm despite his racing pulse. "Morgan, this is my eldest brother, Adapa." He narrowed a glare at his brother. "Adapa, this is Morgan Jackson from the hidden city of Aethralis under Antarctica."

Morgan backed away, taking her weapon with her. She stalked around Adapa, then faced him with a fierce scowl, her own arms crossed. Damn, he loved it when she did that. Even clothed.

Adapa's dark brows rose. "Really? I wasn't aware humans had a base there."

"Humans don't have a base there," Morgan supplied, clipping the device in her hand onto the thick belt she had around her trim waist.

It was then Ari noticed it was her handheld multicorder. Either it could turn into a weapon, or she'd been bluffing.

Ari smirked and leaned back on the pillows with his hands behind his head. "Guess who her great-something grandfather is."

The tension in Adapa's jaw loosened. "Guessing games?" He snorted. "Okay, I'll bite. Who's her grandfather?"

"Rummeh."

Adapa sucked in a breath. "The same Akurn who took Inanna to Earth's surface all those centuries ago?"

"Yeah, that's the one." Ari grinned. "She's a hybrid like we are. Just several generations removed."

His brother examined Morgan with a stern expression.

"Stay out of my head, *ahu*." Morgan warned him in perfect Akurn.

Ari was relieved she at least she called Adapa 'brother' in a friendlier tone.

"I know how to protect my mind from arrogant snoops like you."

Ari climbed out of bed, using his telekinesis to pull on his usual black jeans, T-shirt, and biker boots without a second thought. "I have a feeling you're not here just to give me shit. So, what's going on?" He stepped closer to Adapa and locked gazes with him. "Are the brothers okay?" His throat dried at the thought.

The tension thickened in the air as the words hung between them.

Adapa's face was grim, his usual calmness undercut by a flicker of urgency that Ari wasn't used to seeing in his older brother. It didn't relieve him when Adapa put a comforting hand on his shoulder.

"The invasion has begun," Adapa said quietly, his voice low but weighted with meaning. "The Krystalii breached the dimensional veil. Earth, Akurn, the very seat of the Federation Consortium... nowhere is safe anymore."

Beside Ari, Morgan stiffened. Her gaze darted to him, searching for a reaction.

But his mind raced, making it hard to process the gravity of what Adapa revealed. They had all known this moment was coming, but hearing it was a punch to the gut.

"A small group of us fled," Adapa continued, his arms crossed, the hardness in his voice unmistakable. "Including Asmodel and Abalim, bringing others who slipped through the chaos with them. But it's worse than we thought."

Ari's stomach clenched. "How bad?"

Adapa's gaze darkened. "The Krystalii ship... it's massive, Arakiba. Bigger than anything we've ever encountered. It's like a continent suspended in an impenetrable void. We're talking miles wide, miles high, with its own atmosphere and ecosystem. They're not just invading—they're settling in."

Ari exhaled sharply, trying to imagine the scale. A ship the size of a continent. It sounded impossible, but nothing about the Krystalii ever made sense. They were from another dimension, beings of crystal and psionic power. Their very existence defied the known laws of nature.

Adapa's next words cut through his thoughts like a blade. "Azazel's already inside."

Ari's head snapped up. "What?"

Adapa nodded with a grim expression. "He's gone undercover, infiltrating the Krystalii ship where they hold the woman he was sent to find. When he teleported from FiPan, that's where he went. How he knew where to go is beyond me, but now he's attempting to get them off that ship. But if they catch him first..."

Morgan shifted beside him, her face tight with concern. "This guy Azazel, went to that ship to get one of my friends? Alone?"

Ari's hands curled into fists. The thought of his brother in the belly of that monstrous ship, surrounded by the most dangerous beings in the universe, was a knot twisting inside his chest, making it hard to breathe. Wait... wait. He took in a deep breath. Azazel was the poster boy of calm resolve and clear thinking. The man didn't do anything he hadn't calculated to the nth degree. Nothing ever rattled him. Smart, brave, sure, but this? Hard to believe the unflappable dumbass ran headfirst into something he had no way of foreseeing the resulting outcome.

"I'm sure he's got a plan," Adapa stated in a tone that didn't carry the confidence Ari needed to hear. "But even for him, it's risky. The Krystalii... they see everything, sense everything. One wrong move, and he won't make it out alive."

Great. This whole clusterfuck had the makings of a suicide mission.

Ari clenched his jaw, feeling the weight of the hardship ahead as their entire existence threatened to crumble beneath them. Along with an invasion from another dimension that put the Federation Consortium in chaos, they were missing a key ally, with Azazel trapped inside a spaceship that massive and no way to get him help.

Which gave the Krystalii free rein to close in on every front.

He glanced at Morgan, seeing the worry etched in her eyes. He pulled her under his arm and squeezed her in a tight grip. The path ahead was almost impossible, but what choice did they have? There was no turning back now. The stakes had never been higher, and all they had was each other. No matter how dark or deadly the mission grew, they'd claw their way to victory.

Or die trying.

Look for the exciting series finale in "Azazel"!

A SMALL ASK...

Now that you've finished reading this creation, it'd mean the world to me if you left an honest review wherever you bought it. This type of feedback is an authors lifeblood and helps others find their work.

The adventures can't continue without you!

ABOUT THE AUTHOR

Keri Kruspe, award-winning *"Author of Otherworldly Romantic Adventures"* loves nothing better than writing about romances that feature "feisty heroines who aren't afraid to take a chance on life... or love". Her writing career started when she became determined to indulge in something different in the SciFi romance genre, turning "the alien kidnapping trope upside down" (Vine Voice) in her ***ALIEN EXCHANGE*** trilogy.

After the ***ALIEN EXCHANGE*** universe was born, she created another SciFi Romance series, ***ANCIENT ALIEN DESCENDANTS***, then carried on the adventures in the *ALIEN LEGACY BROTHERHOOD* that continues to mix sensual, romantic themes to otherworldly adventures.

A native Nevadan, Keri is a lifelong avid reader who lives in north-western Michigan with her hubby and ruling member of the family, a Jack Russell Terrier (aka the *Terrorist*) named Hestia. When not immersed in her made-up worlds, she enjoys discovering the fascinating landscape of her home and pairing red wine with healthy ways to cook. Most of all, she loves finding her next favorite author.

If you want to know when Keri's next book will come out, please visit her at her website where you can sign up for her mailing list. You'll get a **FREE** copy of the novella, *The Day Behind Tomorrow* that is a prologue to the **ANCIENT ALIEN DESCENDANT SERIES**. Not to mention being kept updated on the life of a dedicated, obsessed author.

Social Media Links:

Facebook

Pinterest

Instagram

BOOKS IN READING ORDER

Alien Legacy: The Empath

Alien Legacy: The Shapeshifter

Alien Legacy: The Psychic

Alien Legacy: The Vampire

Alien Legacy: The Mage

<u>Novellas</u>
Qhasheik's Pod
Claude & Amata
Lok's Love

<u>Alien Legacy Brotherhood</u>
Abalim
Asmodel